# FINDING FALLEN ANGELS

## THE ERASEHER SERIES BOOK TWO

## SARA NICHOL QUINCY

First published by Milcann Hunnee 2022



ISBN: 978-1-957719-02-3 (Epub)

ISBN: 978-1-957719–03-0 (Paperback)

ISBN: 978-1-957719-11-5 (Hardcover)

SaraNicholQuincy.com

MILCANN HUNNEE
PUBLISHING COMPANY

*For Phoenix*

*The scared little girl that I locked up in a dark place in my mind for so many years because I thought I hated you and that you would never be good enough. I was wrong; you've achieved more than I could have ever imagined and I'm sorry. You are enough; you have always been. This is for you beautiful, be free. I'm proud of you!*

# CONTENTS

# I
## CURSED LANDS

"You're quiet today…" Jake broke the silence that had settled between us.

"I know… I'm sorry." I said softly, hoping he could still hear me.

He turned to look up at me as he took the reins of the horse and brought it to a stop. "You don't have to be sorry," he said, reaching up to gently rest his hand on my leg. "Are you stressed? Is that it? Do you need to talk?" He took my hand and pulled it toward him to kiss my knuckles then held it against his cheek.

I gently shook my head. I probably did need to talk, but I was used to dealing with all my emotions all by myself so I didn't know what to say. "I'm not stressed…" I said, returning my eyes to his.

His eyes softened, but he didn't say anything. He just continued with his gaze, waiting for me to continue.

"I just can't stop thinking about Marcus…" I burst out, hoping he'd understand. "Even when I try not to, I can't stop. I mean… I know he's dead and I'm with you now. I should move on, but—" I paused to look away from him. I knew I was about to cry but I did everything I could to hold it back. "I can't act like I don't still have every single memory of him trapped inside my head… Every time I think about that day on the bridge… It's so painful… I wish I could just block it out and forget what I did but it just keeps replaying over and over in my mind." I paused again. He squeezed my hand a little, letting me know he was still listening. "I loved him, Jake… I loved him and I killed him…" Unable to hold it back any longer, I burst into tears, unable to control myself.

"Come here, baby…" Jake said softly as he reached up to help me slide off the horse. "I don't need you to act. If something's bothering you, it's okay to tell me. We can work through it together." He kissed my forehead as he gently lowered me to the ground.

I leaned my head into his chest as I continued to cry. With everything going through my mind on top of the mental tug-of-war between Eva and Kaleah, I was afraid I'd go insane before we even made it to the grotto lands. *If I'm not already…*

"I don't expect you to be over him…" He said, slowly rubbing his hands up and down my back. "It's not easy, I'm sure."

"It feels like my present and my past have collided and now I have to sort through the wreckage. Like at the same time I remember falling in love with you I also remember loving him and feeling like I should be with him… But I can't because I freakin' killed him…" I said, trying not to cry harder. "My brain can't decipher the passage of time between the two sets of memories… It's like I'm two people now, with two different memory paths, personalities, demons… all crammed into one body… I don't know what to do, Jake. I just don't know what to do…" I leaned into him again, wanting to fall to my knees and cry unabated.

"Shh… baby… it's okay…" He held me up as he hugged me tighter. "You're gonna be okay… I've got you. Just relax."

I didn't say anything else. I just rested against him, letting him hold me.

**The next day…**

It had been three weeks since we'd left the cabin to travel to the grotto lands. Having the horses this time made the journey substantially easier. Even though the weather was still pretty cold, it didn't seem to affect me the same way when I was riding versus when I was walking. I didn't know if it was actually warmer being up on the horse or if it was all in my head, but either way, I liked it very much. I was sure Jake would agree that not having to carry our bags for once had been quite nice.

We could go faster and farther with horses than we could when traveling on foot. I had seen more things in the last two weeks than I had almost the entire four years of being on my own. Knowing curiosity is what killed the cat, I knew better than to ask Jake if we could stop to look at anything. I was drawn to the urban decay, though. It had an enchanting, almost mesmerizing quality about it. It was like staring at a dead body and thinking to yourself about the life it used to possess versus everything it was now—simply emptiness.

Since we'd left, I had found it hard to talk to Jake as much as I had before. It wasn't from lacking conversation topics; I think it was simply because the times I stayed quiet were the only ones I could get my mind to be at peace. When everything was silent, I could rest and let myself zone off and just listen to the sounds of nature. I could tell either Jake had observed that was what I had been doing or he just knew that's what I needed because he had been less talkative as well. The sounds of the gentle wind rustling through the trees soothed me. I would have loved to be able to sit beside a small creek and listen to the subtle gurgling of the water all day as well but I knew that wasn't realistic until spring.

We must have been getting close to the grotto lands. Jake dismounted from his horse and started to walk in front instead, leading it along with mine. He also walked slower and acted more vigilant of the area, which wasn't actually all that remarkably different from the last several miles we'd traveled. The terrain was dense and extremely hilly. The hills reminded me of tiny mountains. They were wide at the base but only tall enough to block out light from the sun until around midday when the valleys between them finally began to brighten up all the way. If we had already arrived and this was it, then I would have been pleasantly surprised, considering the area actually felt rather peaceful. That probably shouldn't have shocked me, but I think I expected more of a sinister, mysterious atmosphere going into it from what Jake had said.

I leaned down a little and whispered under my breath, but loud enough for Jake to hear me past the sounds of the horse. "How do you know we're getting close?" I asked, finally deciding to dampen the silence between us that had been lingering for the last hour or so.

He looked up at me and smiled softly, probably happy I was willing to talk again. "In agent training, they taught us all to look for certain landmarks and signposts for the area. They treated it like it was a forbidden zone. There was no shortage of warnings. So naturally, among the men, it was easy to make up ghost stories and legends about this place and why we should be scared to ever come here." He stopped walking forward and turned to go around to the side of my horse. "Here, let me help you down. It would probably be safer if you walked next to me," he said, reaching up toward me.

"Okay." I leaned down and reached out for him. He took a hold of my waist with both his hands and gently slid me out of the saddle. I noticed as my feet both landed on the ground there was a sharp, burning pain that shot through the leg that had the stitches. I fought the urge to wince, realizing Jake might want to stop and check on it, so I did what I could to hold any sound of pain in and act like there wasn't anything wrong.

He stood there for a moment and looked me in the eye. "I know you haven't wanted to talk much since we left. I realize you're probably stressed about what we're doing but it's going to be all right. We're going to find a place to stay here that is safe, okay?" He asked as he reached up to stroke my face with the hand that wasn't holding the horse's reins. Then he leaned in and kissed me on the forehead. "I promise to protect you," he said, leaning back to look into my eyes again.

"Okay…" I smiled and leaned in to hug him. I wanted to tell him I could protect myself now, though. It should have been obvious from what I was able to do with the two Sicari, but I didn't say it. Not only did I not want to take that from him, I think somewhere inside of me I was afraid it wasn't true. Whether Eva was trained to kill or not, that was never my original job or mission. I was only supposed to acquire and transfer intel, nothing more. Any training I had on how to fight or kill a man was merely for self-defense and solely to keep the intel safe. I never went into that position wanting to be a killer or even thinking I would be. It's not a part of me I liked, and I wanted to resolve within myself to never do it again unless I absolutely had to or unless Jake needed me to. Except for the five men on my shit-list, of course.

We walked for a little while beside the horses. The area we were walking in seemed exceptionally quiet. Whether it was usual for the area during the winter months or not, it didn't take long to notice the peaceful silence slowly morphed into an eerie stillness. It's like the feeling you get when you think someone is watching you but you have no evidence. There was almost a sixth sense within me that was doing whatever it could to warn me. I could feel the hair on my arms start to raise. As we continued, the feeling intensified, and a small chill went down the middle of my back. We were walking into something that was invisible to my eyes but not my subconscious, and my body knew it!

It didn't take long before I could tell Jake was feeling the same way that I had. I watched him as he walked in front of me; he was on even higher alert than before. His stance while walking was almost like he was unintentionally ducking, lowering his head to be shielded by the height of the horse. His steps were more precise and stealthy, each one barely audible to my ears.

He was getting agitated with the sounds the horses were making too, probably because it was something he couldn't control. If he didn't already look tense enough, with every neigh or snort one of them would make, he would quickly turn his head and glare at them, almost trying to hush them with his disapproving glances. I knew even with all the problems they were currently causing, though; they were too valuable for us to part with. That was probably his conclusion as well, considering he didn't turn around and send one away with a smack on the ass.

As we walked further, other things began to change about the area as well. Now the unnatural silence was joined by a dense fog that had settled into the bottom of the valley we were about to walk into. A thought instantly popped into my mind. It's like when you are watching a scary movie and you want to yell at the screen, *"Don't go in there, stupid!"* It's obvious it's a trap, or so you think, and the best way is to just go around. Jake must have been thinking the same thing I was because he stopped and turned around to look at me, his eyes full of uncertainty and trepidation.

He didn't say anything, but began to use hand signals instead. Now that I had Eva's memories back I could clearly understand his signing. He knew as well as I that we weren't supposed to go into that valley and whether it was visibly dangerous or not; we were going to listen to our inner senses. He signaled that we were going to turn back and go around. I knew he didn't know the area any better than I did but I was going to defer to him and trust that he would make the right decision and lead us a better way.

However, only seconds after that decision I found my thoughts swirling with unwelcome memories. These were the same feelings I had that day on the bridge. It was uncanny how silent everything was. Marcus was in the lead when he stopped to turn around the moment he first spotted danger. Riflemen, he mouthed to me… *Riflemen…* Then he was shot.

Instantly, I heard it again, the distinct sound in my memory—a deafening crack that tore through the silence. I looked up at Jake. I felt faint, like every ounce of blood had drained from my face. He looked back at me, his face half concerned and half confused why I wasn't following his signals.

A small quiver began to quake my lower jaw. I was frozen, standing there, staring at him. I looked from his face to his chest. "Riflemen," I said faintly to myself, then hesitated. I couldn't understand what was happening to me. I wanted to follow his orders, but I was trapped in the trauma of my memories. "Riflemen!" I unintentionally said it again, this time without being able to control my volume. I looked back up from Jake's chest to his face. He immediately ducked lower and started to walk over toward me.

"Shh!" It was the only sound I could hear now. "Shh!" He hissed again, trying to keep me quiet without realizing he was being loud himself.

I looked back down at his chest, reaching my hand out toward him to touch it, looking for the blood. "Riflemen!" I said again.

"Shh," he quickly lifted his palm to cover my mouth. "Shush now, there's no rifleman," he said low under his breath while looking at me intently, trying to break me from a trance.

I rubbed my hand around against his chest, up and down, back and forth. After a moment, he let the grip of his hand against my mouth relax. "You've been shot. Where's the blood?" I asked, frantically feeling his torso, trying to pull up his shirt.

"Stop!" He whispered sternly as he firmly took a hold of my wrist, stopping me from searching any more. "There are no riflemen!" He said again, trying to get me to look him in the eyes and not at his chest. "Baby, there aren't any riflemen. I'm fine. Okay?"

I looked back into his eyes like he had wanted. Whatever it was, quickly faded and my mind seemed to return to normal, breaking out of whatever delusion it had fallen into. "Oh my gosh, I'm sorry," I murmured. I didn't understand what was happening to me. I didn't know why I thought he was shot. "I'm sorry I was loud," I whispered, beginning to feel agitated with myself, realizing I could have put us in danger.

He wrapped his arms around me to give me a hug, then turned both of us so he was now facing away from the horse. I leaned my head forward to rest it on his shoulder. I wanted to cry, but I stopped myself, knowing this wasn't the right time or place for it. I stood there for a moment resting against him when suddenly the horse behind him spooked. Jake quickly released his hold of me and took a step around to position himself at my back, between me and whatever he saw behind me.

I spun around, now looking at his back. At first, I couldn't tell what he was doing, but it quickly became obvious. As he reached his right hand behind him to my side, positioning it to show me to stay still, his left hand reached in under his coat to the small of his back, ready to pull his gun.

"We don't mean you any harm. Lower your weapon!" He yelled out toward someone in front of him. I tried to lean over a little to see who or how many there were but I couldn't see past his broad back.

A raspy man's voice hollered back, "Are you Coddymen or Sicari?"

"Gypsyins!" Jake yelled, as he took a small step to his right. "Show him your arm, baby," he said in a softer tone, only slightly moving his head, indicating he was talking to me.

I could see him now. There was only one man standing there. He looked old and worn out, as most Gypsyins did. He was holding a revolver, pointed at us. I reached down and pulled up the sleeve of my coat on my left arm and held it forward with my forearm up, showing him there was no tag. After a couple of seconds, I slowly lowered my arm and pulled my sleeve back down as Jake took a step to his left, returning himself to his original position in front of me, completely blocking me from view.

"See, just Gypsyins! Now lower your gun if you'd like to talk peacefully!" Jake yelled again.

"You think I'm gonna believe you? Show me your arm too, boy!" the man's ragged voice hollered back. I leaned over to see him by peeking through the gap under Jake's arm.

Jake hesitated to respond. I'm sure he was trying to think of a way to get out of showing him his tag. "You've seen hers, that's enough!" Finally, he yelled it back to him.

The man took his thumb positioned on the hammer and slowly pulled it back, engaging it with the sound of a small click. "I'm serious now, boy. If you ain't gonna show me your arm, I'll shoot both you and your little Gypsyin. It won't bother me none."

Before I had a chance to even think about what the man had said and what I would do if I were Jake, I saw the bulge of his coat at his back suddenly flatten followed by the sound of a sharp crack that echoed loudly down the valley. The man quickly fell and started to roll down the hill a few feet before landing face-first in a small drift of fresh snow.

"You shot him!" I blurted out in shock, unable to help myself. I wasn't sure I just saw what I thought I did. "You didn't even warn him, you just… Jake, you just shot him…"

"Don't be so loud, there might be more of 'em," he said through clinched teeth, then returned his gun to his waistband and walked over toward the man. "I know I shot him. He would have shot me first. I had no choice."

"Don't be so loud?" I asked, dumbfounded. "What the hell? If anything is going to tell everyone we're here, it's not me. It's the freakin' gunshot that just rang everyone in the valley's doorbell!"

He didn't respond to what I said. He just reached down and picked up the revolver to inspect it, flipping open the cylinder and spinning it to check for bullets. After a moment, he said a few choice words under his breath that I had never heard him say before. He was obviously upset.

"What's wrong?" I asked, wanting to know what he found that bothered him so much.

He hesitated for a minute as he took the revolver and sharply swung it to the side to snap the cylinder back in place. "It's empty… the freakin' idiot… He didn't need to die!" He rubbed his forehead then looked around as he walked back over to me. "We need to keep moving. Whoever he was, people won't like knowing we killed him." He opened my bag and shoved the revolver into the middle pocket. "There, now you have a weapon. Even if it doesn't have any bullets, you can use it to bluff if you need to, just like he did."

"So I can get myself killed just like he did?" I asked, dryly.

He stared at me for a second, his face stone cold. "Fine!" He said, reaching back into the bag. He pulled the gun back out and with one quick motion, tossed it back over toward the man's body.

"What are you doing?" I was baffled by him.

"You're right. It's not going to do you any favors. Besides, wherever we end up, if we don't want them to know we killed him, then we shouldn't be carrying around the guy's gun. It'll only put you in more danger," he said as he collected the reins of both horses so we could continue walking.

"Do you plan on shooting everyone that wants to see your tag?" I asked, not yet walking with him, only watching as he started to take a few steps.

He turned around to look at me. He didn't respond at first, he just stared like he was trying to gauge where I was coming from. "Look, I don't like killing people anymore than you do. I did what I had to do and now we move on. I don't care how many people I have to kill to keep you safe. I'll do it! So if you have a problem with that, you can keep it to yourself 'cause it's not going to change anything, got it?" The tone of his voice paired with his rigid stance indicated this discussion wasn't open to negotiation.

"Yeah, I got it." I didn't know where I was exactly coming from either so I figured it was no use arguing with him.

"Okay then, let's go!" He said, then turned around and began to walk again.

# 2

## UNVEILING SHADOWS

We turned back and went around the valley, up and over a few large hills, then back down into what appeared to be the only way to go from there—down into another valley. I noticed the same fog had settled at the bottom of this one as well. It didn't have the same eerie feeling as the previous one, however, so neither of us acted like we wanted to stop or go around again.

It wasn't far into the fog that Jake told me he would feel better if I got back on my horse to ride instead of walk. I wouldn't have asked for that myself, but was pleased to do so, considering my leg was now hurting worse from going up and down all the steep terrain.

Jake walked just as slowly and cautiously as he had been before but he acted differently this time. Now he moved with much less stealth and acted more like a normal traveler, moving the way a Gypsyin would. I figured he probably switched up his strategy since his initial one didn't work so well and he already had to kill a man.

We didn't make it far into the valley before I started to feel weird again. It was hard to see very far ahead of where we were walking but there wasn't much we could do about it except keep walking slowly. With each stride the horse took, my eyes tried to readjust to all the different shadows that were suddenly uncovered as the fog's veil thinned. As we moved farther, those shadows became solid objects and new shadows were revealed. Suddenly, straight-ahead standing directly in our path, was a shadow that didn't look like any of the others. It wasn't a tree or a bush; it was another man.

Jake must have not seen it at the same time as I did. It took him a couple of seconds before he stopped and tightened his grip on the horse's reins, stopping his as well as mine from walking any farther. The shadow was just standing there, thankfully, with both arms at its sides. I couldn't make out any features but I was glad it didn't appear to be holding up any weapons like the last guy had.

I looked down at Jake to see what he wanted me to do, knowing I was potentially exposed, sitting so high on the horse. He didn't look back at me but under his breath loud enough for me alone to hear him, gave me my orders. "Stay where you are. He doesn't look armed. You're safer up there right now than you are down here."

"Okay," I said, turning my head to look back at the shadow, seeing if there were any new developments in the clarity of its appearance.

"You a Sicari or a Coddymen?" Jake hollered out. I could see what he was doing, he was asking the same way the last man did, the way a Gypsyin would. He was smart. I wouldn't have thought of that myself.

"I'm a Gypsyin!" The voice hollered back. "But by the look of it, with those horses, I am assuming you are both Sicari. What are you doing in these parts? You know we don't like your kind around here." It was a man's voice, but it wasn't old or raspy-sounding like the previous man's. He didn't have a heavy Appalachian accent like the old man or pronounce his words like most Gypsyins, either. He enunciated what he said very clearly like he was well educated. His voice didn't sound far off from the sound of Jake's, but the man didn't appear to be as tall or as well built as Jake was from looking at the shadowed silhouette that stood before us.

"We're Gypsyins too!" I yelled out to him, hoping if he heard a female's voice it would help ease his suspicion of us. "We came here looking for a safe place to stay. We don't want any trouble either. Here, come closer and look at my arm. You'll see, like you, I don't have a tag." I looked down at Jake quickly after I said it, making sure he didn't disapprove of what I had just done. He briefly glanced at me and nodded his head like he was fine with it.

The dark, misty figure moved a few steps forward toward us, revealing himself finally. His silhouette grew taller with every step. He wasn't as short as I had originally observed. The closer he got, the fog dissipated enough that I could see him as clearly as I could Jake. He was tall like Jake was but that was about the only physical similarity they shared. His hair was dark, almost black. His beard, though short, was thick and full, unlike Jake's, which was just a heavy stubble that had almost a grainy look to it. I couldn't tell his ethnicity but his skin, even against the pale winter light of the day, was a deep, rich olive tone. He walked toward us until he was close enough to see us both clearly. First, he looked over at Jake then he looked up at me; he stared for a moment until I could see his shoulders relax.

"May I see your arm, then?" He asked, keeping his eyes focused on me.

"Sure," I said as I started to pull on my sleeve. "Do you mind if we see yours, too? We don't like Sicari or Coldiers… or surprises really, for that matter."

He nodded and started to pull his sleeve up as well. I leaned down and motioned to Jake to help pull me off the horse. He did all while keeping an eye on the man. As soon as my feet both landed, I felt the same sharp pain shoot through my leg that I had earlier getting down from the horse. I wasn't able to withhold the sound of my discomfort as I had the first time, though. Jake didn't say anything but I could tell he noticed. He was doing his best to keep watching our new friend, so he only gave me a quick glance to acknowledge my pain, then returned his gaze back toward the man.

I walked around to the front of the horse, closer for the man to see my arm, trying to not let my leg display a limp.

His sleeve was rolled up just as mine. I could see his skin better now. His coloring was more of a dark honey tone. I held my arm up to show him. His glance went from my eyes quickly down to my arm and then farther down to my leg where he let it linger briefly before bringing it back up to my eyes again.

He smiled. "It's nice to meet other Gypsyins. My name is Luca. What is yours?" He asked, looking at me intently, then briefly glancing over at Jake before returning his eyes to mine, waiting for an answer.

"Elliceva," I said then looked over at Jake.

His face was stony and cold. He didn't respond immediately. He had his left hand pulled back around at his back tucked in at his waist. "You can call me Miles," he said finally, then looked from Luca over to me. He pulled his hand out from behind his back, took a couple of steps toward me, and put it around my waist. "We came here looking for the caves. We heard it was safe here for Gypsyins," he said, then leaned over and kissed me softly on the side of the head. "If you wouldn't mind showing us a safe place we could stay, we'd be thankful. We don't need both the horses. We could give you one in payment for helping us."

The man looked away from Jake, then back to me for a moment before looking at the horses. "You never said how you got the horses. Generally, only Sicari have horses. Did you trade with them?" He asked, looking straight at me with eyes full of skepticism.

"I killed them," I said. It felt good to get it off my chest. Luca's eyes narrowed as he continued to stare at me. He looked stunned by my admittance. Jake tightened his grip around my waist, trying to tell me to cut it out. "I mean, it wasn't on purpose. They tried to attack me. You know how they treat Gypsyins," I said, holding his gaze, slightly raising my eyebrows to create a pitiful look on my face.

His eyes quickly darted to Jake's, then back to mine, now more full of suspicion than before. I instantly regretted my decision to go down that path. I knew from my espionage training that the best way to create trust, especially in the beginning when you first meet a person, is to be honest with them. Even if you have to tell them something difficult, stay as truthful as you can, only twisting the details.

It was obvious what he was probably now thinking the same thing Jake thought when he first picked me up. I looked to be about as dangerous as a fly is to a horse. How in the world could I kill two men? I spoke up again to quickly correct my error before my honesty backfired and led him to feel he should distrust us. "Once I was able to get one of their guns, I just closed my eyes and shot. I kept shooting until… well, the bullets were gone. But when I opened my eyes and saw what I did. I felt so bad… I mean—"

"I understand," he said suddenly. His face now changed from suspicion to sympathy just as I had been hoping it would. "Sure, I will show you the main cavern. There are a few small chambers leading off from it that you are welcome to stay in."

The heaviness of the fog lifted significantly the farther Luca led us down into the valley, where it ended with a large hole tunneling into the earth. It looked like the hill had a mouth that we were about to walk into. The closer we got, the easier it was to see the area and the entrance. I saw what looked like one person standing close to the side but before too long they disappeared into the blackness of the opening. We stopped where the flat ground of the valley ended and a decently steep slope leading down to the mouth of the cave began.

Luca suggested we leave the horses there at the top of the hill. So Jake took their reins and wrapped them around a small tree before getting his bags. He threw one over his shoulder, then began to carry the other. I grabbed my bag and, after putting the strap over my shoulder so my hands would be free, started to follow Luca closer to the start of the slope, waiting for Jake to follow.

"Here, I don't want you to fall. You'll hurt your leg worse than it already is," Luca said, eyeing me while reaching out a hand to help me begin the descent.

I looked at him, confused. *How did he know about my leg?* I turned to see where Jake was and saw him nod at me, letting me know he was okay with me accepting Luca's offer to help. I turned back and took a hold of his hand; it wasn't as large as Jake's but he had a nice firm grip. I looked down and started to take a few steps, but it was too steep and I didn't anticipate the pain that shot through my leg. I limped forward, trying to continue with another step but the pain made my knee buckle, forcing me to sit down. I leaned back against my bag so I wouldn't roll forward.

"Are you all right?" Luca asked as I pulled my hand back from his to check my leg.

I looked up at him and started to respond, "Yes, I just—"

I was interrupted by Jake as he began to quickly sidestep past me. "Stay there, baby. I'll come back to get you."

I watched as he continued down the slope.

"What's wrong with your leg?" Luca asked, sincerity lacing his voice as he continued looking down at me. "I'm a doctor... or, well, I was. I might be able to help you."

I looked away from Jake and back at him. His eyes again were intently focused on me. "I accidentally cut it pretty deep, so I put some stitches in it myself. It's fine, it just—"

"When?" He interrupted.

I looked away for a second feeling overwhelmed by the intense eye contact. "Ah, it's only been maybe two or three, probably closer to three weeks. But... I mean, it's nothing. I'm sure it's nothing," I said, then looked back at him. "What kind of doctor?" I asked, curious.

"I was going into anesthesiology before the war. If your leg is still hurting three weeks after you stitched it up yourself, you have an infection," he said, as certain as he could get.

I wasn't sure why he was so confident so I ignored his observation and looked away again to see if Jake was close to coming back. "Anesthesiologist... That's interesting. Too bad you're not a psychiatrist," I said, now able to see Jake again as he began his ascent back up to get me.

"I wasn't joking." I could hear a faint accent this time in Luca's voice.

I looked back at him while I waited for Jake to get there. "I wasn't joking either," I said with a small grin. "If something is gonna kill me, it's more likely to be my mind than my leg." I followed it with a large grin, sure to confuse him and make him think I was joking. "You look too young to be a doctor," I said, trying to switch the subject back to him.

He finally broke eye contact and looked back down to see where Jake was as well. "I wasn't able to finish my residency before the war," he said, then returned his gaze to mine. "It doesn't matter. I know enough to know you probably have an infection, and it's going to need to be looked at before it gets in your bloodstream and makes you severely sick."

I wasn't dumb; I knew he was probably right. I just didn't see how he could do anything about it by looking at it. Jake was now getting closer, so we both focused our attention on him and what he was going to do to get me down the hill. He didn't say anything at first as he came up to us. He just eyeballed me then the incline like he was thinking about how he was going to attempt it.

"I can't carry you, baby, it's too steep. I'll have to put my arm around your waist and help you that way, all right?" He asked, looking up at me. "Here, take off your bag," he said then looked over at Luca. "Would you mind carrying it for her?" He asked.

"Sure," Luca said, looking back at me. He smiled, waiting for me to remove it and hand it to him. His smile was different from most other men I had seen before. Maybe it was a Gypsyin thing, I wasn't sure, but it seemed sweeter like he was a genuinely kind person and for once, hopefully, wasn't a man that had bad intentions toward me. I handed him my bag and stood up with Jake's help.

Jake wrapped his arm around my waist as I wrapped mine around his neck. He took a couple of small side steps down the hill in front of me, then pulled me tight almost to lift me as I took the same couple of steps after him. We did that until we made it to the bottom, which at that point I could see we had a couple of onlookers at the entrance of the cave ready to greet us.

"Samuel," Luca said, talking to an older man that was sitting on a large rock when we entered, "this is Elliceva and Mike." He smiled and looked over at me.

"Miles, not Mike!" Jake quickly interjected, to correct him before he continued to confuse everyone. He acted slightly irritated, but no more than usual. He never struck me as the type who would have enjoyed being around a lot of people, but it was hard for me to tell, considering our past circumstances.

"Oh, my apologies," Luca said as he briefly glanced over at Jake then back to look toward an older woman standing beside the entrance. "Mary, this is Elliceva and… Miles." He smiled now, looking over at us again.

"Luca, why would you let more people in? You don't even know them!" A small voice came from a darkened spot near the back of the cave. I couldn't tell anything at first except it was a woman's voice.

Luca's smile quickly dissipated as he looked into the darkness trying to determine where the voice came from. "They're Gypsyins. It wouldn't have been right to send them away. Come out here so we can see you and I can introduce you to them."

Before long, I saw a woman's figure slowly appear as she moseyed out into what little light there was at the entrance of the cave. "Elliceva… Miles… This is Jocelyn," he said now looking at her. She was pretty, which I found odd; likely only because I wasn't used to seeing other women my age, just men. She had long stick-straight dark brown hair and fair ivory skin similar to mine, but a lighter shade, probably from living in a cave.

"What kind of name is Elliceva?" She asked, looking straight at me. I was taken aback by her bluntness. I wasn't sure why she would ask that. It didn't seem polite at all. Maybe her complexion wasn't the only thing the cave had affected. Maybe she'd been in it so long she'd forgotten how to have manners as well.

"You can call her Eva," Jake said quickly with a sour tone before I had a chance to answer her myself. I figured I knew why he told her that and I didn't mind. I realized Elliceva wasn't a normal name. He was right, though. To her I was probably going to be more Eva than anything, especially if she kept it up with her attitude.

"Is this your wife, Luca?" Jake asked him. I didn't think it was obvious that they were in a relationship but I didn't guess it hurt for Jake to ask it. I'm sure he had a reason behind the question.

"Oh uh, Jocelyn… Well, she's…" He began to answer but wasn't all that confident in what he was actually saying.

"No, but we're together if that's what you mean to be asking him," she pipped up to answer the question herself.

I looked over at Luca and smiled. It was obvious that she was more committed to whatever relationship that they had than he was. He responded with a half-smile, then quickly looked away.

After we met everyone, Luca showed us around the large cavern that was at the entrance of the cave. He then picked up a makeshift torch and dipped it into a small fire they had made just inside the entrance. We followed him down the left side of the cavern as he led us back to a narrow passage. After following him again through that, he stopped and pointed us to a small chamber to our left.

"This area is safe to stay in; if you like, you can use it. Be careful exploring past this, though. It can get tight in some areas and you could get stuck, lost, or even fall into the cavern that is back there. Farther on down there are falls where we get our clean water and take our showers. I can show you that area later, after you're settled."

"Thanks, man." Jake said as he set our bags down against a small stalagmite that was rising from the floor. "I'll need to go get some wood so I can make a fire. Are you okay staying here by yourself in the dark?" He asked, now looking at me.

I stood there staring at him, thinking about what he was asking me, trying to work up enough courage to agree and pretend that it wasn't a problem at all.

"You don't want to start a fire in here, Miles. It's not safe. This space is too small to release the heat and smoke. You might heat the limestone too much, which can cause it to crack and break, dropping a slab on you," Luca said still standing there, holding his torch. Jake scowled, probably not enjoying someone else telling him what to do, but he didn't say anything.

"I know it's winter, but it generally stays pretty comfortable in here if you leave your clothes on and lay under a blanket. If you need light, I can show you how to make a torch like this that you can use to come and go with," Luca said, offering more advice. I was hoping Jake didn't take it badly and would accept it without causing problems.

"Thanks but I know how to make a torch," Jake said as he started to reach down and open one of his bags.

"Elliceva, baby, will you stay here while I go get stuff to do that?" Jake asked, now sifting through a couple of pockets, most likely looking for his fire stick.

"She's going to need her leg checked, Miles," Luca said, looking down at Jake. I stared at Luca, hoping he would look back up at me. When he did, I widened my eyes slightly and shook my head no. I knew this wasn't a good time for him to mention it to Jake, especially since Jake didn't know he was a doctor yet and he probably just made Jake feel stupid for not knowing that you shouldn't start a fire in the cave.

Jake's eyes shot from Luca's to mine, then back. "How do you know about her leg?" He asked, furrowing his brow.

"I'm a doctor. From what she told me while she was sitting on the hill, I think she might have an infection. If it gets in her blood, it could turn septic. You don't want that to happen." Luca said again with all the doctor-y confidence he had in him.

Jake stared at me for a second, then let his eyes drift away to think. "Fine, hand me the torch and turn around," he said firmly, looking back at Luca.

Luca nodded, then looked over at me with a smug grin. He knew I wouldn't have let him look at it without Jake asking me to. He handed the torch over to Jake as he stood up, then Luca turned to look away.

"Baby, why don't you take your pants off of that leg and sit down. I will cover you up with my coat. Are you okay with that?" He said as he started to take his coat off with one arm before he passed the torch to his other hand to take it off of his other arm. "He's right. If it's getting worse, it could make you really sick. It won't hurt just to let him look at it," he continued. I think he could tell I was hesitant about the idea.

"Okay," I said softly, then did what he said and sat down. He tucked his coat in under my leg and over my underwear so the only thing Luca could see was my leg from the stitches down.

"All right, Luca," Jake said as he held up the torch for Luca to take back from him. "You can check it out now. You better be the kind of doctor that knows what you're looking at." He said, with a thinly veiled threat.

Luca turned around, grabbed the torch, and squatted down close to look at my thigh. I knew it was bad without him even saying anything. The entire area was red, swollen, and was oozing puss from around the stitches.

"Wow, it's worse than I thought. This is bad, Elliceva," he said, his eyes hesitantly connecting with mine. His face was nothing like Jake's. He showed numerous emotions all at the same time without any restraint whatsoever. I not only saw concern but also worry, tension, stress, and so many others I wouldn't have thought someone who just met me would have had so easily.

"Ok, what can you do about it?" Jake asked.

"She's going to need antibiotics but we don't have any around here. Normally for something little I would use garlic and other herbs, but that's not going to be enough for what she needs. It's past that at this point." The concern in Luca's voice grew the more he shared with Jake how bad he thought it was. "About a year ago, we had a lady here that something similar happened to. I wasn't able to get her fever down… She didn't make it. I *am* a doctor but that doesn't mean I have all the facilities and everything I need to take care of things like this when they happen. Actually, there was another man a couple of years before that when—"

"Enough!" Jake said, cutting him off. "I've heard enough. I get the idea."

"How many of you are there still here?" I asked Luca.

"Well, in this area, right after the war, when we initially gathered, there were seventeen of us. We've lost quite a few people over the years from various causes. There were nine of us still until a few months ago." He stopped briefly to sit back a little, no longer needing to look at my leg as closely as he was.

"What happened to them?" Jake asked, reluctantly.

"We don't know, they just keep disappearing. I don't know where they are going," Luca answered. I could tell by his face he wasn't exaggerating. "Now there are only five of us left. Other than myself, you met three of them already. Arthur left earlier in the day but he should be back later tonight before dark. I can introduce you to him in the morning if you would like. He honestly isn't the most pleasant man to be around but... um, yeah... he is Jocelyn's uncle so we tolerate him."

"All right, I will talk with her about what we can do about her leg," Jake said, looking at Luca as if to dismiss him from our new living space. Then Jake brought his eyes back to mine to see how I was taking the news. It was bothersome, but I'd been in worse situations before so I didn't act like I cared, even though I did. I didn't want it to be as bad as Luca was saying it was. I knew what Jake would want to do, and that was the last thing that I wanted right now.

"Why didn't you tell me your leg had gotten this bad?" Jake asked softly after Luca walked away. "Have you been hiding it?"

We'd been intimate multiple times since we left the cabin, and I didn't realize it until now but I had been hiding it. I wasn't used to having a partner, someone else who cared for me, who wanted to protect me. Maybe I was still having issues with trusting him... it was subconscious if so, because I didn't think I did.

"Eva?" He asked, breaking me from my thoughts.

"I'm sorry..." I sighed, trying to think about how to respond. It bothered me to think that I had been hiding it. Eva had been hiding it, not Kaleah. I wondered if deep down she wanted a reason for Jake to have to leave. Maybe she was still trying to escape again. I pushed out a deep breath when the realization hit me. *Shit, what has she done?* "I should have told you, Jake. I didn't mean to make you feel bad."

He leaned forward, resting his forehead against mine. "I forgive you..." He said softly, staring into my eyes. "I'll do whatever I have to do to protect you, baby, even if it's from yourself. Let's agree, no more hiding things, okay?"

I knew I still had secrets I wasn't telling him. Things about my past, things about the Sicari and my family, but this wasn't the time to bring it up, if ever. I closed my eyes so when I nodded, it wouldn't feel like I was lying. I didn't ever want to lie to him. I wasn't ready to tell him the truth though, and I probably never would be.

# 3

## FEMININE INTUITION

We didn't discuss my leg any more after the doctor left. Jake knew it wasn't the right time to talk about it, or maybe that I wasn't really in a receptive mood. Nonetheless, he knew better than to bring it back up right away. Luca was nice enough to leave us with his torch so we could get the chamber set up enough to stay in it comfortably. We needed a way to navigate in the darkness without somehow accidentally killing ourselves so Jake left me with Luca's torch and gathered some supplies to make us our own torches.

The longer I sat there thinking about the dangers that lurked all around us, not to mention whatever the reason was that made random people keep coming up missing, I wondered if we should have just taken our chances with the Sicari chasing after us instead.

Jake didn't say anything, but I figured he knew just as well as I did that Arthur was probably the man that he shot before we met Luca in the valley. I wasn't about to tell anyone about it and I knew he wasn't either but it was still concerning to think about what they would do if they found out. If they found his body with a gunshot wound around the same time we showed up, I doubted we could convince them to just write it off as a coincidence. It did make me feel a little better hearing

Luca's description of the man and knowing Jake didn't shoot someone that would be missed all that much.

Thankfully, because we had the horses for our trip from the cabin, we were able to bring way more than we would have been if we had had to carry everything. Jake took a couple of the quilts from the cabin that he used as saddle pads for the horses and brought them into our little chamber to help make a softened bed for us to lie down on. It didn't take him long to make the place feel nice and cozy. As cozy as a rocky hole in the ground could feel, anyway.

A few times I thought he was going to go against Luca's advice and start a small fire in the chamber with us, but each time he hesitated then went on working on something else. I knew it bothered him. He wasn't used to not knowing everything there was about surviving out on our own. I'm sure it hurt his pride a little to think that Luca knew something that he didn't. That was probably what made him want to rebel a little until he thought about the consequences and didn't.

"Do you feel comfortable around Luca?" Jake asked, breaking up our random small talk with an unexpected question. I didn't answer right away. Instead, I was trying to figure out why he would ask me something like that and what his motives behind it were.

"Well, uh, yeah... I guess so. Why would you ask me that?" I hoped he would just come out with it.

"No, I really want you to think about it before you answer me. You have been around a lot of men that... well... you could tell. Right? You can tell when they—" He stopped, not knowing how to explain what he was asking, but I knew what he meant.

"Are you asking me if it is obvious? Like if I have some kind of natural instinct to be able to tell if a man is bad or not?" I figured I'd clear it up for him if I was going to answer his question honestly.

He swallowed hard before he answered. I didn't know where he was exactly taking this conversation but he didn't act like it was a comfortable one for him. "Yes, you can tell, right? I think... like a woman's instinct. You knew Seth was... uh... You know what I'm saying... So how do you feel about Luca?" He asked again.

I took a second and let my eyes wander around, allowing my mind to ponder the question, genuinely wanting to determine what my honest opinion was about his character. "Does he have secrets? Yeah, probably, but don't we all? Honestly… yeah, I think he's probably a good guy. I didn't feel any negative… uh, whatever you call it from him so far. I mean that's not to say he isn't hiding who he really is."

"He's a Gypsyin… he's not likely to be hiding anything like that. He wasn't trained to be that way," Jake said, agreeing with my conclusion.

I didn't say anything else. I just stared at him in a way he knew I was expecting him to tell me why he would ask me that question in the first place.

"I'm going to have to leave you here for a few days so I can go to the nearest base and get you some antibiotics." He said, initially looking at me but quickly looked down, trying to avoid eye contact. He knew I wouldn't be happy with his plan.

"You can't do that!" I said the first thing that came to my mind, without even realizing I didn't know where I was going with it. I just knew I didn't like what he wanted to do.

"Don't argue with me, baby. It won't do you any good. I've already made up my mind," he said finally looking back up at me with softened eyes.

"It doesn't work like that. We're a team now. You don't get to just make decisions without me and force me to stick to them. What if these people are—"

"You just told me you didn't feel like he was a bad guy. That's why I asked you before I told you why I wanted to know." Jake quickly interrupted me.

"Yeah, but can't you see it's not a good idea? Why can't I just go with you? I can go just far enough—" I stopped myself this time before he interrupted me again. I knew what I was about to say and how he would counter before I even finished saying it. "Ugh, fine. I get it. I know why you think you have to go and why you won't let me go with you, but what about you? What if something happens to you? What if you don't come back?"

He smiled and crawled over to sit in front of me. "Baby, you don't need to worry about me. I can take care of myself, you know that. You're the one I'm worried about. That's the only reason I feel like I have no choice. I can't let you get sicker," he said as he brought his face closer to mine. Then he leaned in to whisper into my ear, "Besides remember that's why I kept my tag, for times like this when I would need to use it to get us things." He said then gently kissed above my ear.

"Okay, but how long do you think you will have to be gone?" I asked, pulling away and turning my head toward his.

"Well, hopefully no more than three or four days... Max—oh, maybe a week," he sighed, then sat back as he continued to rattle off his exact plans. "I'll have to go to Nashville, that's where I—"

"That's where Miller is!" I said sharply, cutting him off.

"He might be... but he travels around his jurisdiction a lot, so I won't know until I get there. I don't have to see him, though. I'm just planning on slipping in and then back out. It'll be fine." He lifted his hand to stroke my hair, trying to reassure me.

I didn't respond to him; I didn't know what to say. I wasn't happy with it but I couldn't fabricate in my mind exactly what he was able to do about it, so I figured complaining wouldn't do any good.

We agreed he would leave the next morning. He said it would only be after he talked to Luca first and made sure I would be taken care of while he was gone. I knew it was probably to also warn him if he did anything to me, Jake would likely murder him in a slow and agonizing way. If Jake was anything it was protective but possessive came in at a close second.

The next morning, he did what he said. He helped me make myself comfortable out in the large cavern at the cave's entrance and took Luca off to the side to talk to him for a minute before he left. I wasn't sure what he said but Luca seemed to take it well so he must not have been too threatening with him. Luca didn't seem to say much back to him, he just nodded his head a lot in agreement. Jake then returned briefly to me to say goodbye.

"I'll be back before you know it." He smiled and kissed me on top of the head.

I didn't want him to leave, but I didn't want to make him feel bad for having to either. I returned his embrace and pressed my head against his chest one last time. "I love you, Jake." I said softly, trying to savor the moment just in case he didn't return as he promised.

"You'll be okay, baby… You're strong." He hugged me tighter then leaned forward to give me one last kiss. "I love you too, sweetie. I'll see you soon." He held me for a moment like he too was savoring the feeling of our embrace, then he quickly blinked like he was holding back deep emotions before turning to walk away.

Initially, it took Luca a while before he came over to talk to me. Maybe I was wrong and Jake did actually threaten him, possibly enough he was afraid to come straight over to me afterward. I didn't know where Jocelyn or the other man or woman were but I didn't mind having someone to talk to now that Jake had left.

At first, I could tell he felt awkward. He sat down on a rock across from me but he didn't look all that comfortable. He started with small talk, asking how I liked my first night in a cave. I shared with him that I had lived in caves before while I was on my own so it wasn't too awfully different but I preferred the old days pre-war. Nothing was more comfortable than air conditioning, television, internet, indoor plumbing… I went on lightheartedly reciting the list until he began to relax. I was even able to coax a chuckle out of him. He had a pleasant smile. I enjoyed seeing him laugh too, since it wasn't all that common for Jake to laugh at my jokes. I decided I would try harder to be funny. Maybe it would continue.

We talked about our lives before the war, and eventually it felt like he was able to fully relax and feel comfortable talking to me. He shared with me about going through school to be a doctor and that taking care of people was a passion of his. That was one of the reasons he had a hard time picking a side to be on, and why he ended up being a Gypsyin. It could have easily led to why I decided to be a Gypsyin as well but I steered the conversation in another direction when it got to that point since I wasn't a real Gypsyin like he was, and that wasn't actually the path I ever chose.

I wanted to tell him the truth, not because I wanted him to know it but because it felt like it weighed on me pretty heavily. I really meant it when I said I would have preferred him to be a psychiatrist.

I was young when the war started. I wish I had picked being a Gypsyin for the same noble reasons he had, but it wasn't that simple for me. I could still remember the last time I saw my parents. They both decided they were going to be Coldiers. They wanted me to be one as well; I didn't have a choice they said; it was mandatory. In those years, I was rebellious more than anything else. I thought I knew exactly what I wanted, and that was not to be told what I could and couldn't be. I also had no concept of what war was and how that choice would ultimately affect the rest of my life.

Instead of listening to them, I went to the Sicari to enlist. When I went to receive my tag, they pulled me aside and said they had another unit in mind for me that they thought I would be perfect for. If I would agree to it, there would be special benefits, special training and I would receive a title within the units that was reserved only for select individuals that could make it through the rigorous training and testing. I was always up for a challenge so it wasn't a hard decision for me. I wanted in, and that was exactly what I got.

I sat there and listened to Luca as he went on talking about his life before the war and how hard it had been for him after the war as well. He was old enough to be a doctor, though at first I wouldn't have thought so considering he appeared to look younger than he said he was. With all my memory fractures, I didn't exactly know my age but from what I was able to gather, Luca most likely was only about five or six years older than me.

He shared a little about his family and I shared a little about mine and where we both grew up, what I could remember of it, anyway. He admitted he did have an accent like I thought I initially heard the first day. His parents were both Italian immigrants that came over to the states before he was born. That was his reason for being able to hide it so well when he talked. He only grew up hearing it around them. He told me he learned to control it in med school because he wanted to sound more professional. I chuckled at first when he said it, which I think surprised him a bit. So he wouldn't feel bad, I went on to explain that I didn't think he should hide it. It was actually quite endearing to hear it when he talked.

It seemed like we were sitting there for hours just talking, both of us becoming more and more relaxed with the other. I didn't know what Jake told him but I felt whatever it was, if he wanted Luca to take care of me while he was gone, we were on a good path. I was sure with him already having a caring personality it wouldn't be too difficult of a request.

He was such a contrast to Jake, not that Jake wasn't caring, but it was different. I think I could sense the openness in Luca, the part of him, unlike Jake, that wasn't an agent. He didn't seem guarded when he talked to me and he wasn't ever cold or withdrawn during the conversation. In that way, he wasn't anything like Marcus either. I think the only men I had ever known after the war were all agents. I had never been around a legitimate Gypsyin before and it was surprisingly refreshing.

We were both enjoying our chat until Jocelyn found her way over to join our conversation. She sat down next to him on the same rock. Though the way she was acting, if there would have been room, I was sure she would have sat in his lap. It wasn't long before she had completely taken over the conversation.

"Where'd your li'l boyfriend run off to?" She asked with a snooty attitude. I could tell she didn't like me, but for what reason I was unsure.

"He went to retrieve a couple of items from a dead body we passed on the way here. You know everything has value," I said it with an ornery little smile but acted like I was serious.

Luca, knowing I was joking started to chuckle but stopped himself just short of Jocelyn giving him a dirty look.

"Oh, you think you're funny? Whatever…" she said as she rolled her eyes, "You've probably never even seen a dead body."

*Oh, little does she know.* I shook my head. "You're right," I said, letting her believe what she wanted.

"I've seen dead bodies. You know how many people around here have come up missing? It's dangerous. You really should watch yourself. Especially when your man isn't here. Who knows what could happen to you." She said it so I could tell it was a threat without Luca being able to detect it.

"How do you see all the dead bodies if they're missing?" I asked, seeing if I could trip her up a little.

She squinted her eyes, releasing a short, sharp breath as she let a scowl crawl across her face. "I—" She started to respond before Luca answered for her, "Girls, I don't think this is a productive conversation. Maybe we should change the subject."

I took his advice, but at the same time decided I wanted to prod her a little more. "Sure, so how long have you two been together? Did you meet before the war?"

No sooner did I ask it, than Luca's face changed. I could tell it wasn't a comfortable subject for him to talk about, which was exactly the reason I wanted to ask. I was curious what the dynamic between the two of them was, and not wanting to wait over days to observe it, I figured I could force it out all at once.

Jocelyn began to answer but it was clearly a difficult question for her as well. She became a bit tense suddenly. "We're together… But I only came to the cave a couple of years ago." She didn't say anything else. It was obvious they weren't telling me something. The idea that we were all carrying our own dirty little secrets wasn't new to me.

One of my strong suits as an agent was always interrogation, so I thought I would keep probing without it looking obvious. "Oh, I thought you told me you were married before, Luca? Or maybe I got that mixed up with someone else." I made it up. I knew he never said it but I wanted to see how they would respond.

His eyes suddenly widened. He opened his mouth, about to address what I just said but she beat him to it. "Well, he had someone else before me but they were never married. I don't know why you would tell her that, Luca!" she said as she turned to scowl at him.

He cleared his throat a little, then hesitantly looked back at me. "I don't remember telling you that." He stopped briefly to swallow, as if recalling a painful memory. "I was with someone else a few years ago. We were dating before the war and talked about marriage but never got the chance—" He stopped again. He acted like he wanted to go on but it might have been too painful.

"She left him essentially. I'm sorry, Luca. I just had to say it. We've talked about you being honest with yourself about her." Jocelyn said again with a matter-a-fact attitude like she didn't care that it was bothering him to talk about it. I started to feel bad that I brought it up myself.

"Oh, I'm sorry I brought it up. I'm sorry to hear that," I said, looking at Luca.

"It's not like she died… she left him," Jocelyn countered, attacking me for apologizing.

"That's debatable," Luca snapped, then took a deep breath and sat up a little straighter. "You call it that but she went missing just like all the other people around here that have gone missing and we don't say they left," he ended it with a bit of a seething tone.

For a moment, I felt like a marriage counselor, only I wasn't the doctor and they weren't married, but I could sense the similarity. It was a mystery for sure. It sounded like he most likely loved this woman and she disappeared suddenly. *Interesting…*

I noticed the longer I sat there the warmer I became. I enjoyed talking to Luca, but I was beginning to not feel well and I figured it would be best if I went to lie down. I excused myself and painfully standing to my feet, told them I needed to go rest. Luca insisted that he walk me back to the chamber since I probably still didn't know my way yet and it would be easy to miss it and go too far. Jocelyn didn't appear to be happy about it but she didn't say anything. Luca lit a torch and led the way. When we made it there, he told me he would come back by to check on me later that afternoon to see if I needed anything. I smiled to show my appreciation. From what I could tell, he was a sweet man, and it was unfortunate that he had to be paired with a woman like Jocelyn.

# 4

# EXPOSING MORE THAN SECRETS

I don't know how long I had been asleep before I was awakened by a dim glow that began to emanate through my eyelids. I opened my eyes to see Luca standing above me. He had the torch in one hand and something that looked like a plate in the other.

"Are you not cold?" He asked, letting his eyes drift down me. I had pulled the covers off and was laying there in only my shirt and pants with no jacket.

"No," I said, pushing off from the floor to sit up. "I was too warm with all that on." I smiled, then looked at what he was carrying.

"Oh… Well, I brought you some food if you're hungry. I'm surprised you haven't gotten up to come eat yet. It's almost evening," he bent down to hand me the plate. "Also, I boiled some water. When you're done eating, I need to open up your wound and clean it out." He pointed to a pot sitting on the ground.

I looked at the pot of water. I guess my leg probably did need cleaned, but I didn't really like the idea. "I don't really have an appetite, but thank you. I'll try to eat a little," I said, ignoring the wound comment as I looked down at what I was going to have to eat. To my surprise, I didn't see the usual meal of cooked rabbit, but rather a nice portion of perfectly cooked fish. "Oh, I love fish! Thank you! Where do you get it from?"

He smiled, happy to see I was pleased and more likely to eat. "Samuel's usually the one who goes hunting or fishing during the day. He really enjoys it. He told me one time that before the war, when he dreamed of what his retirement looked like, it would be a life full of nothing but hunting and fishing all day, every day. I'm happy to help him fulfill his dream, especially since it isn't my forte." He sat down across from me like he was willing to have a conversation but I figured his real motive was probably making sure I would actually eat.

"So are you the one who cooks, or do I have to worry about Jocelyn poisoning me?" I asked with a tad bit of sarcasm in my voice so he suspected I was joking even though I wasn't.

"Oh… you don't need to worry about her," he laughed. "Though, I know she can be a little… well—"

"Obnoxious," I said, trying to give him the word he was likely looking for.

He laughed again but I could tell he was trying to stop himself from getting too loud. "Well, that's not exactly a word I could use, but yes… she isn't everyone's cup of tea, I am sure. You don't have to worry about her hurting you, though. She is more bark than bite," he said with a smile like he was trying to believe himself.

"Ok, I'll try to believe you," I smiled back, then took another bite of fish.

His face became more serious as he continued. "I think she only acts like she does because she is jealous of you," he said, looking at me with the same intensity he did the first day.

"What do you mean?" I asked. It wasn't like she was an ugly woman. I wasn't sure what she would have to be jealous about.

"Beauty isn't your only endearing quality, Eva," he said it as if he'd read my mind. "You also have the way Miles looks at you. I'm sure she envies that look from a man." He stopped, letting his eyes break from mine for a moment.

"You don't look at her like that?" I asked, even though I knew the answer.

He smiled softly. "No, to be honest, what we have between us is more a matter of convenience than it is love." He smiled again as he looked down at my now empty plate. "Here, I'll take that if you're done. Also, I need to look at your leg now, if you don't mind."

"Ugh… okay," I said, hesitantly handing him the plate.

"Don't worry, I'll be nothing but professional. But if I don't clean it, the infection will get worse."

I didn't reply. I just nodded as I looked away, trying unsuccessfully to think of a way out of this. "Okay…" I said as I reached down and unbuttoned my pants, sliding them off. Then I picked them back up to rest in my lap to cover my underwear. I finally looked over at him again, giving him a look of warning. *Touch me inappropriately and I'll kill you!*

"Why don't you lie back? It'll be easier. I'm sorry I don't have any alcohol to give you to make it less painful." He sounded like he was trying to be professional. Maybe the look I gave him *had* helped.

"It's fine. I can handle pain." I said, lying back. He had no idea what things I had been through before. Pain was an old friend—one I was all too familiar with.

"Okay, just let me know if you need a break," He said softly. Before long, I could feel a gentle pull and tug, accompanied by a sharp shooting pain, likely him pulling out the old stitches. Then, after a bit, I felt the warm water trickling down my leg, running onto a rag he had set beneath me.

I didn't say anything, or make any noises. I just lay there enduring it, thinking about my past and how this really wasn't anything compared to the horrors Miller had put me through.

After a few minutes, he finally spoke again. "Okay, I've done all I can do for it right now. Hopefully, this will help." He said, leaning back and gathering all the stuff he'd brought. "Now, you just need to keep it as clean as you can."

"Thank you. I appreciate you taking care of me. I think I'm going to rest more now; I still feel tired."

He smiled, probably as happy as I was that it was over with. "It's easy to feel that way when you are in such a dark cold place in the middle of winter," he sighed. "When the sun comes back out you should go outside and see if you could catch a little of it, it might help if you are feeling depressed."

I smiled and nodded but I knew even though it probably would be helpful to me, I couldn't. Surely the signal my brain was transmitting was being successfully suppressed by all the surrounding rock, but I couldn't chance it. Even if we were in a danger zone for agents, if they were able to catch that signal again with me traveling around outside, I wasn't certain they wouldn't risk the area to still try to find me.

Luca left, taking his torch with him, leaving me in complete darkness. I never realized I was afraid of the dark as much as I did at that moment. My eyes began to dart around, looking for some object to recognize and cling to, to no avail. I could feel myself becoming more tense so I shut them and lay back down on top of my blankets. I was feeling warmer than I felt the first time when I had come to lie down. I assumed the cave was heating up from the warmth of mid-day, but I didn't know for sure.

As I lay there, my mind thought it would be a good time to go over all my previous thoughts and fears concerning Jake and Miller and everything he needed to do in Nashville. When I realized it wasn't the best path to let it go down, I quickly brought it back to thinking about something else more positive until before long it stopped thinking altogether and I drifted back off to sleep.

I don't know how long I was asleep before I was awakened again by what felt like a cool hand pressed against my forehead. Startled, I opened my eyes to see Luca squatting down beside me.

"Shhh, don't be scared, it's just me. I'm sorry to wake you," he said, looking at me, then down to my body before he swiftly brought his eyes back up to mine. "You have a fever."

I did feel terribly warm, so it didn't take me long to gather what he was trying to tell me and process it. Meanwhile, I sensed something was off about how I was laying. I tilted my head forward and looked down. I was laying there, dressed in nothing but my underwear. I couldn't believe it. I must have removed everything while I was asleep.

"Oh my gosh, don't look!" I said as I began to frantically look around for wherever I placed my shirt and my pants.

"Don't worry about it," he said, reaching above my head and picking up my coat to hand it to me. "I'm a doctor remember? It was normal to see people naked every day in surgery."

That helped me feel a little better but I couldn't control the level of embarrassment that I was experiencing. I grabbed my coat and positioned it as well as I could over the main parts of me that were exposed. He continued to reach around and gather my other loose articles of clothing that I had haphazardly flung about while sleep impaired before handing them to me.

"If you are still feeling hot, you don't have to cover yourself up completely. I really do understand," he said as he lowered himself to sit down across from me.

I was sure he didn't mind, but I was willing to feel overheated for the sake of my own decency, so I continued to replace everything that he handed me. Not wanting to admit the increased modesty was from my own embarrassment, I decided to use Jake as another valid excuse. "Jake'll be upset it if he finds out you saw me like this," I said.

"Jake?" Luca asked, with a surprised look on his face.

"Oh, sorry, I mean Miles… I call him Jake. Jacob Miles is his full name," I said, realizing this was the first time I mentioned him to Luca by his first name.

He didn't say anything for a moment. He just looked at me oddly, then responded, "Right… well, that would make sense with him being an agent."

I started to nod, but before completing a full motion of agreement; I caught it. I realized what he had said and what he knew and what he was and wasn't supposed to know. "Wait… what? Why would you say that?" I asked, giving him a confused look.

"Well, I thought the way he was dressed was a little nicer than what a usual Gypsyin would wear, and he never showed me his arm like you did. Initially, I was suspicious, but because I had no way of defending myself if I was right, I just went along with it. Then when he took off his jacket to cover your leg, even though he had a long sleeve shirt on,

I could see the bump in his forearm... That, and him wanting to be referred to by his last name and seeing you had horses, well I figured it's safe to assume he's a Sicari."

"You're wrong," I said now feeling a bit skittish not knowing if this would change how he treated me. He *was* wrong, but only about what kind of agent he was, so it wasn't hard to say that and look like I wasn't lying.

"You don't have to be afraid of me, Eva. Just because I know what he is, doesn't mean that changes anything between me and you. I don't know yet why you are with him but it's obvious you're a Gypsyin. I will keep taking care of you as I promised," he said.

"Thank you... I guess," I said softly, realizing he was already convinced of what he thought he knew, so for me to try to deny it wasn't likely a good strategy to take.

"So, why don't you tell me? Why are you really with him?" He asked. His eyes were back to the way he liked to look at me—very intently.

I knew it might not help my current situation if I shared that I would stay loyal to Jake no matter what. Luca saw Jake as an enemy and aligning myself with that, making myself one as well wouldn't do me any favors. Until Jake returned and got the whole situation straightened out, I would need Luca to be on my side. So I would have to tell him whatever I needed to achieve that effect.

"It's complicated. We do love each other but... I was his prisoner until he rescued me," I said, giving him full eye contact.

"Are you serious?" He paused briefly, leaving a disturbed look on his face. "Eva... That's not ok! Is he forcing you to be with him? Has he hurt you? Why... What makes you think you love a man that could do that to you?" He asked, obviously taking whatever I said farther than I intended without acknowledging the 'rescued me' part.

"No, it's not like that... It was my fault. He hasn't done anything to—"

"Eva!" He stopped me before I could go on. "I'm not a psychiatrist, but I do know how to identify if a woman is in an abusive relationship."

I stared at him blankly as I silently cussed inside my mind. This isn't what I was intending at all. "He's not a bad guy. Please don't hurt him when he comes back for me," I said not knowing how to proceed without digging the hole even deeper.

I was trying to rely on Eva's training but nothing was clearly coming to mind for this occasion except the thought of using this as an opportunity to deceive him even further. Sicari-Eva wanted to make him believe she was a victim because she could see so much gain from it. The Kaleah side of my brain, however, only felt bad for what danger I had just accidentally placed Jake into.

"Don't worry, it's normal for you to feel that way. I'm not going to hurt him, besides he is the one likely with the weapon, not me. You are who I'm concerned about. It's bad enough you have a fever let alone now I see he probably had some kind of control over you as well," he said, his face was now full of genuine concern for my well-being.

I didn't say anything else out of fear it would be twisted around and used against me again. I just sat there, leaned my head to rest against the wall behind me then looked away.

"I am on your side, Eva. Try not to shut me out. I'm here to help you," he said, seeing that I wasn't all that thrilled with his observation of Jake and our relationship.

I nodded and suggested that I was tired again and that it would be best if I just lay back down. He agreed and said he would go get me some fresh cool water from the falls that were lower down in the cave for me to drink.

O ver the next five days, he visited me frequently, sometimes staying and sitting with me for hours as we talked. My fever began to get worse. Some days, I felt like I wanted to rip all my clothes off again and just lay there naked against the bare stone floor. Other days I felt so cold, not even wrapping myself fully clothed with my coat in both blankets felt like it was enough to warm me up. Luca did the best he could. When I was hot, he would bring me more cool water from the falls and when I was cold, he would heat the water over the fire before offering it to me.

Even though I very much enjoyed the bountiful portions of fish that were available to me thanks to Samuel, I didn't seem to have much of an appetite and it was hard to get myself to eat. Luca did what he could, trying to wake me up frequently to ask if I wanted anything but I often refused anything he brought to me except water.

At first, I was concerned with how Jocelyn felt seeing Luca was spending much of his time with me and not with her. But because I only left my chamber to go to the restroom, I never really saw her, so she didn't have any more opportunities to be bitchy with me. I could only go off of what Luca was saying, and that was that she wasn't a problem and I shouldn't worry about her. I didn't actually believe him, but seeing he believed himself was good enough for me at the time, since I couldn't really do anything about it if she did have an issue and wanted to cause problems.

As the days continued to pass, I grew more concerned with where Jake might be. I had hoped he would have returned by then, since it had been more than the three or four days that he had originally said it would take. So many scenarios circled through my mind. I was afraid he might have gotten hurt or even stuck at the base. I was worried about what would have happened if he did actually see Miller and he asked him about me and where I was and why I wasn't with Jake.

I was anxious to see how Luca would act when Jake returned and Luca told him he knew what he really was. I didn't want Jake to get hurt, but I also didn't want Luca to do anything stupid and threaten him and make Jake hurt him, either.

The time Luca and I had together when I was awake and coherent wasn't all that much, but the quality was there. He was enjoyable to talk to even when I didn't feel well; it was nice to have him there with me as opposed to being alone in the dark. It wasn't hard for me at this point to consider him a friend even if he was entirely wrong about Jake and what his intentions with me were.

Luca was with me once again, sitting beside me while I lay there, resting. I was so hot, not even the cool water he brought me was able to help. He suggested instead of stripping down and laying bare against the stone, as I was doing, that I at least put one layer of clothes on and go outside where there was still snow on the ground that I could use to cool myself off. It was probably an excellent idea except I knew I couldn't safely go that far outside so I told him I'd think about it, fully intending not to. That way, he would stop suggesting it. The smooth stone felt so good against my feverish skin that I just lay there while we talked.

I was feeling very tired again and our conversation was winding down so I figured it would be a good time to try to go back to sleep. No sooner had I closed my eyes than I heard something that didn't sound like Luca. I opened them again to see Jake had returned and was now standing at my feet, staring down at us both. Initially, he didn't say anything he just moved his eyes around, gathering facts before taking action. It was clear he was starting to gather the wrong facts when I thought I would speak up.

"Jake, it's not what you think," I said trying to quickly steer him away from the conclusions he was most likely coming to.

As I did, I could tell Luca likely felt the same way when I noticed him stand up and back away from where Jake was standing.

"Where are your clothes?" He demanded, looking down at me as he quickly began to remove his coat. He was visibly upset, but not necessarily with me.

"I was hot, Jake. It's the best I could do," I said as he bent down and gently laid his coat over me, trying to cover up as much of me as he could.

"Jake, her fever has gotten worse. I hope you were able to bring her the medicine she needs," Luca said flatly, assuming Jake wasn't upset with him but seeing Jake's body language that wasn't the case.

Jake stood up slowly and glared at him. Tension was thick in the air and that look told me he might be about to do something stupid. "I asked that you take care of her! I don't know what you think you're doing in here but it looks like you were doing more than just taking care, you perverted little shit." Jake slowly took a step closer to Luca as he said it.

"Jake, please don't hurt him, he hasn't done anything to me!" I tried, but knew he wasn't likely to hear me over his anger.

"Don't talk to me like that. I haven't done nearly as much to her as you have. You can try to pretend all you want but I know what you really are." Luca just couldn't help himself, he said too much, and I knew it. Jake was already provoked; he didn't need much to push him over the edge.

Jake took another couple of steps and brought his forearm up to Luca's chest to push him against the wall of the cave, then Jake brought his fist back, preparing to punch him.

"Miles, stop!" I screamed, hoping using his other name would make him think about what I was saying.

It did something because he didn't punch him, instead he just stood there, thinking about it. "I don't care what you think I am. If I ever catch you looking at her again like I did when I walked in, I will kill you, do you hear me?" Jake growled. I was happy it appeared he was letting him slide with just a warning.

Luca didn't answer, he just looked at him then down over at me then back at him, and nodded. Jake released him and he hesitantly walked out, only looking down at me briefly before he left.

Jake slowly turned around, letting the tension in his shoulders relax a little as he lowered his gaze to me. I didn't know why but at that moment I felt scared of him. I sat up and started to gather my clothes to put them back on.

"We need to talk," He said quietly. I didn't know what he needed to tell me, or if he was upset with me but that made me feel even more anxious than I had while he was gone.

"Fine," I nodded to the empty spot next to me, "sit down, let's talk."

# 5

## DEEPER THAN A HIDDEN PAST

"Did he touch you?" he asked, still standing stiff, looking down at me. He didn't sit down as I suggested he should. I think he was too upset.

I knew I had to be careful with how I answered as to not provoke him any further. I realized he could still go find Luca and kill him on the spot if he wanted to. "No, never like that," I said, hoping it would help him calm down. "He only felt my forehead one time to see if I had a fever."

He had begun to pace slowly back and forth in a four-foot area. I could tell the torch he brought wasn't going to last long and we would soon be in the dark. He wasn't saying anything, so I thought I would try to explain everything further. "I know why you're upset. I'm sorry I wasn't dressed. I was just so hot, and I couldn't go outside. I didn't know what else to do."

"I understand, baby. I'm not mad at you, it's not your fault," he said finally as he stopped pacing and looked down at me again. "But you didn't see the way he was looking at you."

"What? It was dark. His torch already went out. He couldn't have been looking at me for long... He could only have seen me with the light of the torch you brought in," I said, looking over at Jake's torch, now about to go out entirely.

"It doesn't take long to engrave that image in your head. I know that look. It's the same look that Seth had," he said as he crouched down to his largest bag to get something out of it.

"What? Jake… Luca isn't like that. He used to see people naked all the time during operations. He's a doctor. He understood why I was uncovered. He never even acted like Seth did. If he was going to do something to me, he had his chance, but he didn't," I wanted to help Jake think of the Luca differently without trying to sound like I was defending him, I knew that wouldn't make Jake like him any better.

Jake rummaged through his bag for a moment until he pulled out his fire stick, then used it to light another torch. "You're not a man, Eva, you might not understand that look but I do. He wants you… it's that simple. It doesn't matter if it's for good reasons or bad, it's no different, the look is the same!" He took the now lit torch and wedged it in between a few rocks that were sitting near the wall, then moved over to sit down in front of me.

"Okay, well you're back now and he doesn't get me!" I said, hoping he felt reassured by the confidence I had in my statement.

"I wish it were that easy, baby, I really do," he was starting to sound less uptight, "but it doesn't work that way. This complicates things."

I didn't know exactly what he meant, but I figured he was speaking about how awkward it would be between us all now. I didn't ask for him to clarify, I just wanted to move on to another subject.

"Were you able to get antibiotics?" I asked, looking down at his bag to see what other things he was able to get from the base while he was there.

His eyes widened as he took a deep breath, instantly broken out of an angry delusion and brought back to reality. "Yes, um… here let me get them for you," he said as he pulled his bag over to him. "That's actually what I wanted to talk to you about."

"What…?" I asked hesitantly. I wasn't sure what he was about to say but I got the idea it wasn't going to be pleasant.

He didn't say anything for a moment, he just took a bottle that I assumed was the antibiotics from his bag and handed it to me. He looked down and away like he was trying to come up with the right way to tell me what he had on his mind.

"Spit it out, Miles!" I blurted out without realizing or even intending to say it.

His eyes quickly shot back up to mine with a surprised look on his face. "Fine…" he said still reluctantly, "I just don't want you to take it the wrong way and freak out and do something stupid."

"What, like the way you barged in and was about to murder a man over the way he *looked* at me?" I asked, giving him a flat expression.

"Fair enough," he said with a sigh. "I had to talk to Miller to be able to get your medicine and more supplies." He paused, but only briefly to make sure I wasn't getting mad. "They froze my expense account when I deactivated my tracker. So my only options were to go to him to get it reactivated so I could pay for everything or steal it all and risk getting shot." He had more to say, but he stopped again to gauge my reaction before he continued.

I didn't say anything. I just sat there and stared at him. I had no clue what all this meant for us but I knew the wisest thing was to get all the information before deciding what I should do about it.

He hesitated again, closed his eyes, and reached up to scratch the back of his neck then opened them to remake eye contact with me. "You can imagine he had a lot of questions about where I've been and why I didn't have you with me," he said then looked down again, "I tried my best to only say what I had to, to just get myself back out of there."

I still didn't respond. I was hot; I felt ill and now I was also upset, verging on livid.

"He wanted to reassign me, but I was able to get out of it. He doesn't know I'm with you. I told him the same thing I told the team when we were caught in Charlotte and he believed me. I convinced him to let me keep looking for you. That was the only way I was allowed to leave and come back to you," he finished. He had to know I wasn't happy, he was even more tense than when we started the conversation.

"So they can track you again?" I asked as calmly as I could, still trying to collect as much information as I could before exploding with rage.

"I had no choice, to get the medicine for you, I had to…" he paused then continued, "it doesn't matter though. They won't come after me unless something tells them I have you, besides I don't know of any agent that would follow Miller's orders to go into the grotto lands. Not to mention just being in the caves will help block my tracker to some degree, just like yours."

I closed my eyes, willing myself to relax. I couldn't be mad at him. I wanted to be, but only so my anger over the situation felt justified even though I knew it wasn't. I thought about what Luca knew about Jake and that he was an agent, and wondered if that would compound our problems. I considered telling Jake that Luca thought he was a Sicari, and that he thought Jake was manipulating me but didn't figure it was a good time to bring Luca back up again.

"Okay, I understand. I don't guess there is anything I can do about it now by being mad at you," I said, looking straight at him relaxing the look on my face and any tension I was holding in my body. "I don't feel well. I am so hot. Can I take my clothes back off now, please? I just want to lie down and go back to sleep. The stone against my back is nice."

He initially looked confused, then quickly relaxed and smiled, likely relieved. "Of course, if it makes you feel better, it's fine. I'll just make sure Luca doesn't come anywhere near you while you're undressed again. You should take the medicine before you lie down though, you need to take it three times a day. It should make you feel better before long, hopefully," he said, pointing to the bottle of pills that I now had sitting in my lap.

"Sure," I sighed.

I took the medicine as he asked, then undressed until I didn't feel as hot and lay down again against the bare floor of the cave. It felt magical against my skin, almost like I remember it felt when I took a nice cold shower in the middle of summer. I lay there for a second, not giving any more thought to what Jake was doing or where Luca was or what Miller was plotting. Instead, I just let my mind carry itself away to an enchanted dreamland while allowing my body to surrender to the soothing embrace of the cold stone sucking the excessive heat from my pores.

"Runaway with me, Marcus." I said, looking over at him. His face looked like it was almost glowing from the sun radiating so brightly off of it. Initially, I could tell he thought I was joking until his smile slowly changed into a reluctant frown.

"I would love to, Eva," he said, looking away to refocus his sights on the horizon, "in another life, baby, that's what we would do."

"What's wrong with this life, Marcus? We can make it what we want it to be. We don't have to just keep blindly following orders," I said as I looked back to the horizon myself. The sun was setting in the most splendorous way over Lake Michigan.

"You can't talk like that, babe. One day someone might hear you," he said, true to who he was, the more logical one and I the dreamer.

"I don't want to be a spy anymore. I know you don't want to hear that but it's true. The only reason I'm still here is because of you." I didn't know how he would take it but I was hoping it went over well.

"You know what the Sicari will do to you if you try to get out," he sounded like it upset him to hear it. "Seriously, don't tell me anything like that ever again, Eva. I'm your superior. You know I'm supposed to report it if you start talking like that. Don't do that to me, baby."

"If I can't tell you how I feel, then who am I supposed to talk to?" I asked, hoping he would turn to look at me again.

"We can't go anywhere!" he said finally turning back toward me. "Do you think it's just that easy? Slip away together and live a life happily ever after? That's what I wanted before the war… if I met you then, baby, yeah I would have asked you to marry me. We would have had a baby together. We'd have lived by the lakes someplace like this," he said as he pointed to the shore where we were sitting in the sand.

"Those are pipe dreams now, Eva…" He looked forward and let his head fall a little to look down between his feet, where he was squishing the sand with his toes.

"We can do whatever we want, Marcus. There are no rules. We don't have to live by other people's ideas," I said before he turned and gave me a warning look.

"I told you not to talk like that, and I mean it. That's an order. I won't warn you again." His tone was serious, low, and direct.

"What if I was pregnant? Would that change anything?" I asked, looking away, trying to avoid eye contact.

"It doesn't matter, you're not. I saw them give you the birth control shot when we went in two months ago," he said, completely certain of the fact.

I stood up and dusted the sand off of my butt, then turned to walk away when I felt him grab a hold of my ankle.

"You're not, Eva! Tell me you're not, now!" His grip on my ankle grew tighter as he said it.

"Why? What would you do if I was?" I asked, pulling my ankle away then turning to look down at him.

He rested his arm back on his knee and looked away, back to the horizon again. His face was serious and distraught all at the same time. "I'd report it," he said softly under his breath.

*What?* I couldn't believe he'd say that. "So they can bring me in and kill your baby, all for the sake of a freakin' job?!" I yelled it at him. I felt like I hated him at that moment. I turned around again and started to walk away. I didn't know where I was going but I didn't want to see him or talk to him.

"It's not like that, Eva!" He shouted back at me, "It's not like that at all, I love you!"

"No, you don't! You say you do, but you don't! You love your job, and I'm part of your job, that's what you love!" I yelled back only turning around slightly so he could hear it. "Have me reassigned, I don't want to be under you anymore. Give me to someone else!"

"Dammit, Eva, don't say that! Don't ask me to do that, please!" He stood up so he could follow after me.

"I'm not asking you, I am telling you! I want to be reassigned. Tell Parker to put me under Bennett instead." I meant it but I didn't. I didn't know why I was saying it or if I really wanted him to do it. I just wasn't happy that he didn't want the same life with me that I did with him.

"Bennett is an idiot. He'll get you killed." He began to jog after me, trying to catch up.

"Good, maybe that's what I want. If you don't want me and our baby, then you can just have me reassigned and watch us die, knowing it's your fault!" I said it as hatefully as I could. I wanted it to sting. I was hoping it might wake him up.

"Eva, stop!" He had caught up and grabbed my wrist to stop me from continuing to walk away. "Are you really?" He asked now looking at me dead in the eyes.

"No!" I lied. I wasn't sure but I suspected I could be, but he made it clear I couldn't tell him and he didn't want anything to do with it. I knew we would be heading from Chicago down to Knoxville within the week and he would never forgive me if I screwed up our meeting with our intel contact. We had been waiting for months for that meeting.

"Why would you tell me that, then?" He let go of my wrist, probably hoping I wouldn't walk away from him again.

"Did you mean what you said?" I asked, hoping he was lying to me as well and not actually intending to report it if I was.

He looked down, and away from me, then sat down again in the sand, facing the water. He didn't say anything at first, he just acted like he was thinking about the question, realizing the way he answered mattered more than hypothetically. "If you were then yes, I would run away with you. I would die for you… I live my life for you. Don't tell me I don't love you, I do! But you're not pregnant, Eva. Promise me you're not!"

I sat down in the sand beside him, "I promise you I love you and I will tell you everything you need to know after we get the intel and return to the Praetorium. That's what I can promise." I took a hold of his hand. "Promise me you'd pick us over the job if you had to."

"This job isn't my life, Eva… you are. Right now, that's all I want, just you and me like this. What we have works, I just don't want anything to change that," he said it looking into my eyes, then he brought his hand up to my chin and pulled me in toward him for a kiss.

I woke up feeling like I was in an inferno. I caught myself saying Marcus repeatedly and quickly stopped, hoping no one heard me. I was talking in my sleep again. There was no light in the chamber. I couldn't see anything and didn't know where Jake was and whether he was beside me or not. I reached out with both hands feeling for his body near me, as I softly spoke his name. Then before long, I felt him; he was laying a couple of feet away. I assumed he was keeping his distance as to not make me hotter than I already was.

"Jake, honey, I need some water. I'm so hot!" I said it loud enough it should have woken him up, but he wasn't stirring. "Jake, please…" I shook him just a little, trying not to startle him. "Jake…" I said it again, starting to feel concerned that he wasn't answering me yet. He never slept this heavy. Maybe the long horse-ride on the way back wore him out.

Finally, after another couple of tries, he started to move around. It looked like he pulled himself up from where he was and moved over to where he kept the torch. I heard what sounded like he was striking the rock a few times until then suddenly a little spark started to burn within the torch again. It wasn't bright enough for me to see much but I figured I could tell his shadow what I needed.

"Jake, I need water. I feel like I'm boiling. I have to have something to drink."

He wasn't responding right away. He must have been in a very deep sleep and still trying to gather his wits about him before he could comprehend what I was asking him to do. Before long, the torch's brightness increased as the fire caught more air and fueled the flame to grow larger.

"Eva?" the shadow finally spoke back. "Eva, it's not Jake. It's still me, Luca. Jake hasn't returned yet." The torch's brightness lit his former shadow while he talked and before long I could see his whole face. It wasn't Jake.

"Jake?" Even though my eyes weren't seeing him, my mind believed they must be deceived. It knew what had happened. He was there, he did come back, I remembered it.

"No, Eva, he's not back yet. I'm sorry. I can go get you water, is that what you need?" He asked in the most gentle way, but his face was still slightly confused with how I was acting.

"He was here, I know it. I saw him. Oh my gosh, Luca, you can't be in here. He will hurt you. Don't you remember what he said? If he ever catches you again, he will—" I stopped myself. I didn't want to say anything to startle him if it was actually just a dream and not a memory.

"Eva, what are you talking about? Did you have a nightmare? I'm fine. Jake hasn't hurt me. I don't know why he would." He looked at me the way I remember Jake saying he did.

I looked down to see if I was naked like I had been when Jake returned but I wasn't this time. Thankfully, I still had my shirt and underwear on.

"It's common to have vivid dreams and hallucinations when you have a high fever," he said as he started to reach over to feel my forehead again but I pulled away before I realized that's what he was doing. "Eva, I am not going to hurt you. I only want to care for you."

"I'm sorry," I said, realizing I must have sounded delusional.

"I understand. Let me go get you some water. Don't worry Jake will be back before long, hopefully. I'll take care of you until then. Right now, just try to relax again," he said as he got up and started to walk out. "Would you like for me to leave the torch here? I know you're scared of the dark. I can go get another one. It's no problem."

"Yes, please…" He was right. In that moment, the last thing I wanted was to be alone *and* in the dark with whatever false memories my feverish mind had betrayed me with.

# 6

## FEVERISH DELUSIONS, DISTORTED CONCLUSIONS

The ripples from the sea rose over the shore with a loud roaring sound. I knew then that the tide had started to come in. I stood on top of the rock one last time before leaping off into the water and swimming back to the beach. The water was cool and pleasant to the touch; I didn't know why but I really longed for it. I wanted to take a large gulp and absorb every ounce I could but I knew the salt would make me sick, so I stopped myself from consuming any of it.

I started out of the water to walk along the coast, where the sand hadn't yet lost its feeling of warmth from the sun. Only a few steps in, I could feel its heat radiating against my feet. It was too hot, hotter than it should be at this time of day. I turned to go back to the water to cool them off again, but it had vanished. There was no longer any water anywhere. What was happening?

I yelled out for Marcus, hoping he would come to rescue me from wherever this place was that I had become trapped in. It felt like the sand was beginning to consume me. I looked down. I was right; it was now up to my ankles. I fell to my knees, hoping I could pull my feet free and crawl away. "Marcus," I screamed out again, "help me!" It was beginning to engulf me further. Now I had sunken down into it up to my waist. The sand felt like it was beginning to sear my skin. I started to yell out for Marcus again but stopped when I saw him. He was coming to rescue me finally.

He placed his hand on my forehead. "Eva, crap… you've gotten too hot," he said, staring down at me, his eyes looking intently into mine. "I can't let you lie here like this. I'm taking you to the falls. They'll help you cool down."

"Okay," I groaned. I didn't care what he intended to do with me as long as he helped free me from whatever furnace I had fallen into.

"Can you get up on your own? Or here… let me help you." He stood back up and offered his hand for me to pull myself up.

I grabbed it and tried to pull but I felt too weak. "I can't, baby. I'm sorry." I felt so completely drained.

"I'm not Ja… Oh, it doesn't matter. Here," he bent over and grabbed a hold of me around the waist and pulled me up to stand with him. I wrapped my arm around his torso to steady myself. He bent down and grabbed a torch before we walked into what looked to be a black hole.

"I'm scared," I said as we walked further down a path that looked like it went to the center of the earth. "I knew it. This is hell. I'm in hell. It's hot and dark… I guess I deserve it…"

"Eva, don't say that. Just keep walking. I think you're delusional right now. Your fever has gotten too high. You're going to be fine. Just keep walking." Marcus was so supportive, I didn't know where he was taking me but I figured I could handle hell if he was there with me.

"I love you, baby. Thank you for taking care of me," I said, clinging tighter to his torso. He was leaner than I remembered him being.

"We're almost there. Just hang on. I will get you cooled off." I saw what looked like a small stream of light flowing in from above, like a beam coming down from heaven. The farther we walked the more I could feel a soothing cool mist begin to tickle the hairs on my arms. "Here, it might shock you at first but stand in the falls long enough just so you can get yourself completely wet," he said as he helped position me to stand directly under the beam of light as it showered cold heavenly goodness down on top of me, saturating me with a river of pleasant frigidity.

"Oh my gosh, this is amazing," I said looking over at him as he took a few steps back, trying to stay away as to not get too wet himself.

"You can't stand there long. It's slippery, you could fall and get hurt. Once you are cooled off enough, I will show you where you can sit in the pool of water down there," he said, pointing to what looked like a small disk of pale blue light radiating up from the floor.

"Okay," I said, beginning to brush my hands through my hair, trying to get it completely drenched as well. When I looked back over at him, I noticed he was staring at something. I looked down to see what it was but wasn't sure. My shirt being wet was now sheer. Was he looking at my belly? Marcus never normally looked at me like that, with such intensity.

"Oh my gosh," I said, looking back at him realizing what the gaze was most likely from when he shook his head slightly, blinking free from his trance. He brought his hands up to roughly rub his face, acting like he wasn't just looking at me the way I knew he was. "It's okay. It's the baby. I must be showing already." I said, trying to reassure him that it was normal and that he didn't need to be afraid to touch me.

"You're pregnant?" He asked, seeming clueless. He stood there, his face now full of shock and concern.

I realized I never had a chance to tell him the truth. "I'm sorry," I said, taking a step forward toward him when my foot began to slip making me wobble slightly.

"No, stop!" He quickly walked back over to me and reached around my waist, grabbing me to help me step out of the stream and over to the floating blue disk on the floor.

I sat down in what looked like a shallow pool of light emanating from below me; it was cool and soothing just as the beam of light was. I couldn't help but feel bad for Marcus. He still had no clue. I deceived him... I lied... He was going to be a father, and he didn't even know it yet. I felt awful!

"I lied to you! I'm sorry, baby. I'm so sorry I told you I wasn't pregnant when I thought I could be." I brought my knees up to my chest and wrapped my arms around them, then let myself cry as loud as I wanted. I had been holding it back for so long, I needed to let it out. I felt so ashamed. "I'm so sorry that I lied to you. I wanted you to know, but I was afraid of what you would do when I told you. I was so scared. I didn't think you wanted the baby, and I didn't want you to hurt—" I stopped when I felt him wrap his arms around me.

"Shhh… It's okay. You're going to be fine. No one is going to hurt you or the baby," he said as he hugged me tightly.

I sat there and let him hold me. He cradled me tight between his arms, soothing me as much as the water had. Before long, I felt myself relax and let my weight rest against him, letting him hold me so I wouldn't fall over. I was tired again, but I didn't feel nearly as hot. I closed my eyes and rested, knowing I was safe.


I startled suddenly, awakening from a daze, a dream, sleep, or something. I wasn't sure exactly what had just happened. It was all vague and unclear. I couldn't remember what I had said or exactly even how I had gotten there.

"Eva, do you feel better now?" Luca asked, sitting in front of me, staring into my eyes.

At this moment, there was something different about the way he looked that I had never noticed before.

His gaze was heated… a deep, vivid green ferocity emanated from his eyes, into me. Every second they stayed locked onto mine I could feel the intensity increase like they could soon penetrate my thoughts before going straight to my soul.

"Yes," I said, staring back at him, trying to figure out what this new thing I was feeling between us was. His countenance was enchanting. He had a strong jaw and a nice straight nose that seemed to fit the shape of his face well. The subtle glow from the beam of light breaking through the cave ceiling was reflecting off of the wavy black hair on his head and looked like glowing pixie dust was sprinkled into the coarse black hair in his beard.

There was a moment of silence between us as we just sat there, gazing into each other's eyes. I found myself briefly getting lost, wondering what I was doing and why. Thoughts started to swirl through my mind. I felt pulled to a land of daydreamers and fairy tale whisperers. It was like his eyes had me wrapped in a magical spell and I couldn't break free. I blinked to break eye contact but only so I could look down to his lips…

"Luca!" The spell was broken instantly with Jocelyn's voice after having walked down the narrow passageway leading to the cavern we were sitting in. I looked over and saw a small torch's glow increasing in size as it came closer toward us. "Luca? Are you down here?" She yelled out again. He turned and stood up to face her, leaving me at his back.

"Jocelyn… Yes, I'm down here with Eva, I'm trying to help her cool off, her fever has gotten too high, it's dangerous at this point." He took a few steps toward her, then stopped almost as if to be a barricade so she wouldn't come any closer to me.

She stood there and looked at me for a moment without saying anything. The light from the torch gently flickered off her skin, making it look soft and velvety. I was perplexed at how someone so beautiful could be so ugly all at the same time.

She looked back over at Luca. Her face was now almost twisted-looking with both anger and disgust. "We still can't find Uncle Arty. Me and Mary have both spent the last four days out looking everywhere for him… while—" She stopped briefly to glance at me then back at him. "While you've been doing nothing but sit in here and play nurse to this floozy."

"Don't call her that. She's done nothing to you. I told you last night I would help you look for him but you got upset and told me to go screw myself. What do you want from me, Jocelyn? She has a fever and I am a doctor. I would do the same for you." He said it initially with a tenseness but it slowly disappeared the further he continued to defend himself.

"You don't even know her," she said, then glared at me before looking back to him to continue yelling. "Don't you think it's awfully suspicious Uncle Arty went missing the same day her and her li'l boyfriend came riding up in here like they own the place? I bet she knows what happened to him!" She said as her eyes shot back over to me. "You do, don't ya, ya li'l slut?" She took a step around him to walk closer to me.

"Jocelyn!" Luca turned around and grabbed her arm to stop her from walking any farther. "I'm not going to let you talk to her like that."

"Or what?" She spun around and ripped her arm away from his grasp. "What do you think you're gonna do about it? Slap me around?"

He didn't say anything he just stared at her, giving her a look that most likely meant something to the two of them and no one else.

"Ha! Oh… no, you think you're going to withhold something from me… Oh please, Luca, it's been weeks. I already gave up on the idea of getting anything from you ever again now that this li'l slut is here…" She paused briefly to take a breath. "Fine, you want her? Take her. I'll just have at her li'l boyfriend when he comes back. He's more of a man than you'll ever be!" She turned around and stormed off, back into the dark hole that she originally came out of.

I was taken aback by the idea that either I or Jake were now involved in their little marital—but not really marital—dispute. I wasn't sure how she thought she could just reassign our relationship status to different people but I didn't let it bother me much, knowing that she really wasn't Jake's type. I wasn't sure how this was going to change how Luca treated me, but it did create a slight awkwardness that I was now noticing I had developed when I thought about him.

Even though I hadn't known Luca for long, I could tell she was wrong about how much of a man he was. No, he was nothing like Jake as far as his personality but that didn't make me feel like he wasn't as manly. He was kind and sweet, and attentive… so many things that I found attractive that were also good qualities of a real man.

I sat there and observed him as he watched her storm off, leaving the cavern we were in. I was waiting to see how he would respond to what just happened. He slowly turned and walked back down to where I was sitting. He didn't say anything at first. He just stood there next to me, keeping his eye on where she had just walked out.

"I'm sorry you had to witness that," he said finally, still keeping himself from looking at me.

"Luca, she's wrong about you. Don't listen to her, she's just… You're the kindest man I have ever known, and I hate to see you treated like that," I said, looking up at him.

He sighed. "We all have our own demons, Elliceva. Her's are just more apparent than mine."

"You must hide them well then because I haven't seen any yet," I said it almost as an invitation for him to share with me what his were since I was now curious.

"I try to put the needs of others before myself, but I will admit sometimes my ambition… Well, I can get a little overzealous when I have a goal or a desire for something… or *someone*… It's hurt people in the past." He finally turned to look at me after he said it.

I didn't quite understand what he meant exactly or why having ambition was bad but I trusted the observation he made of himself must have had some validity.

Luca helped me return to my chamber to lie back down and rest again. I hoped I could sleep a little better the rest of the night. Anything had to be better than the previous few. My fever was still high but it wasn't as dangerous as it had been before my bath at the falls. I was able to eat and drink a little before laying back down and felt better thanks to Luca.

I was still concerned about Jocelyn, though. I never knew where she was or what exactly she was up to. Luca, for obvious reasons never really liked to talk about her much, so it was hard to learn anything about her past or very much more about their relationship. I didn't know if what I witnessed down at the falls was them breaking up or just what.

I was eager for Jake to return. I wanted to make sure he was safe and nothing happened to him like what had happened in my dream. I also wanted to get the antibiotic as soon as I could so I would stop having so many vivid dreams. I wasn't sure at what point I would talk in my sleep again and give away too much info to Luca or, worse, someone else. I curled up on my blankets again and closed my eyes, trying not to rehearse the day's events in my head, when finally I felt myself letting go and drifting back off.


I stood there staring out the window at the orchard, waiting for the sun to come out again when I felt large warm hands snake their way around my waist under my shirt.

"Mmm, what do you want now?" I asked, joking.

"You. That's all I want, just you." He said, lowering his head to the nape of my neck, letting the scruff of his jaw tickle me before laying a few kisses along my collarbone.

"Well, I'm yours." I murmured, relaxing against him.

He sighed, "You have no idea how long I've been waiting to hear you say that, how long I've been wanting you... Tell me you've wanted me too. I need to hear the words." He whispered in my ear.

"I want you," faintly rolled off my tongue.

His hands slid lower. "Say it again for me, amore mio. Tell me how I'm the one you chose." He said, kissing my neck again.

"I want you... only you." I said softly, spinning around to look at him, kiss him. But lifting his face toward mine, I didn't see what I'd expected. Instead, hypnotizing rich emerald green eyes flickered up at me, immersing me in an atmosphere of desire and fantasy. "Luca?" I breathed, confused.

"Eva..." His eyes spoke what he did not. They said everything, pinning me with longing and need.

"Luca!" *I can't... Not you... What is this?* I tried to look around, now feeling lost.

"Eva," he said my name again, pulling my arm toward him.

"Luca?" I was more confused than before.

"Eva," he shook me again, hard enough this time I finally opened my eyes. Luca was sitting above me with his hand on my shoulder, looking down at me.

"Luca?" I said, instantly embarrassed. "Oh my go... What did you hear? What was I saying?"

"Don't worry about it. You can't control what you dream and it's common to have vivid dreams when—"

"I know that!" I quickly interrupted him, more mortified than ever. "What did you hear, Luca?" I asked again this time with more force.

He let his eyes trail off as he sat back a little. "You were calling out for Jake again," he said, avoiding looking at me as the words came out of his mouth.

I let my body relax back against the cold floor of the cave. *Shit!* He was lying; I knew it. He had all the classic indications. "Please don't tell Jake what you heard," I said concerned it would cause a lot of unnecessary problems.

"All right, it can be our secret then," he said with a little smile.

# 7

# REJECTED ADVANCES

Silently awakened, I felt a hand gently rest itself against my shoulder, then slowly trail down to my waist. I opened my eyes, expecting to see Luca, but instead, I was greeted by the familiar face I was growing to miss over the last several days.

"Jake!" I sat up as quickly as I could to embrace him.

"Hey, baby," he whispered in my ear. His hug was tight but soothing as he let his hands firmly rub up and down my back. "I missed you too," he said with a slight chuckle, likely because of my overly exaggerated embrace lingering longer than he might have expected.

"Are you real?" I asked, hoping it wasn't another dream.

"Of course I'm real. Why would you ask that? What happened while I was gone?" He pulled back slightly to look at me with a playful grin.

"Nothing… I just had a few bad dreams 'cause of the fever. In one of them, you came back with bad news. It was awful, I thought you—" I stopped and thought about what I was saying. I wondered if what happened in the dreams had some merit.

"Don't be scared, I don't have bad news," he said, reassuring me before I already predetermined that he did.

"So you didn't see Miller then?" I asked, letting myself relax against the wall behind me.

He didn't say anything at first, just looked at me with a bit of hesitation. "No," he said finally. "But I was able to get you antibiotics and some stuff to help clean and bandage your leg. How's it looking?" He asked, looking down at my legs only briefly before his eyes shot back up to mine. "Why aren't you wearing pants?" He sounded more curious than upset.

"The fever," I said, beginning to reply. "I got so hot, Luca had to take me down to the falls where—" I stopped, realizing what I was about to say wasn't going to be beneficial to anyone.

"Where what?" He lost his smile as his eyes narrowed in on me. I wanted to bite myself for the slip of tongue.

"I was getting overheated. I don't really remember much. I think I was a delusional at the time… Nothing happened, I just had to sit in a pool of water to help me cool off. I haven't gotten that bad again since then. That was a couple of days ago." I said, trying to make the whole thing sound way less disconcerting than it might have actually been.

"Where was Luca while you were all wet?" He asked, looking down at my shirt, likely taking mental notes about how thick or rather thin it actually was.

"Jake, I don't want you to get yourself all upset. Nothing happened. Luca has been a gentleman this whole time that you've been gone. All right?" I made sure he was looking me square in the eyes. That way, he could see I was telling him the complete truth so he would drop it.

He didn't say anything, he just looked at me. He knew I wasn't lying but acted like he wanted to still be upset even though I gave him no evidence to fuel it.

"You just can't help yourself can you?" I asked with a small grin. "I know you're a man… and with more than enough testosterone for two… but if you're just itching for a fight, I don't think Luca is the best candidate."

He let his face relax a little before he began to smile back at me finally. "I hate it when you're right," he said jokingly.

"No, you don't. You love it when I'm right. Admit it, you've been miserable this past week without me there reminding you how so wrong you always are and how right I always am," I smiled, then winked at him.

"You're right about one thing and one thing only!" He replied with a small laugh, "I was miserable this week without you." He said, growing more serious as he reached up to stroke my temple. "Not being able to see your beautiful face every morning and kiss those sweet lips every night before I closed my eyes... ugh, it was torture. I missed you so much, baby."

"Well, it's good to hear you didn't find some other poor, lonely Gypsyin along the way to take off with instead of returning here to reclaim this one."

"Never," he whispered, lovingly looking into my eyes, then leaned in to kiss me before setting up straight again and looking at his bag. "I did find a few other things though," he said as he began to dig into it. After a moment, he pulled out some liquor, probably to use to clean my wound out again. Then he pulled out a large white candle and set it in front of me, looking up at me with a big grin, clearly proud of himself.

"Wow, honey, that's a good idea for in here. I'm getting tired of having to be in the dark so much. It's really scary sometimes... and lonely," I said as I began to rub the side of it like it was a genie in a lamp, hoping some magical goodness might escape and help cure all my darkness woes.

"I know," he said as he took his torch and used it to light the candle's three wicks. "I thought about building a fire in here even though Luca said it wasn't a good idea. I still might, I don't know. I would just hate it if he was right and anything happened to you because of it. That's the only reason I haven't yet." He paused to stare into my eyes. "I don't know if it's the light of the candle or what but you're more beautiful than I remember you being when I left."

"It's probably the fever and all my excess sweating," I said with a giggle. "I'm sure it's created a nice shine to my face."

He didn't say anything, he just sat there. His eyes were fixed on me with a grin on his face. Then he leaned in and broke the silent tension with another long kiss. He tasted just as I remembered and I didn't want it to end until I realized I had forgotten to ask him about the thing that had bothered me the most the whole time he was gone.

"Wait," I said, pulling away, "how did you pay for all of this stuff? Didn't they freeze your expense account since you went rogue?"

A large smile crept up his face with a quick chuckle. "What are you talking about? I don't have an expense account. That's not how it works. I traded for it all."

"Traded what?" I asked, happy to see I was apparently wrong in my dream and that it hadn't been an issue.

"Well… it was actually quite convenient you see… On my way there I ran across this dead old guy that had an empty revolver laying on the ground next to him." He stopped to wink at me, knowing I would understand what he was talking about. "With no bullets, the gun wasn't gonna do anyone here any good so," he shrugged, "I used that. It was a good trade too. They are pretty valuable now that they're illegal to be owned by anyone who isn't an agent." He smiled.

"What did you do with the body?" I whispered, realizing he must have hidden it since the girls hadn't been able to find it yet.

"Don't worry about it. I took care of it," he said, leaning in again to steal another kiss. "You have no idea how badly I missed you. All of you…" He said softly, sliding his hand in under my shirt as he trailed his kisses down my collar bone.

"I don't know, I bet I have a good idea. What time of day is it?" I asked, not having yet been out to the large cavern to see outside.

"Early," he said in between kisses as he slowly let his hands slide down my arms to my hands to interlace our fingers.

"So no one is likely to come to visit us anytime soon?" I asked.

"No, my guess is they're all still sound asleep, tucked nicely into their rock hard beds," he said, moving his kisses down to my neck.

"Okay," I said, looking down at the only thing that was creating any light in the room. "Why don't you show me how much you missed me then." Then I leaned down and blew out the candle.

.   .   .

After spending some quality time together catching up, Jake helped me walk out to the large cavern where he got me something to eat before sitting down beside me next to the fire. He was right. The revolver must have been worth a pretty penny seeing all the things he was able to bring back for us both. I told him it probably wouldn't be long until the first round of Samuel's fish came in for us to cook but he didn't want me to wait and gave me a large helping of trail mix that he had brought back with him. I hadn't had dried fruit in so long; it was a nice treat after what I had to deal with over the last week. He also seemed pretty proud of himself when he pulled out a new set of clothes for me. I'm sure I acted quite giddy over them. It wasn't every day that I got doted on with gifts.

We weren't sitting there long before I saw Luca walk out from the other side of the cavern where he generally stayed when he wasn't in my chamber with me. He initially looked surprised to see Jake, but it didn't take long for him to act normal again. I didn't know with what I had accidentally let slip, and what he thought he knew about Jake and our relationship if he would mention anything and try to cause problems. To my surprise, however, he didn't say a word about what he thought Jake was or how he thought Jake treated me; he just acted like he knew nothing and was as pleasant as normal.

Jocelyn, in good Jocelyn fashion, exited her side of the cave, a good deal later than Luca did. I had never been on their side of the cavern so I didn't know what it looked like and if they had been staying together or not, despite their little breakup. Luca seemed to be in decent spirits even though Jake had returned so I assumed they most likely made up but I didn't actually know that for sure. Jocelyn wasn't as grumpy as she normally was either so I felt it was a safe assumption to make of the two of them.

At first, between the four of us, it was awkward, but only briefly, as we sat there and had a bit of small talk around the fire. Jake knew not to say anything about Arthur or where he had been, but that didn't stop Jocelyn from trying to bring up both subjects, likely to cause tension. Luca didn't say much and I could tell he was trying his best to look at

Jake or Jocelyn while they were talking but I found him often letting his eyes drift over to mine even when there was no reason to.

Everything seemed to go surprisingly well until the real Jocelyn started to show herself. She was a charmer for sure, looking at Jake with intensity in her eyes, giving him excessive attention. Too bad for her, I knew he was oblivious to that kind of magic. I could see her frustration as she began to realize her run-of-the-mill flirtation tactics weren't working very well for her. The look on her face indicated that she wasn't about to give up and she intended to up the ante. I had half a thought to step in and foil her plans but I didn't, since I figured it would be more fun to see him downright reject any passes she intended to make at him.

She tried giggling, then she tried fluffing and tossing her hair a few times, but he continued to ignore any signals she was sending his way. She tried acting like what he was talking about was something she enjoyed hearing and that they had something in common. Then she said she was getting hot and started to lift her skirt slightly to show more of her legs. Before long, I think Luca could tell as well as I what she was trying to do. It was so obvious to everyone except Jake, that is. Luca looked at me a few times with concern in his eyes, probably for Jocelyn's safety rather than mine, maybe wondering if I would soon have enough and attack her.

Not too terribly long into the exhaustive ordeal, I think Jake finally caught on. He's more of a blunt person than most so he cut her down a bit more direct than what was probably helpful in that situation. I believe it was the fourth, maybe fifth, time she threw her long brown mane around when he finally asked her if there was something wrong with her neck.

I wanted to laugh; it bubbled up inside me quickly but I was able to suppress it. Luca, on the other hand, didn't do as well and burst out with a loud cackle before she sent a sharp glare his way. I could see she was instantly embarrassed. That was precisely what I had been waiting for and why I didn't say anything myself, though it wouldn't be long until it was obvious it backfired on me.

Seeing the way Luca reacted, she quickly gathered what pride and dignity she had left and set her intentions to get back at him, and probably me as well.

"What do you think you're laughing at?" She said, scowling at Luca, "Why don't you and your new girlfriend go back down to the falls again? You seemed to be enjoying yourselves last time I saw you two down there together."

Luca quickly stopped laughing. At the same time, he lost all color in his face. "What? Why would you say that?" He asked, looking at her, then brought his eyes to meet mine.

Before she could answer Luca, I looked over at Jake to see how he was reacting to her claim. "What is she talking about?" Jake asked calmly now looking back at me.

"I have no idea," I said, narrowing my eyes at her. I gave her the same look as Luca just had, insinuating she would do well to recant her lies.

"Don't give me that look," she said now returning my glare. "Do you think you can whore around and get away with it?"

At that moment, my brain emptied itself of all non-essential thoughts and set a fire within me, releasing me to attack. It gave me permission to leap across the fire to her, throw her against the ground and straddle her, then wrap my hands around her idiotic little neck and see how well I could do at choking the life out of her. But I wasn't able to take more than a small step forward before Jake's arms wrapped around my waist holding me back from being able to grant my own wish.

Jocelyn's face quickly developed a look of surprise as Luca piped up, trying to verbally stop my attack. "Eva, no! Not in your condition, stop!" He shouted, then stood up and put himself between us.

"Eva, you can't!" Jake said, pulling me back toward him, making me sit and rest against his lap. Then he wrapped his arms completely around my waist just in case I tried to lunge for her again. "Luca, control your woman and her mouth," he said, looking over at them both.

No sooner than Luca could turn around to address her, she stood up and began to storm off. He stood there for a second to watch her, likely making sure she was good and gone before turning back around. "I'm sorry," he said, looking at us. "Miles, the things she said aren't true. You must know that. Eva and I—" he paused for a second and focused his eyes on me, then looked back at Jake, "you know how much Eva loves you, she'd never—"

Jake interrupted his defense of me to agree. "I know!" He said, gently tightening his arms around my waist and pulling me closer to him. "I'm going to warn you though, the next time she calls her a name, I won't stop Eva. Her self-control is unmatched, but when she snaps, if she gets to her, there won't be much of a fight. Eva will win. So, unless you want one less woman around here, you better get her mouth under control."

Luca appeared to take the warning seriously. He stood there for a second about to say something else, then looked down at my stomach, pausing briefly before looking back up at my eyes. "It's not good for you to get so upset," he said as he let his look linger so I knew what he meant, even though I didn't. Then he turned and walked back the same way Jocelyn did, most likely returning to the same chamber where they would share a few choice words with each other.

"What's he talking about, baby?" Jake asked, turning me around to stand between his legs to face him.

"She's a liar, Jake. We didn't do anything down at the falls, you know I wouldn't—"

"That's not what I was asking," he stopped me. "Why would Luca tell you it's not good for you to get upset?" He looked as if he already suspected the answer before he asked the question.

"I have no idea," I said. Since it didn't make any sense to me when Luca said it, I didn't take it all that seriously.

"All right," he sighed, looking down at my waist with a brief pause before continuing. "You know you can tell me anything, right? You don't need to hide things from me."

I didn't know where that was coming from or why he was saying it, but just the insinuation that I *was* hiding something started to irritate me. "Jake, it's not like that. I don't know what you think but—"

"Okay," he interrupted, "I wasn't saying you were. I just wanted you to know you didn't have to. I won't be mad at you if—" he stopped again and pulled me down to sit on his knee, "I just want you to know that I love you and you can tell me anything without being afraid of how I will react, that's all."

"Fair enough," I said with a smile, then leaned in to give him a kiss.

# 8

## KISSING FALLEN ANGELS

"The Marigolds are blooming nicely." Marcus was trying to create small talk, but I wasn't ready to speak to him again yet. I was still upset about what he'd said during our rendezvous meeting with Puckett. I just gave him a cross look, so he knew I wasn't in the mood.

"You're going to talk to me. If I have to make it an order, I will!" He said, returning my look. He liked to pull that out anytime I wanted to give him the silent treatment. He thought he could order me to do anything, and I'd just have to blindly obey, which was partly true but I didn't like it.

"Fine, make it an order. But you can't order me to tell you what you want to hear, you freakin'—" I stopped, I knew I couldn't just say whatever I wanted and I probably would get in trouble if I went too far with the derogatory conduct.

"Eva, it doesn't need to be like this. Come on! I know you're upset about what I told Puckett but it was necessary to get the intel," he said, trying to calm me before I became more upset.

"It wasn't necessary to get the intel. You just wanted him to think you were more important than you are. Why did it even matter when you were just going to kill him after he gave it to us, anyway? Look, I know I don't have a Sicari tag like you but I'm not a real Gypsyin. You referring to me like you did was insulting and demeaning and I don't appreciate it." I snapped back, refusing to calm down.

"Eva, hang on!" He stopped walking beside me like he wanted to stand there and talk, hoping I would stop as well but I didn't. "Eva! I only said what I did to get the intel."

"Bullshit, Marcus!" I said, looking back at him. He now started to take larger steps to try to catch up with me. "That's bullshit and you know it. I know why you said what you did. You don't like that I don't have to have a tag when you do." I stopped to yell it at him.

"You better stop raising your voice with me before I have to reprimand you," he growled. I doubt he knew what he was getting into when he asked for me to be assigned to him. I could get pretty feisty at times. "You're wrong! I don't want to be a Gypsyin. They're filthy idiots that don't know how to pick a side. I'm happy I have my tag," he said all proud and smug.

"If you have such a problem with them, why did you have me assigned to you, if I am just a filthy idiot then?" I asked, intentionally twisting his words.

"That's not what I said, Eva. You're not a Gypsyin, so—"

"But you treat me like that's the choice I made!" I interrupted him. "You don't act like I'm a Sicari like you. You know the unit I came from is superior to yours, and you can't stand it!" My voice was loud but not so much that I would get in trouble for it.

He didn't say anything at first. He just gave me a look like he knew I was right, but refused to admit to it.

"If that's the case, why did you even ask for me to be assigned to you, Marcus? I wanna know!" I said, demanding he answer me.

He hesitated, "Some days I wonder that myself," he sighed. His eyes looked like it hurt to say it but he did it anyway, then he turned to walk again.

That's not what I wanted to hear nor what I thought he would say. I wanted to hear what he told me every other time we had that same argument, that he thought I was the most beautiful, talented agent he'd ever seen and that he couldn't help but ask for me to be assigned to him. Apparently, before my initial assignment to Marcus, multiple senior agents put in requests for me to be their partner but Marcus always got what Marcus wanted... now he wanted to act like he regretted it. I knew he didn't mean it, or I hoped that was the case at least. I figured he'd just said it to hurt my feelings, which, if that was the effect he was going for, it worked.

I continued to walk just not as quickly, following him. His pace had picked up a little, probably because he was now upset as well. I was waiting for him to turn around and tell me he didn't mean it, tell me he was sorry he'd said it, but he didn't. He just kept walking.

I felt weird... *Someone's staring at me...* My mind was trying to wake itself up while I was still lost in its dream world. I must have fallen asleep sitting next to the falls again. I opened my eyes, and sure enough, my instincts were correct. Jocelyn was standing at the entrance to the cavern, staring at me like she had been watching me intently, but for how long, I didn't know.

"Jocelyn!" I said instinctually. *Holy shit, was I talking in my sleep again? If so, how much did she hear?* I started to ask but before I could get another word out she quickly turned and vanished into the darkness of the passageway.

Jake warned me about coming down to the falls. Too bad he had only mentioned the danger in me slipping and getting hurt, not falling asleep. I hadn't even thought about what could happen if I did that and someone heard my dream talking again. Not that I ever liked it, but most of the time my dreams were rather innocuous. Unfortunately for Jocelyn, this particular dream had information in it that would get her hurt if she decided to try to use it against me.

I sat there a bit longer, trying not to doze off again. I really did love being there. The falls were more than soothing, in a lot of ways they felt quite enchanting as well. Considering I couldn't really go outside, I enjoyed the beam of sunlight that made its way drown from heaven, resting itself against my shoulders and lap. Not to mention how soothing the sounds of the large chamber were as the water, running down and splattering the cave floor, echoed against the walls and seemed to swirl around me. It had a nice calming effect on my mind, the same effect that I had been looking for when we traveled to the grotto lands. I needed something to tell it to stop thinking and relax.

It wasn't long before the chamber garnered more attention than just Jocelyn when I looked up to see a torch glow preceding Luca as he entered.

"I was looking for you," he said with a large smile on his face, clearly happy to see me. He was carrying a cup as well as his torch. I assumed he was bringing me more of his elderberry tea that he'd had Mary make for me to help with the fever. "Where is Miles? I didn't see him when I passed your chamber?" He asked as he came closer and handed me the cup.

"He went to catch some rabbit. He appreciates the fish Samuel has been getting but I think he just prefers rabbit. Or maybe he just likes to hunt. Some men are like that I guess." I took the cup of tea from him and set it down beside me on the floor as Luca sat down on the other side of me.

"Good. I was hoping I could talk to you about a couple of things. Also, I wanted to check on how your leg was healing now that you've been on antibiotics for a few days. I'm sorry again about all the pain you went through when we cleaned it out." He said, then he re-positioned himself a little to look at me more directly.

"It's fine. I have a high pain tolerance." I picked up the cup of tea and started to sip on it while I thought about what he might want to talk to me about. He sat there and stared at me, waiting for me to agree to have this conversation before he continued. "Thank you by the way," I said, lowering the cup from my lips just slightly before setting it back down. "My leg is better. I can show you later in my chamber when Jake gets back if you'd like."

He smiled as he looked up at my hair then back down to my eyes, "The light from above the falls makes it look like you have a halo," he said, changing the subject.

I knew that wasn't what he came to talk to me about but I figured I might as well go along with it. "Maybe," I said with a faint laugh, "but believe me, I'm no angel."

"You are to me," he said, still smiling. I was beginning to see more intensity in his eyes the longer he sat there looking at me. "Like you fell from heaven right into my life."

"So I'm a fallen angel now then, huh?" I said sarcastically, knowing that wasn't what he intended for me to glean from his comment.

He let his smile relax a little. "I guess if you want to call it that."

I didn't know if he realized fallen angels were actually supposed to be another term for demons, and that was why I referred to myself like that but I didn't figure it mattered to share that part with him. I didn't respond. I just smiled, then tried to look away briefly to let my eyes rest from all the intense eye contact he was excellent at.

"Elliceva," he whispered, trying to bring my eyes back to him.

In that moment, that one word sent a spark through the air that sent chills down my spine. As I turned my face back toward his, he quickly leaned in and kissed me. It was nothing like I would have expected coming from him. It was bold and strong. I wanted to pull away, but I caught myself letting it linger, feeling trapped by the magic of the moment. I felt his hand rest against the side of my head. Again, I knew I needed to pull away, but I couldn't, for whatever reason I didn't. Then, before I completely lost myself, my mind reminded me of Jake and what I was doing to him. Suddenly, that was enough. I pulled away from him and looked down, now afraid to look into his eyes again.

"Elliceva," he said again softly, trying to get me to look at him.

"No! Luca, you can't do this to me. You need to quit," I said, trying to get him to realize what he was doing wouldn't benefit either of us.

"Why? I know you feel something, too. Why should I stop?" He asked, still calm and solemn.

"Because I love Jake. I don't love you!" I said, hoping that answer would be definite enough for him.

"I don't believe you," he said, lifting his hand to my chin gently, trying to get me to look at him again. "How can you love a man that would take you as his prisoner?"

"It's not like that, Luca," I said finally looking back up. "He isn't the person you think he is. It was my fault." I stopped, afraid to give him too many details.

He leaned back a little, probably gearing up to try to break me free from a delusional state. "You're wrong. He isn't good for you. He is controlling you but you can't see it. Just that you think it's your fault says enough for me to know he's manipulated you to believe that. You might call what you have love but—"

"It is, Luca, stop with this, please! You can't have me. I'm his. You don't even understand… Do you realize what he would do to you if he knew you kissed me, let alone if he saw you were trying to turn me against him?" I asked, trying to plead with him to think of his own safety.

"I don't care. Tell him if you want. I promise to keep your secrets, but you don't have to keep mine," he said, letting his eyes settle back into their mesmerizing state.

"That's not fair… you know that was a dream." My stomach began to churn. I was so upset.

He reached up and moved the strands of hair that had fallen into my face and tucked them behind my ear. "It was enough for me to see I wasn't the only one who felt like this," he said, returning his gaze from my hair to my eyes.

"I don't…" I looked away again. "You're wrong, Luca!" I was beginning to breathe a bit harder, at the same time I felt my heart start to beat faster. I picked up the tea and finished drinking it, trying to give myself an excuse to not continue what I was trying to say.

"If that were true you would tell him. You wouldn't care if it hurt me, but you do," he said, as he reached down and took a hold of my hand.

"I think I'm going to throw up," I said as I began to quickly look around for where might be a good place if I did.

His face quickly changed as he moved forward to wrap his arms around me and help move me to position myself over the flowing water near the bottom of the falls.

"This is normal. You're likely to experience more of this and that's okay," he said as he brought his hands to move my hair completely over to one side of my head.

I didn't know why he thought that it was normal for me to feel nauseated, but maybe that was true with the stress of thinking about what Jake would do to him if he found out about the kiss. I was feeling bad enough that I didn't really want to think about that. I just wanted to puke and get it over with.

"Luca, I won't tell him, but only because I don't want him to hurt you. You have to promise me that you will leave it alone. We can't be together, you have to realize that," I said, still looking down at the water. I thought maybe if the nausea was due to the stress, it would go away if I cleared it up between us once and for all.

"I can't promise that. I'm sorry. Don't worry about that right now, we can talk about it again when you feel better," he said now letting his hand rest against my upper back.

"Luca, please…" I started to say it when suddenly I couldn't finish. My stomach had had enough and was ready to purge whatever I had in it. I heaved, and it came forth, flowing out of me. Part of me wanted to feel embarrassed. Just as I would feel if someone were standing above me watching me use the restroom, I wasn't fond of the idea that he was watching me puke my guts up, either.

I sat there as long as I could, waiting for it to all be over and for my stomach to have finally emptied itself before I felt like I could sit up again. I wiped off my mouth, then rinsed it out with some clean water before asking Luca to hand me the cup that I had used for tea so I could fill it up to drink. He moved quickly to grab it, then reached down beside me to fill it for me. I sat back against a stalagmite that was rising from the floor and rested. Surprisingly, all the heaving had worn me out quite a lot, and I felt like I could fall right back to sleep if I stayed there much longer.

"I'm sorry if us talking about this upset you," Luca said, taking a seat back down in front of me. "I should have known it would be too stressful for you right now. I'm sorry, upsetting you was never my intention."

I appreciated his apology, but it didn't do me any good now that the stress had already made me throw up. "Okay, so promise me now then, you won't try to kiss me again… you won't try to make me pick you," I said, as I leaned my head back to rest, closing my eyes.

I didn't hear him respond right away. I just felt him place his hand on my knee. "Eva, I want to promise you what you're asking because you're asking but… I would be lying to you."

I took a deep breath in then released it, hoping any residual stress would leave with it. I didn't respond; I didn't know how and didn't have the energy to keep going.

"Eva, open your eyes… look at me and tell me you don't feel for me like that. If you do, I will promise you what you are asking for." His words were soft and sincere sounding.

I opened my eyes and looked at him. I tried to work up the courage to tell him what he needed and ask for the promise again but it was too hard. I couldn't get my mouth to say it. I just sat there and looked at him. He leaned in and brought his hand up to my cheek to wipe away a tear that had begun to run down it.

"I can't love three different people," I said, looking at him. Finally, my mouth let me express what I was really feeling. Until I thought about it and realized he didn't know about Marcus. I shouldn't have said it and wished I could take it back.

Surprisingly, he smiled like he understood and didn't look confused at all. "Well…" he looked down my torso briefly, then back up to my eyes again, "one of them is a given. You will always love whoever it turns out to be. As for the other two… you can… You have to eventually pick one, but you can love both." His smile disappeared as he said it.

I was now confused by him not being confused and I didn't know what he meant by 'whoever it turns out to be' but I put the thought aside to try to think about what he was really trying to say about having to pick one. I knew what he meant by that and internally agreed. I realized it wasn't the fear of loving more than one that was debilitating for me, it was the realization that at some point I would have to choose one over the other and I didn't like that. I didn't want to hurt anyone.

I looked back up at him and nodded like I understood and agreed with his conclusion. "Will you help me go back to lie down?" I asked.

"Of course," he said, then stood up and leaned over to help me stand. "You're likely to be more tired now, too. It'll be good for you to rest."

# 9

## WRETCHED TEA

Having to stay in the cave was starting to bother me. Days passed as I sat there at the entrance watching people come and go, in and out, as they pleased. The weather was beginning to get nicer. Most days, if it did snow any, it would warm up enough by mid-day for it all to melt off. Now and then there would be a really nice day where it was only mildly chilly. I could tell spring was coming around and part of me was excited since I hated winter, but part of me wasn't because I knew I wouldn't be able to leave the cave and enjoy the change of weather like the everyone else.

Luca had started to ask more questions about my routine and his perception of the lack of sunlight I'd been getting. I couldn't help but think about how valid his concerns were. Jake and I never really had the best game plan as far as what we would do once we got to the grotto lands and how it would help protect me. We never thought of the long-term effects it might have for me to never be allowed to leave the cave.

I could already feel those effects both physically and mentally and we hadn't even been there all that long yet. I didn't know if it was the boredom or always being in the dark but I'd felt depressed more lately. It was easier when I had the fever to allow myself to lie around and sleep all day, but now that I'd been feeling better I wanted to do more than that. I'd thought about trying to express how I felt to Jake, but I hadn't yet since I knew there wasn't anything he could do about it.

I thought it might make me feel a little better if I could cook some of the meals for all of us, but Mary was the one who normally did that, and she didn't seem to take it well at all when I tried to help. Just like Samuel, they each had the one job that they had self-assigned and they didn't want anyone to take it from them. I wasn't sure what Jocelyn's job was yet. I did see her frequently leaving the cave and returning with herbs, shrubs, plants, and all kinds of other random crap. She took it all with her back to her chamber so I had no idea what she did after that. I half expected her to have a cauldron she stood over, stewing up magic potions to use to curse me with.

If Jake wasn't needed by me for anything, he generally liked to go and do what Samuel did. Even though Samuel did a decent job, I doubt he minded having the people that brought more mouths to feed, also feeding themselves. The times that Jake did stay in the cave with me when he could otherwise go hunting, I think was mainly so I didn't spend all my time sitting around talking to Luca. He still didn't know about the kiss but I think he did suspect Luca was growing rather fond of my company.

I asked Luca one time what his role was, being curious about what he actually did all day before we arrived. He said unless someone got hurt or was ill; he hadn't really had one except maybe keep an eye out for intruders. The real security force for them, though, was originally supposed to be Arthur, although since he had come up missing, it was obvious he wasn't the best at what he did.

Now that my fever had pretty well passed, it seemed Luca had devised within his mind other ailments he perceived me to have. I think he wanted me to be needy. Not only did it make him feel useful, but it gave him a reason to spend more time with me. He kept talking about how tired I had been, and how that was normal. I guess I could see how it would be normal if I felt depressed as well as not getting much sunlight or fresh air.

Even though my leg had healed rather well over the last couple of weeks, he still kept trying to bring me his elderberry tea. The first few times I drank it I didn't seem to have any issues but I haven't been as fond of it since the night I threw it up at the falls. I hated the idea of having to tell him to stop bringing it to me since he seemed so satisfied with himself when he thought he was making me feel better, so I hadn't. I just took a sip or two, then let it sit while we talked, then I would toss it once he wasn't looking.

Until today… maybe he was becoming suspicious that I started to do that because today he prodded more, making sure I drank it, all of it, while he watched. I didn't know if it was in my head because of my new negative connotations with it but I didn't feel so well after drinking it this time either. We only chatted for a while until I had to excuse myself to go lie down.

I slept, but it only felt like maybe a few hours until Jake came in, returning from his hunt again with a couple of nice rabbits and this time a ground hog as well. He mentioned if I was having issues with boredom, then he could clean the hides and dry them for me if I wanted to use them to make things like more blankets for us to lie on. It was a good idea, so I agreed and he said he would start doing that with all the new hides he caught.

I told him I hadn't been feeling well since earlier when I drank the tea. He acted as if he understood and was sympathetic, but didn't say anything past that. I wasn't having trouble keeping down any other food so I thought he would be at least a little curious as to the reason I couldn't stomach it. I was certainly confused by it and his reaction (or lack thereof) as well. He didn't act like he was curious at all. He almost acted like Luca and that he figured it was normal behavior.

I knew it wasn't normal, though. I rarely remembered ever being that sick and throwing up and the few times it had happened there was good reason. The first couple times I didn't cook my game well enough, and I paid for it for a few days. Then there was the time I thought I was pregnant when I was with Marcus. Even though the Praetorium supplied us with quarterly injections for birth control, I remember being sick for a while then, too. But the way I'd been sick this time was different, and I knew I couldn't be pregnant again. I had just had my cycle before we arrived at the cave. Granted, even though it was extremely light like usual, it *was* still there, so I figured I could rule that out. I didn't know why I had felt so sick lately but I wasn't enjoying it and I hoped it would stop.

It wasn't long before Jake lay down beside me ready to go to bed. Even though I got to see him throughout the day, I still often felt like I missed him. Neither of us said much. We just lay there and cuddled a little, enjoying each other's warmth. He brought his hand around and gently rubbed my stomach for a while. I knew it wasn't likely to make me feel any better, but it was a sweet gesture and I didn't mind.

I don't know how long I was asleep, but I was awakened suddenly by Jake springing up away from me. I heard him rustling around for a second like he was getting his fire stick to relight the torch. I initially felt a little concerned, wondering why he was awake and what could have caused it. He lit the torch and looked over at me. His expression was hurt and confused like I had done something to him in my sleep.

"What's wrong, Jake? Why are you awake?" I asked, wondering not only that but also the reason for his look.

He didn't say anything for a moment, he just sat there, studying me almost as if in shock. "Eva, I'm going to ask you something and I need you to tell me the complete truth, all right?"

My concern increased. I wasn't sure what the issue was but the idea there even was one was starting to bother me. "Of course! What?"

"Has Luca ever touched you?" His expression hardened as he asked it, bracing for the answer.

"Well..." I hesitated but only because I felt the question was so open-ended I was trying to think of all the innocent ways he had so I could use those as an example. "Well, when I was at the falls, I told you he was there when I got sick. He held my hair back and rubbed my back," I ended it with a high inflection like I wasn't sure if that was the answer he was looking for but I wasn't ruling out the idea of their being more that I wasn't telling him.

"I told you not to lie to me," he said, still obviously upset.

"I didn't… I don't know why you're so upset. I'm telling you what you want to know. I'm not lying!" I said, fully believing it since I really wasn't lying.

"Dammit, Eva! Did you forget you talk in your sleep?" He knew I wasn't telling him everything.

"Ugh… Jake… Okay, just calm down and I will tell you everything. But I don't want to while you're mad at me. I don't know what you're going to do," I said, moving a little farther back from him as I spoke.

He looked down as I scooted away. He saw I was frightened by his aggressive tone, so taking a deep breath, he made himself relax before saying anything else. "Elliceva, baby, I'm sorry. I'm not mad at you. Unless you lie to me, I can't stop myself from being mad if you're going to lie. So please don't do that, all right?" He asked, and I nodded to agree with him. "Okay… What has Luca done with you?" He continued now more calmly, looking at me in the eyes, confident he'd know if I didn't tell him the absolute truth.

"He kissed me," I said slightly under my breath, "but you don't have to be mad. I told him to never do it again," I continued more rapidly as to stop him from taking it and running with it. It didn't work though because as soon as the words 'he kissed me' left my lips Jake stood up and turned to walk out to find Luca to address it.

"Jake… Stop!" I yelled as I reached to take a hold of his ankle, trying to prevent him from leaving.

"Eva…" he sighed loudly, then stopped trying to pull away. "He's not going to touch you again," he said, looking down at me. "Let go," he said more like a request, knowing he could just force himself free if he wanted.

"You can't…" I pleaded with him, then before I realized what was happening or how to avoid it, I pulled my arms back and heaved, turning my head to look down at the floor. Nothing came up but I could feel my body wasn't done. I heaved again, then again. There was nothing in my stomach but that wasn't stopping my body from trying to expel what it thought there was down there.

"Oh, baby…" Jake got down on his knees and lowered his face to the level mine was at, placing his hand on my back. "Are you okay? Is it the ba—" he stopped. "Here, let me take you down to the falls." He stood up, then bent down to help me stand as well. Without me saying anything further, he bent forward to scoop me up in his arms, quickly snatched up the torch, then carried me deeper into the cave.

When we got to the falls, he sat me down where I had been sitting the first time I felt sick, after Luca kissed me. I turned around and aimed my face at the water, waiting for when my body would heave again. Jake wrapped my hair in his hand and held it up off of my neck and out of my face as he sat down next to me.

I didn't know why this was enough to stop him from continuing to go and drag Luca out of bed to beat him but I was thankful that it was. I was happy it was the least I could do to stop whatever onslaught of carnage would have taken place otherwise.

I began to heave again, but still wasn't able to bring anything up.

"I'm sorry, baby," Jake began to rub my back as he said it. "I'm sorry I did this to you."

"No, *I'm* sorry," I said in between heaving, trying to accept some of the blame for the kiss. "I felt so bad…" I couldn't help but begin to cry as I said it. I really did feel bad. I should have pulled away sooner than I had. "I love you, Jake. I told Luca that I love you and only you and that you would kill him if he ever did it again," I said, then heaved again.

"Shh, baby, don't cry. You're fine, just try to calm down," he said now trying to pull more hair back that had fallen into my face again.

"I didn't mean to lie to you. I only kept it a secret 'cause I didn't want you to hurt him," I was trying not to heave again in the middle of saying it.

"Okay… If it'll make you feel better, I won't kill him," he said almost begrudgingly, willing to agree even though I'm sure he didn't like it all that much.

"Or hurt him?" I asked, hoping he would agree to that as well even though I wasn't all that confident that he would.

"Fine… but only because I don't like seeing what you're going through… and if we need a doctor later, he won't do us any good if he's dead… or maimed."

"Thank you," I said, finally hoping the churning in my stomach might slow down and let me breathe a little. "Please don't say anything to him. I don't want it to be awkward between all of us." I knew that might be a lot to ask, but I hoped he'd be willing.

He let out a deep sigh. "Fine, but do you promise to tell me if he ever tries anything like that again?"

"Yes," I said, trying to keep from heaving again.

"Okay then, baby…" Jake reached up to rub my back again softly. "Don't worry about it then, just relax. You're dealing with enough. You don't need to worry about that too."

The next morning began later than usual, likely due to the events from the previous night. Jake didn't rush off to go hunting. This time he stayed with me as we went out to the main cavern together to get our breakfast cooking and enjoy a little warmth from the fire. Luca, already up and active, didn't take long to come and sit with us to chat but only after he got me some of his tea again, then made sure to watch me as I drank it.

Initially, I was concerned with how Jake would act around him now that he knew about the kiss that we shared, but like clockwork, he didn't bat an eye. He'd mastered the art of hiding his emotions and it showed. I thought at that moment about how well he would have done if the Coldiers had made him a spy like myself instead of a track and capture agent. He could have rivaled the best of them.

It was obvious that Luca was clueless. He didn't change how he was acting at all, which in some ways I thought he should have. He had a bad habit of looking at me with a little too much intensity, even with Jake sitting there talking to both of us. I had hoped he would let it ease up a little just for the sake of not feeling so awkward while trying to talk to me around Jake, but that didn't appear to be happening.

The tea Luca brought me this time smelled a little different, I wasn't sure how he was having Mary make it but I thought maybe if the last couple batches were bad and that was what was making me sick, this new smell was a good sign. I still didn't really want to drink very much of it, being a little gun shy and all but I didn't have an opening to dump any of it out as I usually did when he wasn't looking. I took a few sips and let it sit in my lap, holding the cup between my palms. I enjoyed the heat coming off of it.

It wasn't too long into our conversation when I noticed Jocelyn walk in. I hadn't seen her much since our last encounter, but was hoping she wouldn't come over to sit and try for a round-two; I wasn't in the mood. She wandered around for a minute or so, then from the other side of the cavern yelled out to Luca, asking him if he'd seen Mary yet. He turned to respond that he hadn't but she was probably close, considering she didn't really ever venture far from the cave.

Jocelyn acted like she agreed, and that she would just wait and see if Mary turned up, but it wasn't much longer until she hollered over to Luca again. She told him she was concerned, and she was going to go look for her outside. She would go ask Samuel and see if he knew where she had gone. Luca turned and hollered back, not really acting like he much cared to be broken away from his conversation but that was fine and to go for it. He turned back around and rolled his eyes a little, enough to give me the idea she had likely already irritated him earlier that morning and he didn't really want to talk to her.

Jake was getting more antsy the longer we sat there as well. He didn't mind having conversations, but he didn't really like feeling idle, not when there was likely something he could do outside. Instead, he probably felt like he was being forced to sit there and babysit Luca, monitoring him to make sure he didn't do anything else stupid, trying to steal Jake's catch away from him.

I assumed it was a male thing; the hidden rivalry they both knew existed but didn't speak of with each other. Part of me didn't really like the idea that they were at odds and it was because they both wanted me. Deep down, though, there was a part of me that reveled in the idea that I was desirable to them both.

The idea of having not one but two men that I could pick from was actually comforting to me when I thought about it. Then the feeling was quickly dashed when I was brought back down to earth. I knew that relationships didn't work like that and I couldn't have them both; I had to pick one and stick with him. Ultimately, that wasn't a problem. I loved Jake and Luca was just a good friend.

I sat there and sipped more of the tea, very slowly, waiting for a chance when Luca wasn't looking to dump a little of it. Before I realized it though, I had already drank a decent amount. It was easy being lost in conversation to not realize how much I was drinking. I immediately stopped myself and set it back down in my lap, making a mental note that at that moment I was no longer thirsty.

# IO

## DEATH'S KISS

I felt sick again… *Dammit, what was in that tea?* I sat there, trying to collect myself, thinking of what I needed to do next. I had been alone for about ten minutes after Jocelyn came back in and asked Jake and Luca to go help her look for Mary. I picked up the cup again and smelled it. After Luca left, I finished dumping what I had so I couldn't inspect it now, unfortunately. The longer I sat there the worse I felt. I knew I couldn't leave the cave to look for either of the men so I'd have to figure out what to do about it myself.

If I went down to the falls, I thought the fresh water might help me. I stood up to start that way, then stopped. My head was spinning, my pulse was racing, and I felt like I was about to puke again. I leaned against the rock that I had just been sitting on, hoping if I sat there long enough the spinning would stop. My stomach, wrenching itself a few times to prime the pump, finally propelled forward whatever was ailing it. It was severe; I had never thrown up this hard before in my life. I felt like I was dying, but surely that was all in my head.

After a few large productive heaves, in the corner of my eye, I saw what looked like two feet standing close to me. *Shit, those aren't men's feet.* Before I looked up to see who it was, I was praying they were Mary's.

"Aww… someone is a bit sick, huh?" It wasn't Mary's voice, it was clearly Jocelyn's.

"What do you want, Jocelyn? Now isn't a good time." I tried to say it with a threatening voice but it wasn't easy to do while holding myself back from puking more.

"I know what you are," she said, still standing above me. I was afraid to lift my head to look at her. I didn't want to incite her to make a move against me in the state I was in.

"So what… just leave me alone, now's not a good time," I said, hoping she'd listen but pretty sure she had other plans.

"Oh, I know! You and your little puking problems…" she said as she let out a large, exaggerated sigh. "You know I wondered when you might figure it out. That's what made me realize it was taking too long, and I just needed to finish it."

I finally looked up at her, confused. "What are you talking about?" I suspected what she meant, but I wanted her to clarify. I was still hoping that I was wrong, and she wasn't actually trying to poison me.

"I see you finished the tea Luca gave you," she smiled, looking down at the cup. "I knew if he was the one giving it to you, then you would drink it, even if it kept making you sick." I began to heave again as she continued talking. "But it was taking too freakin' long, and then when I realized what you really are… I knew I had to make it look like an accident. I just needed to speed it up a little. So I had Mary add a little extra to it this morning to help push you over the edge, just a little white snakeroot, I figured would do. Right before I sent her off on a little mission and told her not to be found for a few hours."

I knew why she was doing it; she hated me, that was obvious enough. However, I realized if she was right; I was almost dead and there was nothing I could do about it, except hope that Luca or Jake walked in while she was confessing. So I decided to keep her talking. "Why?" I asked.

"Why… well, why not?" She said with a smug grin, still looking down at me. "With you gone, not only do I get Luca back but then I could have Miles too if I wanted. Two men to be at my beck-and-call, that sounds like heaven. Besides, this whole killing thing has become a little addicting. See, 'cause I've been the one who's helped most of the people go missing around here." She stopped briefly to nudge me a little with her foot, probably to check and see how close I was to being done for.

"Ugh… you are just like that li'l wench, Bria, that Luca had before me. She was a hard one to get rid of for sure, but I did it… never regretted that day either. The only thing I regret was not showing Luca her dead body. It took him forever to move on. He couldn't just get over her and let me have him. Until when he finally did, then you came along and screwed it all up, you li'l whore."

I could feel my heart beginning to flutter in a way that wasn't usual. I had to make her keep talking. "Was… Luca… in it too?"

She gave me a confused look but proceeded like she thought she knew what I meant. "Do you mean was Luca in on me poisoning you?" She let out a small chuckle. "Oh, I wish. That would have been great, but no. He didn't know anything about it. He just thought he was trying to help. Poor idiot, that's all he thinks about—*you*." She stopped to nudge me with her foot again.

I couldn't hold myself on my hands and knees any longer, so I lowered my body to lie against the ground, if nothing else, hoping the cool floor of the cave would help soothe the distress of dying.

"Luca had the idea of me collecting the elderberries for him but well… when I realized who they were for, it was my idea to tell Mary not to cook them, and the idiot didn't even see it coming. He helped poison you… kill you and he'll never even know it."

"Jocelyn!" a man's voice called from behind her. It sounded like Luca but I couldn't determine it for sure.

She spun around. "Luca?" She said with a loud gasp. She knew she'd been caught.

"What have you done?" He yelled. It was the first time I'd ever heard him angry. He quickly began to walk closer to us. She didn't say anything, but swiftly turned to run out of the cave. He acted like he was about to run after her when he caught me in his peripheral vision and stopped himself to come address me first.

"Eva…" He turned me over to rest on my back, looking up at him.

His eyes were as intense as always but this time I could see what looked like anger mixed with sorrow. They quickly became glossy the longer he looked at me.

"Oh my god, Eva... I don't... I don't know how to fix you," he said hopelessly as he started to look around frantically, probably thinking of what he could do. He then looked back down at me as he moved closer to pull me up into his lap and cradle my head.

I wanted to talk to him. I wanted to tell him I knew it wasn't his fault and to tell Jake that I loved him, as well as so many other things that were going through my mind. *You never know how much there really is to say until you know you're about to die.* I couldn't say any of it, though. I couldn't get my mouth to function. It's like my brain had resorted to being in only-do-what-is-necessary mode. I just lay there, looking up at him. I could feel tears as they started to roll down my cheeks. I wanted to see Jake. I wanted Jake to be the one who was holding me, kissing me as I went.

"Eva, I'm so sorry," he said. His eyes were now watering more than mine. "I'm sorry she did this to you. I'm sorry I didn't know..." He stopped to make sure I was looking at him, and I could understand him, "I didn't know! You believe me, right? I didn't know!"

I nodded my head the best that I could.

"Luca!" Jake growled from behind, likely unsure about what he thought he was seeing.

"Jake, come here. She needs you," Luca said, looking up and behind him.

"What?" Jake said as he came closer, now looking down at me. His face was instantly full of confusion and torment. "Why is she like this? Eva... Look at me, baby... What's wrong?"

"Jocelyn poisoned her. I came in on her telling Eva what she did. She ran out. I don't know where she went." He hesitated before he finished. "Jake, I don't know how to fix her..."

Jake got down and pulled me into his lap. Now holding me as Luca had, he looked down into my eyes, "I love you, baby. I love you, you know that, right?" He asked now with tears in his eyes as well. I nodded. "Okay, I'm going to fix you. We're going to fix you. You're not going to die… you're not, dammit! Not if I have anything to do with it!" He looked over to Luca who was still on his knees watching Jake talk to me. "Go get me my medium duffle bag, now! Run!" He said, ordering him to hurry, then looked back down at me.

He didn't say anything else for a second, he just let his eyes gaze into mine. It felt peaceful at that moment. I could feel my heart starting to slow down, letting me relax.

"Baby, don't leave me," he said softly. "Not like this…" he swallowed, then brought up his arm to wipe his eyes with his sleeve. "Not like this, baby… please… stay with me."

I knew why he was saying it. The longer I lay there, the more relaxed I felt, the easier it was to let my eyes close with long, slow blinks. Each one seemed harder and harder to recover from.

I felt his lips against my forehead with my last blink. He pulled me closer to him and began to rock me slowly. "Elliceva… Not like this, baby. Don't go to sleep. Stay with me, please… stay awake. I'm gonna fix you. Please stay awake," he murmured into my hair, holding me close.

"Luca, get your ass in here!" He cried out suddenly. The intensity broke me from the peaceful state I had begun to fall into, making me open my eyes again.

"I'm… I'm coming… Here!" Luca stammered breathlessly as he ran up to us. His voice was shaky and fast, likely breathing heavily from all the running.

"Inside, reach into the first bottom pocket on the right side. There is a glass jar. Pull it out!" Jake said as he watched Luca fumbling around, trying to follow orders.

"Here," Luca said, quickly pulling it out. It was a small glass jar full of black powder.

"Good, now go get some water for her to drink. Over there, I still have my canister." He pointed at the rock where he had been sitting before they both left to go with Jocelyn. "It should be half full!"

Luca ran over to grab it, then came back and handed it to him. "What is that stuff?" He asked, referring to the black powder.

"Activated charcoal," Jake said quickly as he took the jar and opened it, then carefully dumped the powder into the canister. "Quick, shake it up. I need her to drink it."

Luca did as ordered, though still with confusion on his face, then handed it back to Jake.

"Here, baby, sit up just a little if you can. I need you to drink all of this, all right?" He said as he tried to get me to sit up with the arm that he had underneath me. It was hard for me to respond, but I tried to do what he asked. "Eva... come on, baby... you're not dying today, now sit up... please!" He tried to speak to me stronger to see if that would help, but I just couldn't do what he wanted.

He brought the container to my mouth and started to slowly pour, probably hoping I could still swallow, and I could. "Good girl, baby, that's all I needed. Just keep swallowing. This will help."

"What kind of person carries that stuff around with them?" Luca asked, likely trying to take his frustration of not being able to help me, out on Jake.

"I'm an agent! I keep it on me because you never know who's going to try to poison you," he snapped, giving Luca a dirty look. "But you already knew that, didn't you?" He stopped to concentrate back on helping me drink as much as I could. It still must have been bothering him after a few seconds though because he felt the need to verbally attack back. "What kind of person lets his girlfriend poison people?"

"She's not my girlfriend and I hope I never see her again," Luca said brashly, letting himself relax a little and finally sit flat against the ground.

"You better hope *I* never see her again," Jake said still focusing on my drinking while talking to Luca. "You know what, I can say the same for you... If this ends up killing my baby, you're a dead man, hear me? There will be no reason to keep you around if that happens. That's the only reason I haven't hurt you yet!"

Luca didn't respond. His eyes widened as his mouth closed, forming a thin line. He nodded like he understood, then looked back down at me. I finished drinking everything in the canister, now I just hoped it was going to work. At least Jake seemed confident it would. After I finished, I relaxed back against his arm and let my head sink into his thigh. I knew there was nothing more I could do but rest at that point so I let my eyes close again while my mind reentered whatever peaceful state I had been previously feeling.

"She looks pale, Miles," Luca muttered, still concerned.

"Shut up, it'll work!" Jake barked back, clearly upset. "It's gotta work…"

"E va, open your eyes, baby, look at me. Eva? Eva, baby, wake up!"

"Miles… she's not looking good, she looks…"

"Shut up, Luca!…… Eva, look at me, open your eyes, Eva! Baby, come on, don't leave me… Not like this. It can't be like this…"

"Miles…"

"Dammit, Luca… Open your mouth one more damn time and you'll see what hell looks like before she sees heaven!"

"I got you, baby, I'm right here. I got you… You're gonna be okay… you're gonna be *okay*… just wake up for me, Eva. Open your eyes… please baby, don't leave me… Please!"

I woke up to the pitch black of hell, though it wasn't as warm as I thought it should have been. I must have died. I knew I had. I had hopes that when it happened, I would have gone to heaven but I wasn't surprised this was where I ended up. I didn't do anything in life that earned me an entrance anywhere else but here.

It was quiet. There was no noise except the faint murmur of what sounded like people but I couldn't make it out. I couldn't move. My body felt like it was still reeling from my death. I tried to talk but I couldn't do that either. I wasn't even sure if my eyes were open or not. Maybe the blackness was actually the inside of my eyelids, or was it? *Do you still have eyelids when you're dead?* Maybe that's why I couldn't feel anything, maybe I didn't have a body and it was just my spirit laying there, lingering in place.

*Was I a ghost? How did all this afterlife stuff work?* Maybe I was in purgatory, if that even existed. I didn't know. I lay... rather uh, lingered there, thinking... letting my spirit ponder what all was happening with me, and where I might actually be.

Jake... My mind emptied of all but that one thought, no more about me, only Jake. Where was he now? How did he take my death? Did he blame himself? It wasn't his fault in the least, but maybe it wouldn't have happened if we had never come to the grotto lands to begin with. If he would have just let me erase myself again like I had wanted, maybe none of this would have happened.

The longer I lingered there, the more sensations I felt returning to my body... uh, *spirit.* Maybe it was how the spirit realm worked. Maybe there was an acclimatization period. I knew it was all new to me but it really felt similar to being alive. Too bad there wasn't a manual for how to pass over when the time came, or maybe there was. It would have made this whole process easier, surely.

I moved my hands around in the space above me, feeling for whatever I could, but nothing. I moved them around to the space next to me but again I felt nothing. I tried to pull myself to where I thought I was sitting up, but I couldn't tell if I was. *Does hell even have gravity?*

The longer I sat there the more my eyes began to acclimate to my surroundings. Then finally I saw it, a little glow of light coming toward me. It wasn't the large bright white that I had heard about but I would take it. Maybe God had changed his mind. Maybe he was coming to give me a second chance. I sat there and watched it as it got closer but it wasn't coming as close to me as I thought it should before it looked like it was passing again. "God," I called out. Finally, my voice was working. The light stopped moving away and slowly crept back over to me.

"Miles!" the voice screamed right before the light fell and hit the floor along with whatever entity was holding it.

*Wait... Miles? He said Miles... Was I not dead? What?* I tried to process what I thought I just heard when I saw another light quickly enter the room. It was Jake, holding a torch, standing above me looking down. He was frozen, standing there, staring, like I was a ghost just like I had thought I might have been. I looked over to see Luca on the floor, passed out beside his torch.

"Eva?" Jake said, his mouth hung open as he blinked a few times slowly.

I didn't respond. I was in about as much shock as I thought he was.

"Eva… but you're dead…" he said still standing there, trying to comprehend what he was now seeing in light of what he thought he knew to be true.

"I am!" I said in full agreement. I knew I was dead too, though I wasn't sure how I could still be sitting there talking to him.

"No… you w… you were dead. I saw… you… you're dead," he began to breathe faster, as he brought his hand up to run it through his hair.

"I know, I am. What are you doing here?" I said, confused why I would see him in hell.

He let out a low laughing sigh, like whatever I said broke him from his delusion. He dropped the torch to the floor and got to his knees, quickly positioning himself at eye level in front of me. "God, please don't be playing games," he said as he brought both hands up to cup my chin, lifting my face to look at him. "Eva… look at me," he said, bringing his face closer to mine, then looking me in the eyes, almost as if he was trying to examine my soul and see if it was still there.

"Jake?" I mouthed, trying to ask what he had concluded of my condition. Was I dead or not?

His face instantly broke like I had never seen it before, and he began crying, almost sobbing, as he wrapped his arms around me to embrace me. "Eva… you're alive! Oh my god, thank you God… thank you!" He kept repeating himself as he hugged me tighter and tighter.

I looked over to see Luca was now beginning to stir and wake up. "Jake," I said as I pulled away from the hug slightly, "How dead was I?"

He let go and sat back a little, resting one arm on his knee while still keeping the other wrapped around my waist. He didn't say anything, he just looked at me, overwhelmed with unbelief. Then finally he answered. "It's been hours, Eva. Luca couldn't feel your pulse anymore so… we brought you back here to lay you down…" he started to cry again in the middle of his words. "Baby, I lost you! I totally lost you. You were there, then you were gone. I've never felt the way I felt at that moment. I wanted to die. I wanted to dive in after you. I wanted to save you," he began to sob again. "I don't want to live this life without you. I'm not me when you're not mine. I never want to lose you again. I can't! I can't, baby, I can't!" He said as he pulled himself closer to me again, then brought his arms around me to hold me tight. "I've never thought of myself as incomplete, but today… without you… there is no heaven, there is no hell, there is no life, there's no wrong or right, there's no beauty, no love… it's all nothing. I might as well live in a black hole without you." He ran his fingers through my hair and we sat there holding each other as tight as we could, for as long as we could.

"Eva?" Luca was now awake and sitting up, looking at me. "You… you were…" his eyes fluttered for a second then rolled up as he passed out again.

"Eva, baby, I love you." Jake said, ignoring Luca and continuing with our embrace, "I love you more than you'll ever know. Never leave me again, promise me, baby, you'll never leave me again!"

I nodded as I pushed my head into his chest. He ran his hand through my hair, pulling my head tighter toward him, then leaned down and kissed me on the crown.

# II
## MISPLACED CONFESSIONS

"Eva, baby, you need to hold still. I can't get any sleep like this." Apparently Jake wasn't seeing my excessive readjusting as I had intended—attention seeking. I needed attention, physical touch, cuddles, anything!

I moved my hand from gently resting at his navel up to his chest. With the temperature of the cave, it was rare for me to get to sleep up against his bare skin, and I missed it terribly. I wanted him to touch me. I wanted him to cuddle me... love on me. It'd been almost a month since I had been poisoned. I felt fine now, but for whatever reason, he still acted skittish of me, and wouldn't let himself give in to any of my many daily advances. I knew he could be dense, and he didn't always see when I was throwing myself at him, but this seemed different. He was holding back, but why?

"What if I don't want to hold still?" I asked, trying to lure him further.

"What? What's wrong, baby? Can you not get to sleep?" He stirred slightly, talking to me with his eyes closed, probably trying to get himself to drift back into sleep.

"It's been so long... Why won't you touch me? What have I

done?" I asked, feeling relieved that I finally had enough gumption to just come out and say it.

"Oh, baby, is that what's bothering you?" He asked groggily as he rolled over to his side to face me. "Don't worry about it, it's not you. I'm just… I have a lot on my mind."

I didn't say anything, I just lay there trying to stare at him in the dark. I was upset. Whatever he was trying to say wasn't a good explanation and didn't make me feel better at all. I was frustrated now as well.

"If you won't give me any attention, I bet I know someone else who might…" I said it. I shouldn't have. I didn't mean it, but I said it. Whether it was a joke or not, I hoped it would provoke him to about what I needed from him.

"Eva, why would you say that?" I couldn't see his eyes but I felt them now glaring at me. His voice was stern and harsh. It was obvious he didn't appreciate the comment or think it was a joke. "If he touches you again, I'll hurt him this time. I don't care if it's your fault." He pulled away from me as he said it.

"What are you afraid of?" It came out without me thinking about what I was saying. After hearing it myself though, I thought it was a good question, and I was happy that my mouth said it.

"What are you talking about? I'm not afraid of anything." I heard him strike his fire stick.

"It's not a coincidence what all happened to me and now you won't touch me anymore," I said, raising my voice. I couldn't hold back my emotions.

"That's ridiculous, Eva." I could see him now that he'd lit the torch. He didn't even know how badly I needed him. He enticed me just by sitting there with his well-formed muscles, calling to me, convincing me they needed my touch.

"No, it's not. We can talk about it. We can work through whatever it is you might be scared of. Talking helps. We need to communicate better," I said, trying to keep my voice down.

"I'm not scared. I don't know why you're saying that." His voice was now beginning to raise but I could tell he was trying to keep it low enough to not temp Luca to come and *check* on me. "If I'm scared of anything, it's definitely not touching you."

"Where are you going?" I asked, seeing he had stood up, about to walk out.

"I'm just going to the bathroom. I'll be back. Can you keep yourself together while I'm gone or are you going to run over to seduce Luca?" He said it sarcastically but it hurt.

I didn't say anything. I just narrowed my eyes at him. If I had been standing, I would have slapped him. Part of me entertained the idea of running off to Luca just to get back at Jake for inferring I would do such a thing and then the other part of me felt like he was allowed to be upset considering I was the first to reference Luca like that in the first place.

"Just stay here. We'll talk when I get back," he said as he started to walk out.

"I don't want to talk to you anymore," I yelled back at him as he walked away. "If you're gonna infer I'm loose, I might as well play the part," I said, trying to upset him further. I wanted him to feel like he made me feel when he said what he did. I knew I was being childish but I couldn't help it. I didn't know how else to express myself.

He took the torch with him, leaving me again to lie there in the darkness alone. I thought for a second about what I should do. I didn't want to involve Luca even though I threatened to. I didn't mean it. I just didn't know how else to get Jake to see my side. I just wanted him to be open to telling me what his problem was. I knew I wasn't the best communicator myself. Maybe that was making it worse. Maybe if I made him feel more comfortable talking to me he would give in and feel free to express himself.

I crawled over to his large bag, looking for the alcohol he brought back when he returned. There should have still been a lot of it left, considering he always took it away from me before I ever got more than a couple of swigs in. I reached into the bag and searched for it, sifting through all the various items that he kept in there until I felt it and pulled it out. I opened the bottle and lifted it to my mouth. I had no idea what kind it was, what the proof was or anything about it. I never got to drink alcohol. Before the war, I was too young, and Marcus never allowed it.

I knew it wasn't the best idea, and he wouldn't be pleased with me, but I'd hoped if I was able to drink enough to relax, then he could let his guard down and finally talk to me. I didn't know how much to drink but I figured a few good gulps would suffice. I lifted it to my nose to smell. It was strong. *Just do it...* I started to take a sip when I decided it'd be best to just commit before I changed my mind. It tasted like shit and burned like hell but I kept the rim to my lips and continued to drink when suddenly I saw the glow of his torch returning to the chamber. I looked up at him, feeling caught like a kid with their hand in the cookie jar.

"What the hell do you think you're doing?" He scolded, way more upset than I actually expected he'd be, but I had drunk enough that I really didn't care much at that point. "You know you shouldn't be drinking... Oh my gosh, Eva. Why? Stop it, now!" He quickly moved over to me to snatch it out of my hand and replace the lid.

*I shouldn't be drinking? Why not?* "I'm sorry..." I said, but I wasn't. I started to crawl back over to the bedding, taking the opportunity to meander as slowly as I could, giving him the chance to watch me. I hoped it would entice him to finally touch me. It must have worked. He swatted my ass briskly before he sat back down.

"Oh... you wanna play that way?" I said playfully, hoping he would get the idea.

"You're not supposed to be drinking right now, Eva," he said still upset, now sitting across from me.

"Why the hell not?" I asked, getting frustrated again that he kept refusing me.

"Why?... Are you serious?" He asked, his face genuinely looking confused by my actions.

"Whatever, Jacob." I pushed myself up to stand to my feet and walk out.

"Where the hell do you think you're going? You don't even have a torch… or any pants… get your ass back in here," he was serious. I didn't know what I was doing either. I was just letting the alcohol take over and move me to where it wanted, which at that moment was to go talk to Luca just because I knew it would make Jake mad.

"I'm going to talk to Luca," I said, apparently already having lost my normal verbal filter.

"Like hell you are!" He quickly brought himself to his knees to reach out and grab a hold of my thigh with both hands.

"You can't stop me," I said, trying to pull my leg free from his sturdy grip.

"Fine. Is this what you want?" He asked as he slowly slid his hands up my sides.

Before I had a chance to answer him and tell him that was precisely what I had been wanting, he grabbed a hold of my wrist to pull me down to sit in his lap.

"You shouldn't get yourself drunk like this, Eva, even if you are mad at me," he said softly, looking me in the eye as he gently brushed the hair off my face. "You'll go do something stupid and end up getting Luca killed."

"I just—"

"Shh, don't talk," he said, staring at me for a minute before he rested his forehead against mine. "I get it. I'm sorry…" Rubbing his hands up and down my back, he leaned in to kiss me soft and slow.

I couldn't help but feel ecstatic. I was finally about to get what I had been longing for since my emergence back from hell. I pulled back to look at him. His face and body both were glowing from the illumination of the remaining embers of the torch. He was so handsome. I couldn't help but remember how it felt to have his stubbly little beard tickle my neck as he laid a trail of kisses along it. I brought my arms up to rub my hands along the stoutness of the two large muscles holding his neck to his shoulders as we continued to gaze into each other's eyes.

"You get it?" I asked, hoping he'd continue.

He nodded, "I know you're more likely to be emotional right now, maybe a little irrational—" He stopped to hold up his hand when he saw my furrowed brow with a look of confusion. "Don't say anything for a minute, just hear me out."

I tried to let my face relax, but it was difficult.

"I know you're going through a lot... *physically* and probably emotionally, too. You haven't really acted like you want to talk about it so I haven't said anything. But I just want you to know I'm here for you, baby. Whatever you need, I'm here... I'm not going anywhere. We'll get through this together."

I was still confused, but appreciated him being open to talking. "Okay," I said as I ran my hands through his hair. Now I was beginning to regret the alcohol a little as well, considering it made it hard for me to think about how to respond to him. "It just feels like you... uh... you've been so distant from me. You know, ever since I was poisoned. You haven't wanted to do anything. You've barely touched me. You haven't... um... you know haven't wanted to cuddle like normal, be playful, intimate... nothing."

"I can cuddle with you, baby." He said, leaning in to kiss me again.

I wanted to address why he'd been distant so we could fix it, but didn't want to refuse the offer so I just nodded and leaned into him, resting my face against his chest.

"Here, why don't you lay down on your back and I'll move over to lie against you." He said as he began to unbutton his shirt. "We'll cuddle as much as you need."

"Okay," I did what he asked and watched as he pulled his shirt open, lay down next to me so his bare chest was up against my arm, then he draped his shirt over my torso and rested his arm against my chest. "I like this. This is good." I murmured, turning my head to nuzzle it against his neck.

After we lay there like that for a while with him softly rubbing circles over my belly, he finally spoke again, whispering softly against my ear. "Was this what you wanted?"

"For now," I said with a quiet giggle. I could tell the alcohol was setting in nicely and I was beginning to feel really excitable and quite mellow all at the same time. "I'd like you to do other things, too. I miss your body." I said, feeling unashamed and uninhibited.

"This is enough for now. You're drunk, I won't do anything else with you drunk," He said coarsely.

I didn't understand him but I didn't argue. I got what I wanted; I was happy enough at that moment to take it and rest. I didn't have to have anything else from him.

He took his hand away from my stomach and pulled my shirt down. I could tell he was right. I must have been drunk because I was beginning to ramble at him, not realizing what I was saying or why.

"Eva?" He asked, interrupting my rambling, as he sat up next to me leaning against the wall of the cave, bringing my head to rest in his lap so he could stroke my hair.

"What, baby? You ask and I will deliver. What do you want? You want the world, Miles, I will... the world... I'll world you, baby," I couldn't tell but it was getting more difficult to distinguish my speech and how well I was speaking to him.

"Are you going to remember any of this tomorrow?" He asked.

*Shit...* It worked to make him talk but if I didn't remember anything he'd said that wasn't well planned out. "I do... n... not... no... yes, I member ever... thing you say, baby."

"Ok, good. I know you wanted to talk. You're right, that's what we need. And I have some things I need to tell you."

"Okay... shooter." I giggled. What I said was funny. I didn't mean to say it but it was funny.

"You don't have to respond, just listen... I will tell you everything, okay? Everything that's been going on with me... why I've been so distant."

"Roger me, Charlie..." I answered, giggling again at myself. "Okay... okay..."

"All right..." he hesitated for a moment, then proceeded, "I lied to you, baby. I lied and I'm sorry. I promised I would never lie to you but I did because I thought I had to and it's been eating me up inside," he paused again probably waiting for my reaction but I was feeling sleepy so I just closed my eyes and tried to listen, hoping I'd remember in the morning.

"I saw Miller when I went to Nashville. I know I told you I didn't, but... I was so mad at him for what he did to you. I couldn't stop myself. I was going to go in there and kill him. I hate that man. I just wanted to rip every limb off of him and make him suffer like he did you. But when I got there, I couldn't... He... Oh my gosh, baby... He knew things about you he shouldn't know. He said you weren't who I thought you were... I didn't care, though. I didn't care; I was still about to kill him until... he stopped me, holding up a picture of this little girl.

"She looked like she was four, maybe five. She looked just like you, baby; I mean just like you. He said she was your daughter and that he wiped your memory and sent you away after you had her. I don't know how that could be true because you've never said anything about her... you don't look like you've ever had a child either... but then I thought about all the other things you still couldn't remember and I was confused. I didn't know what to do. He said he would kill her if I didn't cooperate with him or almost as bad, he would raise her himself. The perverted bastard... I wouldn't want any baby raised with the likes of him as their father.

"I didn't want to believe him, baby, but I didn't know what to do. He said if I just got him the intel he would let her go. He would give her back to you... to us... He said he didn't have to have you brought in. He knew I wouldn't do it, anyway. I wouldn't do anything that would compromise your safety again.

"He made me turn my tracker back on so he knew I wasn't going to do anything tricky and get her away from him another way. That means he knows where we're at now... I'm sorry, baby. I don't even know if you're hearing any of this but I had to let it out. It about killed me already, thinking I lied to you when I found you poisoned. I didn't want to hold it in even longer.

"I know that you're pregnant. I don't know if the poison killed our baby, but I didn't want you to lose another one of yours just because of me. Luca said we will just have to wait and see if you miscarry. That's why I haven't wanted to be intimate with you, baby. It's made me scared to touch you… I didn't want to hurt you any more than I have already. I just need the intel, and it can all be over with. I know I told you I wouldn't ever ask you for it but… I'm only doing it 'cause I don't feel like I have another choice… Eva? Are you still awake, baby? Eva…"

# 12
## TREACHERY

I woke up to the distinct sound of the hammer being pulled back on a revolver. I opened my eyes to see Luca standing above both Jake and myself. It looked like the sound woke Jake up at the same time as it did me. He instantly placed his hand over me and sat up, positioning himself between me and Luca.

"What the hell do you think you're doing, Luca?" Jake was upset, very upset.

"I don't want to hurt her." Luca said, pointing the gun at Jake with one hand and holding a torch with the other. "Eva, sweetheart, come here. I don't trust him anymore. You'll be safer with me." He looked at me with his intense green eyes like he always did. I didn't know what made him act this way suddenly, but I could tell he was serious, very serious, and it was beginning to scare me.

"You'll have to shoot me before you think I'm just gonna let her walk over to you while you point a gun at me," Jake said, keeping his hand across my stomach, stopping me from standing up. "What's this about Luca? Where'd you even get that gun?"

"Miles, let Eva come to me. I don't want her on that side of the barrel. I know you don't either. Please, just let her come to me," Luca said as calmly as he could be, like he'd held a gun and used it to threaten someone before.

Jake didn't say anything. I could see he was trying to calculate what Luca was doing and how to out-whit him.

"Jake… it's okay," I said softly under my breath as I rubbed my hand against his lower back, trying to feel for his gun but it wasn't there. He must not have had it on him, or even close or he would have already pulled it. Or maybe he hadn't because he knew how dangerous it was to shoot inside of a cave. "I'll be okay, Jake. He won't hurt me," I said softly, then looked back at Luca. "Right, Luca?"

"Eva, of course, that's not what I want. That's why you need to move. This is between me and him." He didn't take his eyes off of Jake. He said it all still staring at him, knowing one wrong move and he wouldn't still be standing.

Jake didn't lift his arm to let me up, he kept it firmly against my stomach. "Luca, talk to me. We don't have to have a problem between us. Please, just put the gun down, you're scaring her. I won't hurt you if you just put it down. We can talk like men."

Luca's eyes twitched slightly over to me, then back to Jake. I could tell he didn't want to be pointing it at us either but he must have had a good reason since it seemed so out of his character. "Miles, I found two dead agents out in the woods today. One was a Coldier and one was a Sicari. They shot each other. Agents don't come into the grotto lands, not until you showed up here. She isn't safe with you. Now, that's all I am going to say until you let her come over here to me." I could tell Luca was starting to get nervous. He didn't act like he was lying but I knew this was a bold move on his part. Something I was sure he probably never thought he would have the courage to do.

"Jake, I'm not scared. I'll be okay," I said, trying to get him to listen to me. I thought maybe if I was standing by Luca I could disarm him myself. I was concerned if I did though, Jake really would kill him this time, which I didn't feel was fair even if Luca was stupid enough to point a gun at us. Albeit idiotic, he was doing it out of selfless motives and didn't deserve to die.

"Okay, I understand. Okay, Luca? Let me explain it. Just put the gun down and we can work through this. You know you don't want to hurt us. We're on your side even if it looks like I'm not." Jake didn't move. He ignored any suggestion I made that I would be okay to go over to Luca.

"I'm not going to put the gun down because I don't trust you, but talk. Explain it. What are both side's agents doing here? Why are they looking for you?" Luca pulled his finger out of the trigger guard and rested it along the side of the gun, letting Jake know he was willing to listen.

Jake was silent for a moment, probably trying to gather the right angle to take with Luca.

I decided to say something, hoping he might believe it coming from me. "I'm an agent, Luca. It's me they want, not Miles. Please, just put the gun down and we'll explain everything to you. We aren't here to hurt anyone. We just wanted to be left alone. You have to believe me." I tried to match the intensity of my eyes with his so he'd listen and know I wasn't lying. As soon as I said it, I felt Jake's hand against my stomach tense up. I didn't know if he was upset with me telling him, but he didn't look back at me, so I couldn't tell.

"What?" Luca let his eyes linger on mine longer than he had been at that point. "But you don't have a tag. Eva, I told you he's manipulating you, please, you can't lie for him. I won't believe you."

"It's true, Luca… Please just let us explain." Jake's tone was now calm and relaxed like he was taking a different approach with him. "We can work out all the details together. No one has to get hurt. No one has to have a gun pointed at them." He paused again as he swallowed. "Come on man, you're pointing a gun at my baby… Please put it down."

The words hit Luca more true than when I tried to talk to him. He hesitated only slightly, then nodded and slowly bent over to place the gun against the floor in front of Jake, conceding his position of authority.

I was instantly nervous not knowing what Jake might do next. If he would do as he said or if he lied and he intended to actually pummel Luca instead.

"Thank you," Jake said as he leaned forward to pick up the gun. He released the cylinder and spun it slowly as he ejected each of the six bullets that had been loaded into it. One was just a casing, likely the remnants of the shot fired to kill one of the agents that Luca had found. "I meant what I said Luca. We'll tell you everything. I don't appreciate you pointing a gun at us. That was foolish and dangerous, but I understand your concern for Eva. Thank you for putting it down." Jake finished as he took the bullets and dropped them at my feet, then took the gun and tossed it over by his bag.

He was trying to show Luca that he meant it when he said he wouldn't hurt him. I was surprised, but extremely thankful. I didn't want to see either of them get hurt, so I liked the idea of them being able to talk and hopefully get everything out in the air so they could get along better than they had up to that point.

"I meant what I said, Miles. I only did it because I'm concerned about her." Luca looked back over at me almost apologetic that he'd just put me in the cross-hairs.

"Sit down. If we're going to explain everything it's going to take a minute. I hope you're ready to listen." Jake motioned to him to take a seat in front of us, then he slid the candle over to light it.

W e sat there for a couple of hours, telling Luca everything we could without telling him too much. He now knew about my memory loss and gain, what the Coldiers had done to me, who I was as a Sicari, why we needed to hide and why we came to the grotto lands instead of using the serum we took from the Sicari. Jake explained to him better how we met and the circumstance behind why I was his prisoner. Luca still acted like he didn't totally agree with all of Jake's methods but he at least understood. We didn't tell him about the intel. Thankfully, Jake did a good job of keeping both that and Marcus my secret. I think he knew that both were memories of mine that I would only share when I felt comfortable enough to, and this wasn't the time for it.

It was easy for us to conclude why the Sicari had come to the grotto lands to find me. I explained to them both about Jocelyn catching me dream-talking and what she likely learned from her eavesdropping. After that, it was a shared consensus among all of us; she was likely the culprit and probably ran to them to tattle, ensuring that if she hadn't been able to kill me with her poison that something or someone else might still have a chance to.

Jake didn't say much about why the Coldier would have been here, he kind of glossed over it but we both got the idea it wasn't a good thing. I let Jake do most of the talking. I didn't want to bring anything up that he didn't want Luca to know about just in case. I also didn't know if he intended to lie to Luca about anything, in which case I didn't want to intervene and ruin it for him.

After most of the information came out and we'd all sat there digesting it, we were left with the same conclusion. What were we to do now? If both sides now knew where we were and both sides were now willing to come to the one place that we didn't think they would go, we knew we were no longer safe. *I* was no longer safe. It was easy to see that I was the one that they wanted. It was the intel that was inside my head that they were both searching for. Intel that could change the course of the war in favor of either side. Intel that had been the death of everyone else that had known it except me. I decided if I had to remember it I might as well take it to my grave because it wasn't going to do anyone else any favors knowing it.

It was getting late in the morning by the time we finished telling Luca all that we thought he should know, and *only* what he should know. Jake suggested we go out to the cavern to get a bite of breakfast and let everyone cool off before we talked any further about how we would proceed. He said it wasn't likely that they sent more than one agent from each side as initial scouts. It was just our luck that they ran into each other before they ran into us. He said it would be at least a week or more before either side knew their agent was dead and would send more after them, so we should have more than enough time to sit and come up with the most viable and safe option going forward. Luca and I both agreed and followed him out to the cavern.

"Here, baby, you need to eat," Jake said, offering me some nuts that he had reserved from his pack.

"Oh, I didn't know you had any of those left. It's okay if you want them. I'm fine just eating more of Samuel's fish," I said, trying to politely refuse since I knew the nuts were Jake's favorite.

"Eva, you need the fat. Eat them," Luca said, chiming in. I looked at him from the corner of my eye, then I looked down at myself. I guess I had gotten a bit gaunt since we'd been in the caves. Still, I didn't need him telling me so. I would have at least liked to think I was still relatively healthy-looking otherwise.

"Fine," I said as I took them out of Jake's hand. He smiled like for the first time he was happy that Luca agreed with him, making me comply without fighting.

"I was thinking," Luca decided to jump into the subject of all of our future plans, "If she needs to stay in the cave to keep the signal blocked, that shouldn't be a problem. She can just stay here with me. Miles, if you leave for a little while, you can probably lead the trail away from us and they won't be able to find her. Then you come back when you think it's safe again. She should be safe here with me, you can leave me the gun... Then if they do come around, she just looks like any other Gypsyin. They won't know who she is. I can say she's my wife."

I looked over at Jake completely flabbergasted, fully expecting him to be outraged and about to stand up to strangle Luca any second for even alluding to such a horrible idea.

"I hate to say it, but you might be right," Jake said calmly, looking down, then over at him.

"What?" I said, now totally taken aback by them both. *How dare they agree on what to do with me! I can decide what to do with myself!* "Uh, I don't think so, Jacob Miles. If you're going anywhere, you're taking me with you, Mister."

Jake looked up at me, his expression distraught. I bet he knew I wasn't going to be happy with what he already decided though he'd probably try to put his foot down and make me do it whether I liked it or not. "Eva, baby—"

"No, Jake," I didn't let him finish. I knew what he was going to say. What he would tell me, what he always thought he got to tell me every time we disagreed, the same ole—I've already decided—bullshit. "You're not leaving without me. You could get hurt or die. If the agents are chasing you, who knows what could happen. I don't want you out there alone."

"That's exactly why you're not coming with me, baby. I don't like it any more than you do, but I won't risk it. You're not in any condition to be out running around the countryside being chased by agents. Especially not around the grotto lands," he said, with his same stern, hard-ass stare, like I wouldn't get my way no matter what I said to try to persuade him otherwise. I was irritated that he kept bringing up my '*condition*.' It'd already been over a whole freaking month since I was poisoned. I felt fine now.

I didn't even look over at Luca. I knew it was exactly what he wanted so he wouldn't be on my side even if I tried. "But aren't you afraid Luca will kiss me again?" I asked, knowing it would likely stir shit up, but I didn't care. I wanted my way and I would say whatever I needed to get it. I didn't want Jake to leave me. I didn't want to be stuck in that cave any longer and I didn't care if I had to fight off some agents. To me it sounded like it could be a fun little adventure, like we could be Bonnie and Clyde without all the robbing and criminal crap they did.

I had expected what I said to ignite Jake into a fury, hoping it woke him up to the idea that what Luca suggested wasn't the best option, even though I hadn't come up with a more suitable one yet myself.

"Eva, I don't want to leave you. I know it bothers you, but there's no other way to keep you safe," Jake said, looking straight at me, then turned to look at Luca. "Besides, Luca knows better than to try anything with you. He knows I will be back and I won't be happy if he has—" he stopped suddenly like it was uncomfortable for him to say it.

"I won't touch her like that, Miles, you have my word," Luca said, looking at him, creating this kindred brotherhood bond or some shit like that I didn't appreciate at the moment. They were teaming up against me, dammit. It wasn't fair.

"Are you freakin' serious?" I said, standing up looking back and forth at both of them. "Where is Mary? She'll agree with me. I need someone on my side." I began to look around exaggeratedly.

"Baby, calm down, it's not good for you," Jake said as he stood up and took a hold of my arm to try to gently settle me down.

"Stop treating me like I'm a freakin' child," I'd had enough. I couldn't help but yell at both of them. I wasn't okay with them deciding for me what I was going to do. I picked up a torch and lit it then turned around to head back to our chamber.

Luca stood up, ready to calm me down as well until I heard Jake address it. "Just leave her alone for a little bit. Let her go and cool off. She's upset but she'll get over it. When she knows we're only doing what's best for her, she'll come around."

I didn't know what I intended to do when I walked into our chamber but it wasn't going to be 'cool off and get over it'! I lit the candle with the torch and sat there, thinking, trying to come up with another way. It wasn't just not wanting Jake to leave me; it was also not wanting to continue staying in the cave indefinitely for nothing. The weather was getting nicer, and I wanted to go outside. I couldn't stand what it had been doing to me. I was bored and depressed. Even thinking about how long I would be there alone with Luca, not able to let him touch me, all while he tried to keep his word—I knew it wouldn't last. I knew the moment Jake left, Luca's word would be as good as horse-shit on a sundae.

Jake's bag caught my eye the longer I sat there, thinking. *The vial!* We still had the Sicari's vial of serum that I wanted to take at the cabin. I knew it would make Jake upset, but I didn't care. This was my choice. I wanted to be free again. I rummaged through the bag looking for it, and without too much work there it was. I pulled it out and held it in my hands, staring at it just as I did the day I pulled it out of the Sicari's pocket.

I wanted a new life with Jake. I wanted free from my past, free from anyone knowing who I really was to the Sicari, free from the cave, free from my tracker, and free from the burden of keeping the intel and all my other secrets. All of it, I wanted all of it gone!

Before I had a chance to change my mind, I quickly took the syringe, drew up the serum, and slowly stuck it into my arm. My mind shot through a series of emotions, fear, pain, grief, but they were all suppressed by one—relief. I didn't know how long it would take for it to hit me but I was relieved and knew it meant freedom. I took the empty vial and walked out to Jake to show him what I had just done, hoping he would understand and somewhere deep inside, ultimately forgive me.

"Jake," I walked over to him, his face looked happy to see that I was no longer upset. "I'm sorry, baby. I love you but I had to." I said as I opened my hand. His expression quickly changed when he looked down to see what I was holding.

"Eva, no! No… Eva, you didn't." He said hushed, almost under his breath like he was in disbelief. He was a little less upset than I thought he might be but I realized it still was a little early to tell. He stared at the empty vial in my hand for a moment, obviously still in shock and not sure if he could believe it. "Are you freakin' serious, Eva? Why the hell would you do that and not talk to me first?" He snapped, now acting as upset as I had expected.

"I'm sorry," I said, taking a step back. I was beginning to feel slightly faint.

"Holy shit…" Luca said as I looked over at him. He was in shock, too. Apparently, he didn't think I was capable of such treachery against them and their decisions.

"Eva, how much did you take, baby? Not the whole thing, right?" Jake asked quickly, calming down, likely realizing he might not get much chance to talk to me before I was lost to him.

"All of it…" I said hesitantly. I knew why I did and that he didn't agree with my methods but I wanted to be sure.

"No, Eva! No, baby!" He closed his eyes tightly and ran his hands roughly down his face as his whole body instantly tensed up. Saying he was upset would be an understatement.

I took another step back; the dizziness was getting worse.

"Eva, sit down." Luca stood up to help direct me to a rock where I had previously sat.

"She needs to lie down, Luca," Jake said as he quickly moved over to me to help me lie against the stones on the ground. "She's gonna be out soon." There was so much pain in his voice, I almost regretted what I'd done. He sat down in front of me and put my head in his lap so he could look down and talk to me.

"Why, baby? Why would you do this to me?" He asked, holding back tears.

"I didn't want to lose you. It was the only way I could stay with you. I love you, Jake… I didn't want you to leave me." I looked at him as best as I could in the eyes, trying to let him read my soul again as I said it. "I didn't do it *to* you… I did it *for* you. Hopefully, someday, you will understand." I said softly, trying not to shut my eyes but my lids were feeling heavy.

He shook his head, then brought his face down to rest his cheek against mine. "No…" He groaned softly, his tears now mixing with mine.

"Love me like you did Kaleah. Let me be your Kaleah again. All yours… only yours, baby, only yours…" The words drifted from my mouth like a song in a fairy tale, faint and sweet. I knew they would be the last that I would be able to say as Eva.

"Eva… No, baby…"

"Eva…"

# 13
## WHO'S BABY?

I felt heat radiating against my face. I opened my eyes to what appeared to be the bright light of mid-day. The sun was warm and soothing against the skin of my cheeks. I lay there enjoying it until I realized there was something amiss in my mind. It felt like an absence of thought. There was a clarity I didn't remember feeling before, an intense atmosphere of peace. It felt like when you let your mind drift away to a serene place while you lay on the beach, listening to the roar of the waves as they crest the sand. I'd almost thought it would be close to what heaven felt like, except I knew I wasn't dead. The sun's warmth was too intense against my skin for it to be heaven. I sat up to look around as random thoughts floated through my mind. I didn't know where I was but I felt so relaxed and tranquil that I didn't care.

Suddenly two voices spoke, both at once. "Eva?… Kaleah?"

I looked over to see two men both standing now, walking toward me. I watched as they came closer, both walking with a similar stride. One of the men was larger and considerably more muscular than the other, clothed in nothing but all-black attire. His gait was strong and commanding, likely being the one in charge. His eyes were sweet and pouty looking, but so heavily hooded I couldn't see the color even as he got up close. I couldn't gauge his demeanor by looking at him. He acted like he was open but his face read closed and serious; he was a man meaning business, surely.

They came closer to talk to me, standing above me, both staring down like they didn't know what to say or who should speak first. The second man was almost as handsome as the first. His skin and hair were both darker, and his beard fuller. Unlike the other man's, I could see this one's eyes, since they weren't as deep and hooded. They were a magical green, and the way he looked at me felt like I could get lost in them. I could go swimming in their vast intensity and never look back if they tried to pull me in. He started to speak to me but I wasn't listening to what he was saying; I was too lost in the pull of his eyes to care.

"What do you remember?" The other man spoke finally, breaking me from the trance of the darker man's eyes.

I hadn't thought about what he had asked; the question was a good one. I sat there for a second gazing at him… "I don't know," I said finally, realizing that I couldn't remember anything that had happened to me before the moment I woke up.

"Uh, okay…" He said as he ran his hand through his shiny light brown hair. I didn't know why but I felt drawn to him. There was a mystery about his face. Where the darker man seemed open and enchanting, this one felt mysterious and alluring.

"Why can't I remember anything?" I asked, feeling calm, realizing that was probably an unusual feeling for whatever state I was in. I surprised myself with the lack of anxiety I felt not knowing anything about who I was or who these two men were. I wasn't scared or agitated… maybe a bit confused, but it felt so peaceful. None of those things seemed to have much of an effect on me.

"I'll explain everything to you, okay? You're going to be fine." The beefier man spoke like he'd done this before.

"I already feel fine… but what happened to me?" I asked, now looking over at the green-eyed man, secretly wanting to fall back into the same enchantment his eyes had on me the first time I saw them.

"Eva… how are you feeling? Are you hungry or sick?" The man

asked as he let his eyes slowly wander downward finally settling on my torso. I tilted my head down, wondering what he was looking at, then looked at my chest.

"Why? Was I shot or stabbed?" I thought maybe he was looking at some sign of what caused me to be like this.

He smiled, "Oh, no…" he said with a light chuckle. His smile was sincere and handsome. I enjoyed him looking at me like that. "You're pregnant," he finished, then looked back up at the other man as his smile relaxed.

"What?!…" I knew I must have looked shocked. As soon as I said it, they both jumped a little like they were about to go into a pre-planned action they previously discussed if and when I responded a certain way. "What the hell?" I said, feeling more overwhelmed by that than not having any memory. "I don't even know my name… or either of yours… oh my god." I felt myself beginning to freak out. If I hadn't felt sick before that I had now.

"Oh… right. Sorry, baby. I'm Jake. He's Luca." The taller man spoke now as he squatted down to place his hand on my back lightly in support.

"Baby? Why did you just call me baby? Does that mean that you're the father or has there been some weird shit happening between us all?" No sooner had I said it, they both burst out laughing. I didn't realize it was so funny, but I still wanted an answer.

"Uh," the darker man sighed before he spoke again, "I knew this was going to be rough."

"It's fine Luca, we'll just explain it all to her and she'll be fine, just like last time."

"Last time? What the hell?" I pulled back, making him drop the hand that was resting against my back. "Answer me! Which of you got me pregnant?" I said now looking back at the taller man. He must have been afraid to answer me, considering the way he looked at my face and hesitated.

"I did," he said softly, probably hoping I wouldn't be mad at him for it.

I swallowed, keeping my eyes straight on his, hoping I could find it in me to relax and accept what had been done. "Are we married?" I asked finally, trying to give him a chance to calm me.

"No…" the other man quickly spoke up. I turned my head to look at him, now more confused than ever.

"Oh my gosh, so am I with you, then?" I asked as I let myself gaze into his eyes.

"No…" the larger man spoke. I turned my head back to look at him. "You're with me… you're mine, and that's my baby." He said firmly.

"I'm yours?" I asked, not liking the way it sounded. I wasn't keen on feeling owned.

"Yeah… you're my Kaleah," he said now showcasing a bit more intensity in his eyes. I was starting to feel more drawn to them with this new unveiling of emotion he was expressing.

"Then why did he call me Eva? Who am I? I can't be both…" I was trying the best I could to not let myself get flustered and upset as I felt more and more confused.

"Kaleah Eva… That's your full name… well for right now… Shit, this is—"

"Confusing her!" The shorter, darker man interrupted him.

Everyone paused for a moment, feeling the tension, when I finally spoke up again. "I don't remember your names. You said them too fast. Is it Jake and Luke?" I asked, looking at the darker man, the one I thought I remember being Luke.

"It's Luca… I'm Luca," he said, smiling at me.

I felt the hand from the first guy return to my back and he began to talk again. "Yes, my name is Jacob Miles, but you called me Jake. We aren't married… you can't really get married out in the woods… but we're together. We've committed to each other and you're carrying my baby, not *his*." I could detect something in the way he had said it like there might have previously been an issue with them knowing who's it actually was. *Oh my gosh, was I cheating on him?*

"Let's go sit down in the cave, baby, and I will answer all your questions and tell you anything you want to know. You've been asleep for hours. You need to eat and drink something," Jake said as he took a hold of my hand to help me stand up. I allowed it but I still had my own trepidation about what I thought our relationship would be like going forward. *Did I love him? Had I wanted the baby?* Realizing that if I had, I no longer felt the same way about it and maybe not about him either.

We sat there for a very long time, talking. At one point, there were other people who had come into the cave that the men quickly rushed away, like whatever they were telling me was a secret and they didn't want anyone else to hear it. Apparently, I took a medicine that made me forget everything. They weren't clear with me about why I had taken the medicine, though. Jake did most of the talking and even though he appeared to be telling me everything, somehow I couldn't help but feel like he was holding back a lot of important information.

Jake was calling me Kaleah Eva but my real name was Jordan Ellice Eva. Jake found me lost in the woods and rescued me. He said I called myself Kaleah, and we fell in love. That was why he wanted to call me by that name even though Luca was still choosing to call me Eva. We came to the caves to find safety from both sides of the war. He said both the Coldiers, and the Sicari were after us. Especially me because I was a Gypsyin, and they thought I had information that they wanted. Jake assured me though, that I didn't have what they thought I did.

He said he was a Coldier agent, but I didn't need to be scared of him. He still had work that he needed to attend to in Nashville and then he would be free to take me wherever I wanted to go for us to be free again and live together, just the two of us.

Luca sat there and didn't say anything. Now and then I would look over at him while Jake spoke. He seemed to be taking in all the information as well, like some of it was new to him, too. Sometimes I would also see a look on his face like what Jake was telling me didn't match up to what Luca already knew. I suspected it wasn't all the truth, but I felt a little grace for Jake, knowing it would be hard to try to sum up so much of our history together in one little conversation. So I sat and listened and tried to glean everything I could from it.

He told me more about myself. How I was raised and more about my parents. They were Coldiers, just like he was. Just from the little bits of things he was saying I felt like I missed them and hoped someday I would get to see them again. I didn't have any siblings and both of my parents worked a lot growing up so I didn't see them all that much. When I asked him why I was a Gypsyin and not a Coldier like them, he said that was more detailed of a story that he would have to tell me later when we had enough time. I knew there was so much more that he wasn't saying, maybe even because he didn't want Luca to know but I was starting to feel more comfortable with him and looked forward to talking to him further, alone.

After telling me he was an agent, he further clarified to say he worked in Track and Capture. It sounded exciting and dangerous. I think it also helped him on the whole hotness factor scoring that I caught myself doing with both of them in my head. So far he was winning but to be fair to Luca he hadn't had much of an opportunity to talk at that point. When he did, I was eager to see what his profession had been before the war. Maybe it was something exotic that matched his eyes, like a masseuse, though he acted more like a businessman.

I couldn't tell for sure but to me, he looked to be more brains than brawn. There was an elegance to the way he spoke and the way he used his words, not to mention the accent that I could detect in his voice was nice and thick. He wasn't as muscular as Jake but he wasn't scrawny and pathetic by any means either. He looked like he could hold his own relatively well if he needed to.

Jake, on the other hand was obviously an athletic man. The build of his body was strong and toned. He was tall and stout, but in all ways well proportioned. The muscle he held seemed like it was put to use and he didn't have any in excess of what he needed. If Luca's eyes were what drew me toward him, likewise, it was Jake's muscles that I knew were the most attractive thing about him. I caught myself staring at their form as he sat there talking to me. The long clean lines of his shirt tightly held against his chest and arms. It wasn't long before I felt a bit giddy with the idea that he was the one who had claimed me.

"How are you feeling?" Luca finally decided to speak up now that Jake had let there be a small lull in the conversation.

I realized he was most likely asking because of the pregnancy. Something to which I had tried not to give much thought after they told me, considering it bothered me more than anything else they had divulged. "How far along am I? Do you know?" I asked.

"Well, it was a little over a month and a half ago or so when you told me you were. For you to have known about it, you had to have missed your menstrual cycle, which meant you were probably five or six weeks at that point. So I am guessing you're maybe close to twelve weeks along now. But that's good… you won't experience as much morning sickness now and you'll probably start showing soon since you're relatively thin already." His answer was extremely detailed. I was surprised by how he knew as much as he did.

"And you're sure it's his?" I asked Luca, pointing at Jake, trying to trip him up to see how he would respond. *How did he know so much about it if he didn't have anything to do with it?*

"Huh," he laughed slightly, then looked up at Jake to see his reaction to my question. I looked over at him as well. He didn't say anything he just looked at Luca waiting for him to answer just as I had.

"Well, of course, it's not mine. You would have already been pregnant when you got to the grotto lands. So unless you were with someone other than Jake beforehand, it's his," he said with a straight face. I got the idea he wasn't all that thrilled with the idea that I had been claimed already and now something in me was holding the claimer's place.

I looked back over at Jake to see how well he liked Luca's response. He smiled and nodded like a man that was proud of his good fertility. His response was quickly extinguished when I asked my next question. "Why would you do that to me, Jake?" I couldn't help but ask. Not only had I wondered if we'd previously discussed having children, but if not then I wanted to know why he wouldn't have protected us from it, seeing this wasn't the best time to go about having babies and all.

"What?" His face froze suddenly, then relaxed as he took in a deep breath. "Baby, I didn't do anything *to* you. Life happens, and that's okay, it's beautiful."

I didn't say anything else not wanting to ignite an argument, but I hadn't felt the same way as I could see he did.

"You didn't answer my original question, Eva… How are you feeling now? Are you tired, still hungry… do you need anything?" Luca asked, looking back over at me, complete with his intense eyes and all. I couldn't help but wonder why he was so concerned about my health. If the baby wasn't his, why did he care?

"I feel fine, maybe a little tired. I don't want to sound mean but why do you care?" I asked, keeping my eyes locked on his, trying to determine the real reason he was asking.

"I'm your doctor," he said with the smallest little twitch of his eyes down to my body then back up. "Well, I mean I am *a* doctor, but I'm devoted to being yours until you have the baby."

*So that's what he was before the war.* My mind felt the clarity as all the pieces began to organize themselves within my head. It was beginning to make more sense now, the way he was acting with me as well as his upscale mannerisms and intellect.

"How does Jake feel about that?" I asked Luca, then looked back over at Jake, waiting for his response. I wasn't trying to incite a feud between them. I was just generally curious how this whole relationship between the three… err I guess now *four,* of us was going to work out.

"He's a respectable doctor. He won't touch you anywhere he isn't supposed to. He knows better than that," Jake said, looking up at me, then quickly glancing at Luca. He looked like he was trying to believe what he was telling me but his facial expression gave away that he wasn't completely sure that he did.

Luca didn't say anything, he just smiled as if agreeing to the conditions.

"Can I go lie down somewhere now? I'm tired," I asked, not particularly looking or speaking directly to either man but suddenly they both stood up at the same time like they each intended to show me where I could go.

"I got it," Jake said firmly, giving Luca a look that silently ordered him to sit back down. I couldn't help but feel a little aroused by his bossy demeanor. His hotness at that moment was scoring pretty high on my mental ledger.

Jake took me back to a little chamber in the interior of the cave where he showed me our bed. I hesitated, feeling a little awkward being in the room alone with him for what felt like the first time. Even if we had been together before, I didn't feel like the same woman and I hoped he knew I wasn't just about to jump back into the sack with him without a little time to become reacquainted first.

"I…" I felt quite shy at that moment, even though I knew all he was doing was showing me where I could lie down to rest. I swallowed hard, then tried again. "I… well, I'm a little…"

"Nervous?" He asked softly, trying to help me find my words.

"Yes," I said quickly, without any hesitation. That was precisely the word that I was looking for.

"Don't worry, baby. I know this is all new to you. I won't touch you until you ask me to. Does that make you feel better?" He asked. His tone was sweet and his eyes were soft, laced with sincerity like he meant it and he cared.

"Yes…" I said, looking down at the bed, trying to figure out how it was large enough for both of us to sleep in it without being crammed right up against each other.

"Just lie down and rest. Don't worry about anything else for right now. I'll talk to you later before I lie down next to you." He stopped and swallowed, almost like he felt a bit nervous at that moment as well. "Don't be scared of me, baby. I wouldn't ever do anything to hurt you. All right?" He said as he gently took a hold of the top of my arms with his hands, then leaned in and kissed me on the forehead.

I looked back up at him and nodded.

"Good… now rest then." He said, as our eyes locked again. Even though his weren't as easy to see as Luca's, when I stared into them they seemed deeper, like so many unsaid things were radiating from them.

"Okay…" I said softly, trying to blink out of the silent conversation our eyes were just having. Then I turned to lie down as he left.

# 14

## NO TAKE-BACKS

One day turned into the next. I slept, then slept some more. For a couple of days, I was overwhelmingly tired, then I began to feel a bit better and liven up some. Jake spent almost every waking hour with me, only leaving when he needed to use the bathroom, take a shower or go get food or water for us. He started to grow on me the more I talked to him. He was sweet and charming, and rather witty as well. Once he got going, he could really make me laugh. I caught myself often just staring at him, wondering what our relationship was like before I lost my memory. How much had I loved him, and how much had he loved me?

He hadn't touched me sexually or even tried to make any advances toward me, just as he said he wouldn't until I asked him to. Every night he'd lie down with his back against mine, expecting nothing, only wanting to protect me if I needed it. The last three nights I couldn't sleep. I just lay there awake, wondering what it was like when we were together intimately.

I tried to consider if I should just tell him that I was ready or if I should wait, but I didn't really know what I would be waiting for. He had made me feel comfortable with him and I had nothing else to look forward to during the day. I found myself getting lost in all the contemplation. *Why couldn't I just make a decision and go for it?*

Was it Luca? What was it about him that intrigued me so much? Was it the draw of wanting something that wasn't being offered up to me on a silver platter like Jake had been? Was it his eyes? Surely not… How could eyes have such a strong effect on me? I continued to lie there and considered my options.

With no memories, my mind felt like a blank slate. I didn't know who I was before or who I was supposed to be now. I didn't even have the same moral compass as I probably did before my mind was lost to the world. I felt like a child in a way, uninhibited and free. But still with the intellect of an adult, to know that such lack of inhibition can come with severe consequences. Such freedom isn't really freedom as much as it is the absence of safeguards. I knew I could do whatever I wanted but what scared me was the feeling of not knowing why I would choose to want something over something else. How did I know if my *wants* were really my true desires or just a byproduct of this new twisted sense of freedom that I had?

The longer I lay there thinking, the more anxious I felt. I didn't like that feeling. It was new to me, or well, in this new mind space I was in, it was anyway. I didn't know who I wanted to love. I knew who they said I loved before, but why did that mean I needed to love him again? How did I know he was really the one that I wanted now? Ideally, I would just give myself time to get to know both on a deeper level. Morally though… well, I wasn't sure, but I thought morally that probably was unacceptable. *Should I care what's unacceptable, or should I just do what my mind and body wanted me to do—explore my options?*

"Jake?" I knew he was likely already asleep and I would be waking him up, but I wanted to talk.

"What, baby?" He answered relatively quickly, without sounding groggy or sleepy, whatsoever.

"Where you awake already?" I asked, thinking maybe I hadn't actually awakened him.

"No… I'm just a light sleeper," he said as he rolled over to face my back. "What do you need, baby?"

"I don't know… nothing really, I guess." I didn't actually know what I wanted to say to him when I woke him up. I just wanted him to talk to me. Maybe he could help settle my thoughts.

"Ok… well, why don't you tell me what you were thinking about when you woke me up then? Something was on your mind. Share it with me."

I appreciated the invitation, but I wasn't sure he would love what I had been thinking about. "I don't think you really want to know what I'm thinking," I said softly still keeping my back to him.

"Your thoughts don't scare me, baby. Tell me," he said, as he lifted his hand to rest against the top of my arm.

"I don't know if I can love you again," I said it, whether I really wanted to let out with it or not. I did, and it felt good to have it out.

"Kaleah… turn over, please. Look at me while we talk."

I hesitated, then did as he asked, knowing it was likely the best way to communicate how we both felt. It was dark and I couldn't see much of him as I turned, but just knowing we were facing each other was helpful. I didn't say anything else; I was waiting for him to first. I could feel the warmth of his breath as it slowly drifted over and settled against my face. He didn't say anything for a minute either, then he pulled away and sat up.

After a few seconds, I saw a spark and then the light from the candle as it set a small glow cascading through the chamber. He turned around to lie back down just as he had been, facing me with his eyes now even with mine.

"Okay… let's talk, baby," he said, staring into my eyes. I could see the color of his eyes now. They weren't brown or green, but both. The two colors almost appeared to have collided into each other, creating a magnificent starburst effect around his pupils. They were beautiful.

"*Are you* scared of me?" He whispered softly, as he brought his hand back up to rest on my arm again.

"Yes," I was, and I wasn't. I wanted to be honest, but didn't know how to tell him how I felt. I knew he wouldn't hurt me but for some reason, he made me nervous.

He reached up and tucked my hair behind my ear, probably so it was easier for him to see into my eyes.

"What are you afraid I'm gonna do to you?" He asked, moving his hand to rest just below my ear.

I closed my eyes, trying to not get lost in his as I thought about how to answer him. "I don't know… I just… it's hard for me to breathe when I look at you. My heart starts racing and I feel—"

"Nervous?" He asked, completing my statement again as he did the other day.

"Anxious…" I whispered, opening my eyes to look down, staring at his mouth, then slowly I let them drift back up to his. I blinked a couple of times when suddenly he looked down at my lips, then leaned forward, closing the gap between us, covering my mouth with his.

I couldn't remember what his kiss felt like but at that moment I realized this was like our first kiss all over again. He slid his hand from over my ear to behind my head, cradling it as he gently pulled me towards him. Every ounce of nerves I had been feeling quickly dissolved away as our lips sank into each others. It felt passionate as if he was kissing someone he loved right when they returned from war. I let it continue even though I knew I hadn't asked for it. It felt so good I could feel my body becoming overwhelmed with a unique sensation I didn't recognize, like a spark of electricity.

"Am I still scaring you?" He asked as he briefly let up before continuing.

"No…" I said, pulling my lips away just for a second. It hadn't taken me long to see what I probably saw in him originally. I wanted whatever that was to take me again, as he had the first time. I wanted to see what he had to offer.

"I'm ready," I whispered, finally giving him full permission to show me why I had loved him, and convince me why I should again.

"Are you sure?" He asked, closing his eyes and leaning his forehead against mine.

"Would you stop if I wasn't?" I asked, knowing I was very sure.

"No take-backs," he laughed under his breath as he began to pepper kisses down my cheek. Then he pulled back to look at me, sincerity lacing his words. "I'm joking. Of course I'd stop, baby. I'd never do anything that would make you uncomfortable."

"Then show me why I should love you and not someone else," I said softly.

He hesitated slightly, looking at me more earnestly. "What about the baby?"

"What about the baby?" I asked, then quickly realized what he meant. He must have thought he could hurt it somehow. "You won't hurt the baby," I said, hoping it eased some of his fears.

It worked. His lips found my neck again. "I didn't know that," he said, now working his hands around to my back. "In that case… do you mean it?" He asked.

"Mean what?" I said, now caressing the prickly hairs along his jaw as we spoke.

"That you're really ready? That you know what you're asking… You don't need more time?"

"Yes, I mean it." I breathed. And I did. I wanted to see what we were like together… all of it without any reservations.

"Okay, sweetheart…" He leaned back to look at me again almost like he was in disbelief. Then, after a couple of seconds, he smiled. "I love you so much, baby." He said, leaning back in to kiss me again.

The next morning, I had a bit of a rough start, but there wasn't an ounce of regret from the night before. The connection Jake and I shared was undeniable. We were made for each other. He was now at the top of the top of my mental ledger and I didn't see him going anywhere. This must have been why I chose him. He was magnificent. His body was a gift from God, bestowed upon me. Who was I to deny God's gift? I would accept it, it would be mine and I would let mine be his, just as he said it was.

After we got up and got dressed, Jake and I went to the large chamber to have breakfast, then I went and lay out on the rocks just outside the cave to let the sun settle on me as it had the first day I woke up. The weather was nice; the birds were chirping, and the leaves were beginning to glow their majestic spring green colors.

I wanted the baby to get all the glorious sunlight as well, so I pulled the top of my pants down to my pelvic bone then lifted my shirt a little to let the sun bathe my stomach just as it was doing my face. Then I heard Jake yell over to me. "You're showing too much skin, Kaleah," he said, suggesting I lower my shirt back down.

I looked down to see. I did have a lot of skin showing but nothing inappropriate so I respectfully disagreed with him. "No, I'm fine, but thank you," I kindly shouted back as I lowered my head back down against the rock, closing my eyes to let the sun continue its absorption into my skin.

"I'm serious," a deep voice growled suddenly right above me. I startled as I opened my eyes again to see Jake standing there staring down at me with a super serious face.

"Oh my gosh, you scared me… What the hell, Jake?" I said, trying to stop myself from breathing faster.

"I know you don't know all the rules yet, but you can't just lay yourself out here like bait to a hound. I don't mind you getting some sun. It's good for you, but there are limits to how much of you Luca should see, and this is pushing it."

"Man, don't be so controlling… in about six months Luca is going to see a whole lot more than this. Hell, he'll probably be all up in there helping me get the baby out, so you can just calm down. I'm fine." I said, letting myself relax again against the rock.

"You didn't mind me being in control last night," he said slightly squinting his eyes. "I'll deal with Luca and the baby in six months. That doesn't mean he needs to see anything right now."

"Whatever…" I said, looking back at him, not knowing how else to combat his valid argument.

"Tomorrow we need to leave here and head toward Nashville. I have business there that I need to handle. You're going with me, so if you need anything done today to get ready for it, then I'm letting you know now, so you have time." He reached up and ran his hand through his hair as he said it. I couldn't help but feel attracted to him when he did that.

"Fine…" I said, giving in to him, trying to stop myself from fantasizing about more of the night before.

"I'm going to get the horse ready to go," Luca yelled over to us.

"Oh, is he going too?" I said a little too enthusiastically, then caught myself and tried to relax my face to rein it in a little, hoping Jake didn't notice.

He did notice. He stood there and looked down with a slight furrow to his brow, clearly unenthused by my comment. "Yes, he is going. But only because he knows this area better than I do and it's dangerous to travel through it, especially alone with a beautiful woman… and one that's pregnant with my child. Believe me, if I didn't think he would help me keep you safe, he wouldn't be going."

The way he said it confused me a little. "Oh… but I thought you liked him better than that, like I thought you were friends?"

He didn't say anything, he just looked at me with his stern stare, then he looked up to watch Luca off in the distance with the horse. "Baby, the only reason he is still alive is because you might need a doctor in six months." He sighed, returning his eyes to mine. "He's not everything you think he is… You let me know if he touches you, all right?" He said in a way to warn me, not scare me.

"What? Why would he… has he—"

"Once… he kissed you after we first got here. But he knows you're off-limits now so you don't have to worry about it again," he said with a small smile.

I looked over at Luca like he had. I couldn't help but let my mind frolic about as it had previously. *Kissed me, did he? That's interesting…*

# 15

## FOX TALES

The next morning, we got started very early. Not only had the sun not come up, but the moon was still bright in all its glory. I didn't know if I was an early person yet or not but it was obvious that Jake was and Luca wasn't by the way they lightly bickered back and forth. Apparently, Luca was upset we had to walk, and we didn't have enough horses for everyone to ride, but Jake wasn't in the mood to argue and quickly cut him off with the idea that it was actually his fault there was only one horse because his woman was the one who took the other horse.

I felt a little beside myself not knowing who or what events they were talking about, but let it go quickly considering I felt freedom in not caring. Then they argued about whether it was safe for me and the baby to ride. Luca didn't think it was but Jake said he was just making things up to slow us down. Whether Jake wanted to believe him or not, he listened and loaded the horse with the bags instead, declaring it was his idea and that way no one got the horse to ride if I couldn't have it.

The farther we walked from the cave the creepier the area became. Maybe it was because the sun still hadn't risen but I couldn't stop myself from imagining that the different shadows I was seeing out in the woods were moving.

"We're the only people out here, right?" I asked Jake, thinking maybe having open dialog would be less scary than walking in silence.

"I'm sure we aren't totally alone, but you don't need to worry about it, baby. I won't let anything or anyone hurt you." His response was reassuring, even though it wasn't what I originally expected to hear.

"There's more out here than you think there is, Miles. We shouldn't have started out before the sun came up. I told you, I don't think this is safe." Luca apparently wasn't done bickering about what we should and shouldn't have done. He hadn't agreed with Jake about anything all morning.

"You're just paranoid because you can't defend yourself, let alone her. Nothing is going to bother us," Jake said, sounding rather confident in his conclusion.

"I'm not paranoid, Miles. I've lived here for years now. Everyone knows you're not supposed to be out at night. Have you never heard of the Fox Tales?" Luca grumbled. I could tell he was irritated with Jake for not listening or heeding his warnings but also probably for insulting his manliness.

"Well, this isn't night, it's morning. The sun should be up in the next couple hours or so and yes I've heard of the tales. But they're just exaggerated stories that the people who live here started to keep the agents out." Jake said it forcefully, probably to put an end to the discussion and move on but now I was curious and wanted to know more.

"What are the fox tails?" I asked, turning around to look at Luca, knowing Jake wasn't likely going to tell me.

"It's nothing, Kaleah. You don't need to hear about them. It'll just scare you," Jake answered me instead.

"I'll tell you," Luca responded probably enjoying being defiant to Jake's wishes.

Jake turned to give him a dirty look, then looked back over at me. "Do you want to be scared?"

I shrugged, giving him a tiny grin. "Sure, it's exciting… I think…"

He rolled his eyes and kept walking. I turned back to Luca as I slowed my pace a little for him to catch up with me.

He walked with me for a second, making sure Jake had conceded and he was indeed allowed to tell me, then smiled and began. "The first few months after the war started were chaotic. You probably rememb... ah... no you don't, never mind. People were leaving the cities to try to find refuge in the country. The deeper into the woods they could get the better, or so they thought. Ideally, you would have three sides, the Sicari, the Coldiers, and the Gypsyins... right?" He paused. I nodded, letting him know I understood so he could continue.

"Right... okay... Well, the Gypsyins were never supposed to be their own side. Neither the Sicari nor the Coldiers wanted a third rogue party. Both sides knew if it existed and got large enough, the other side could use it as an allied force and potentially leverage it to fight against them. So when the Sicari initially found out that there were a ton of Gypsyins that came to this area to live because they could take refuge in the caves, they sent an army to try to wipe them out." He paused again to take a deep breath.

"Oh my gosh, did they kill a bunch?" I was surprised by what he was saying.

"They did... they killed thousands of us. It was a massacre. The creeks ran red with the blood from all the bodies for weeks."

"How did *you* stay safe?" I asked.

"A lot of the people hadn't found a cave to stay in yet. The ones that were here from the beginning, like me, already had their place established. When the army came, we just hid deeper in the cave. There were chambers deeper down where the agents couldn't find us. The spring that made up the falls in our cave never turned red, so we still had fresh water, unlike most." His face looked like it grew grimmer and grimmer the more he recounted all the memories.

"Ok... so it's basically like the area is haunted now, then? Is that why all the agents stay away? Odd... I don't know why you'd call it fox tails?" I said, thinking out loud.

"No... I can't say the area is haunted. I mean, if you want to believe in that stuff, then sure, it feels like it is sometimes but that's not why the agents stay away. Most agents are more practical than that. I mean look at Miles. He's not the superstitious type, right?" He asked as he motioned up to Jake. I nodded, realizing he was right and there must be more to the story.

"It's what happened after the massacre that kept the agents away, and why we call them the Fox Tales… Have you ever heard a fox's scream?" He asked as he briefly looked at me, then back to where he was walking.

"Um… I don't know… I can't remember," I tried to think hard but nothing was coming to mind.

"Oh… right, sorry. Well, it's one of the creepiest sounds you could ever hear. It's like a screaming howl. They make that sound mostly when they're in their breeding season, which is in spring, and it's horrible. It sounds like a shrill… a baby crying out in anguish, or like a woman being tortured. I think the sound is used by the female foxes to lure the males in for mating…"

"Okay…" I said, getting the idea, trying not to let it creep me out too much.

"That's enough, Luca," Jake must have been listening as well and decided that Luca shouldn't continue when he turned around to tell him to stop.

"Jake… I want to know… Please?" I said, looking up at him a few feet ahead of us. "I'm not a child. I can handle it."

"Then I'll finish the story," Jake said as he stopped walking and looked back at me. I couldn't help but feel like there was something Luca might have told me that Jake wanted to keep a secret. "All the dead bodies drew foxes to the area, then coyotes, and other predators. You didn't have to worry about other humans anymore. If you tried to walk through the area, you were more likely to get attacked by a stray mutt instead. That's it, it doesn't have to be a freakin' ghost story!" He acted upset as he said it, but I wasn't sure why.

"That's not it! You weren't here, Miles. Every night I'd sit in that cave and have to listen to them howling… The foxes screaming to one another, it sounded like women and children screaming, like they were being tortured. It sounded like the massacre all over again. We couldn't leave the caves… You leave and you go missing. I had so many friends that I never saw again. Whatever it was out here, foxes or wolves, big-ass cats… I don't know, but they were stalking us, eating us! They started eating everything in sight. We couldn't find any rabbits, we couldn't go to the lakes to fish, we were starving to death… There are more stories, this is just the tip of the iceberg. Weird things kept happening, whole groups of people have disappeared—"

"Just stop! You don't need to scare her with shit from your past. She just got rid of her own," Jake said, cutting him off.

I looked at him, wrinkling my face a little. *What's he talking about?* He looked away from Luca back at me, now realizing he opened a box of secrets that I wasn't about to let him shut without extracting the truth. "Eva, don't look at me like that… Now isn't the time." His tone was now a bit harsh, and I didn't know why. *What was he hiding from me that he felt so defensive about?*

"I didn't say anything. I just looked at you. Why are you so irritated? What are you hiding?" I asked, starting to feel defensive myself.

"He feels guilty because his people were the ones who came in after the Sicari to finish the job. Or maybe it's because he knows what you really are and he hasn't told you yet." Luca said nonchalantly.

"What? What I really am?" I paused, narrowing my eyes back at Jake.

"Dammit, Luca, you had to do this right now?" Jake said, glaring at him.

"Yeah, I think she should know. You can't just keep all her secrets to yourself. You're not protecting her when you do that. She's not your child. She had a right to know her past, what she did, what she was a part of. She can't atone for her sins if she doesn't know she has any." Luca was becoming more vocal now as well.

"You're wrong. She is like a child. Until she relearns how this world works, she isn't going to know what is dangerous and who to stay away from. The last thing she needed right now was for you to bring up shit from her past." Jake got closer to him as he raised his voice.

"You're lying to her. She deserves to know the truth!" Luca continued.

"It's none of your business what I tell her, when I tell her. She's not yours to make decisions for!" Jake snapped back.

I didn't like how it felt when they argued. Maybe Jake was right, maybe I was like a child even though I didn't like thinking of myself that way. Standing there listening to them felt almost as if they were my parents and I was watching them fight over how to raise me. The longer I stood there, the louder and closer they both got, yelling into each other's faces. I took a few steps back and turned around to walk away. I didn't want to be around them when they got like that. I just wanted to go sit down somewhere and rest until they worked it out. I walked down a small hill, trying to look for a stump or something I could sit on. I kept going until I couldn't hear them any longer. I didn't want to know what they were saying about me.

I don't know how far I wandered, lost in my thoughts, but I finally found a place that looked comfortable enough to sit. It was a large tree with a small hollow at the base where the roots were. I sat down and leaned up against the beefy trunk, letting the concave of the earth below form against my butt. It was cool and relaxing. I leaned my head back and closed my eyes. I figured it wouldn't be long before the sun was up and they would come to find me when they were finished.

I woke with a start. It felt like something was watching me, but I couldn't see anything there. I must have fallen asleep as I waited for the boys to come get me. It was still dark but now it was silent as well —eerily silent.

"Jake!" I hollered out as I stood up. I looked around, trying to remember the way I had gotten there but all the shadows were different and I couldn't tell. It was so silent, the hairs on my arms began to stand up. I started to walk back the way I thought I came from, but the farther I went the more I could tell it wasn't right, it was getting darker, not lighter, like I was walking deeper into a valley not back up a hill like I had come from.

I spun around looking for a hill as I called out for Jake again, then Luca, hoping someone would come to find me. Whichever it was, I didn't care. After a minute, I heard something. *Finally!* It sounded like someone calling out for me, but because it was echoing off of the hills and down the valley, I couldn't tell which direction it was coming from.

"Jake!" I tried calling out again, but I didn't hear any reply. The longer I stood there trying to decide which way to go the more it looked like the shadows were moving again as they had when we were walking earlier. I could feel my heart start to beat faster. My eyes were now seeing more things too, likely the work of my imagination, but I wasn't sure. The shadows got larger as they moved from behind one tree to the next. I turned back toward the valley. I knew it wasn't where I came from but I didn't want to go near the shadows.

"Luca," I tried yelling out, but part of me felt like I should stay quiet not to entice the shadows to come closer or follow me. I began to walk faster into the darkness of the valley. I didn't know where I was heading but I just wanted to walk until I didn't feel the same eeriness like something was watching me. With each step I took, it sounded like there was a step that echoed mine from behind me. I stopped and turned around to see, but there was nothing there so I continued. Before long, I could tell it wasn't an echo; the sound wasn't mine. It was something else, so I moved faster.

The shadows were back; they were in front of me again, right where I was heading but I knew I couldn't turn around because there was something behind me as well. I moved even faster toward them; I didn't know what else to do. Then, suddenly, my foot hit a rock or a root. I wasn't sure, but it knocked me to the ground.

"Jake," I called out frantically, as I tried to push myself back up, but it was too late. As soon as his name left my mouth, a hand from behind quickly covered it, muffling my cry for help. Then another hand grabbed me around my waist to hoist me up.

"No!" I tried to scream through the hand but no sound came out. He held me tight against him so I couldn't turn my head to see who it was.

"Stop…" the man whispered. "Stop, Eva, don't fight me."

He knew my name. I stopped and relaxed, hoping he would release me to turn and see him but he didn't.

"I need to get you out of here. It's not safe. We have to move. Let's go." The voice whispered again still holding my mouth with one hand and now had his other firmly on my shoulder. His grip was tight so I couldn't turn to see him as he pushed me to walk deeper into the valley. I began to writhe again, trying to make him release me so I could talk.

"Stop it, now! You're going to make me hurt you. Walk and I'll let go when I know you won't scream," he said still whispering.

I did as he said, but I still couldn't tell which of the men it was. He didn't have an accent like Luca but he didn't sound like Jake either. I wasn't sure why either of them would say I was in danger. I wondered what happened after I walked away when they were arguing.

I walked until I saw an end to the valley; it was brighter than the middle. *The sun must be beginning to rise.* I slowed down a bit and began to wiggle again, hoping he would finally let go of my mouth.

"Eva, keep walking… I'm not letting you go yet, so stop it!" He said as he tightened his grip against my shoulder.

I stopped walking. I didn't like being told what to do when I didn't even know who it was ordering me around. I didn't care if he hurt me. I wanted to see who it was and make him let go of my mouth.

"Eva, walk! Now!" He said louder like it might help me listen to him, but it didn't.

"Ugh, why won't you just listen to me?" he asked as he finally spun me around to see him. It was Luca. I'm sure he saw the surprise in my eyes. I wasn't expecting him to have been the one to find me, and what happened to his accent? I wondered.

"Nod and promise me you won't yell or scream," he said now looking into my eyes.

I nodded in agreement. I didn't know why he wanted me to be quiet but I figured I would listen to him since I trusted him.

"Okay, good girl," he said as he slowly released his grip from my mouth.

"Where's Jake?" I asked as soon as his fingers left my lips.

"You're not safe with him… right now, I mean… right now… He is going to catch up with us later. We're going to go to a place where I have some people I know. It'll be safe there." His eyes stayed locked on mine other than a few times he let them dart around while he said all of it. I didn't know if he was telling me the truth or not.

"Why, what happened? Where did he go?" I asked, trying to get more information out of him.

"He got upset that you walked off the way you did. I told him it wasn't your fault, and you didn't know any better, but he was really mad. He said we should just leave you out there to teach you a lesson. Maybe if you got scared enough, you wouldn't do it again. That's when I heard other agents coming. He said he would talk to them and then come find us, but I knew it wasn't safe, so I came looking for you. That's why you need to be quiet. If the agents find you, they will hurt you. Agents don't like Gypsyins. You're safe with me, all right?"

I didn't understand all of what he was saying or know if it was the truth but I didn't figure I had any other options but to listen to him and hope he wasn't lying, even though somewhere inside me, I felt like he wasn't being totally honest. I nodded in agreement.

"Good, the people we're going to meet can't know who you really are because it'll be dangerous so I am going to tell them you're my wife. But don't worry, Jake knows about it. It's for your safety. They won't bother you if they think you're mine."

I didn't say anything. I just nodded again. He turned me around and began to guide me once more in the same direction we were heading, towards the light at the end of the valley.

# 16
## WHO AM I?

"Where are we?" I asked Luca as we came up over a hill to the entrance of what must have previously been a state park. We'd been walking for hours, and my feet were beginning to hurt. I wanted to be done and not walk any further.

"There's an inn here where a Gypsyin faction stays. It's heavily fortified so we shouldn't have any issues with agents coming for you," he said, offering me his hand to help me down a step to stand next to him.

"Then how will Jake find me?" I asked, looking out over the broad hills and valleys that now lay between us and this apparent inn.

"He won't… be here for a while. Just don't worry about him right now. I have a lot I need to tell you. After we get there, you can rest, then we can talk."

"But—"

"Eva!" He interrupted me, "I'm in charge now, do you hear me? You're going to do what *I* tell you. You're going to listen and follow *my* orders now." He spoke to me harshly like I was a child and he was scolding me. I furrowed my brows while looking at him. I didn't like how he was talking to me. Then he relaxed and brought his hand up to remove an imaginary strand of hair from my face. "It's for your own good, sweetie. Just trust me, okay?" His tone softened and was now calmer. He acted like he wanted to lean down and kiss me but he didn't. He quickly looked away in the direction he intended for us to keep walking.

I didn't respond. I didn't nod or agree; I didn't do anything but continue to follow him. We walked until I saw it—a beautiful large stone building. It had windows and columns galore, all adorned with a scattered maze of ivy creeping up the walls and spilling out from various cracks. There were men stationed at every door and a few randomly mulling about here or there in the large open space that sat between the building's columns and a paved area that likely used to be a parking lot. Every man had some sort of object they were carrying with them. A few looked like they had knives tucked into their pants. One had a gun sitting on his hip but most had a bat, some wood, some metal, all probably lethal with the right blow.

They noticed us as we walked toward them. Two left their post and came to stop us from getting any closer. One man was larger and the other smaller but neither were as tall as Luca. The only distinctive thing they seemed to share was a large dark mark on their arm that I couldn't distinguish until they got closer. They both had a large elaborate G tattooed on their left forearms. I probably wouldn't have been able to see the tattoos if it hadn't been such a nice day, but most of the men had their jackets off since it was already warmer than it had been the past few days.

"Tags?" The shorter of the two men spoke first as he looked at Luca then turned to eyeball me.

"Show him your arm, honey," Luca said as he pulled up his left sleeve, insisting I do the same.

"Good, now what do you want?" The shorter man spoke again after we had both brought our arms up to display our bare, tag-less skin. The taller of the two didn't say anything. He just stood there with no expression, staring at both Luca and me.

"I'd like to talk to Chet," Luca said as he lowered his sleeve and re-buttoned the cuff.

"Chester isn't letting any more Gypsyins in right now." The taller man spoke this time looking straight at Luca.

"Let me talk to him and we shall see," Luca retorted with an air of authority in his voice. "He's an old friend. He also owes me a debt, so I'd like to speak with him."

The shorter, thicker man quickly relaxed and turned to the taller one, motioning for him to lean in so he could whisper something in his ear. Then the taller one nodded and walked back across the tall grass and into the building. Another man came over to take his place, standing in front of us while he was gone. This man was about my height and thin. He had a noticeable scar down the side of his face that pulled the corner of his right eye down a little lower than his left.

"Who do you got here?" The new man asked, looking at Luca as he motioned to me.

"This is my wife, Bria. She is carrying my child. I need to speak to Chester about his protection. We've seen an increase in agents the last few weeks at the Freedom Caverns, where I've been posted."

"Agents… from which side?" the man asked, briefly letting his eyes stray from Luca's over to me again.

"Both!" Luca said with a level of anxiety in his voice, indicating he really was concerned for our safety.

I didn't say anything to contradict him even though I wasn't sure if he was telling the truth or making things up about the agents. I knew my name wasn't Bria though, or at least I assumed it wasn't unless Jake hadn't been honest with me. I was beginning to feel more confused the longer I stood there listening to them all speak.

"Chet!" Luca said like he had seen a long-lost friend. An older, rather rotund man slowly walked out of the building and over to us.

"Luca, my friend, what brings ya here?" The man spoke quite demonstratively but his voice was pleasant, nonetheless. He looked over at me and before Luca could answer he continued, "Oh, did you bring your w… is this Br… I'm sorry I can't remember her name, it's been ages since I've seen ya!"

"Yes, Bria, my wife! I know, it's been a while. We've been married since we were last here. She's carrying my child now." Luca didn't miss a beat. He spoke his introduction of me so quickly and with such ease, I was starting to wonder whether he was an adept liar or maybe I was actually misinformed about who I really was.

"Oh, well… I thought she looked different from the last time I saw her," Chester chuckled to himself as he looked at me, "I figured my eyes were getting worse as I was getting older, but I'm sure it's the baby, not my eyes," he said as he laughed, again with a great deal of volume.

"That's why I'm here, Chet. I need your help," Luca said, letting his expression look a bit more distressed than it had.

Chester nodded, then turned to the shorter man that was standing behind him, caressing his bat, and whispered something to him. The shorter man then motioned over to the other two and all three of them turned to walk back inside. Chester turned, motioning for Luca to follow him. "Well, if that is indeed the case, then we shouldn't be standing out here in the open," he said loudly over his shoulder as he began to walk back toward the building as well.

Luca started to follow him, then turned toward me when he realized I wasn't moving. "Bria," he said with a wink, "let's go inside, honey." He reached out, offering me his hand.

I looked down at it, still hesitating to move or speak. I felt frozen, not with fear, but confusion.

"Take it, now! We need to go inside," he said curtly.

I didn't do as he said. I didn't know what I was doing, but I turned to walk away. I was going to go back and look for Jake, even though everything inside me knew it wasn't a good idea.

"Dammit, Ev… Uh, Bria! Come here!" He moved to get in front of me so I couldn't walk away from him.

"Is everything all right?" Chester hollered back to us from near the doors.

"Yes, we'll be there in a moment," Luca shouted back to him before looking down at me and clenching his jaw, clearly unhappy with my defiance. "Don't make a scene. We are going inside. After you've had a chance to rest, we can talk about all of this. I know it's probably hard on you, but you need to trust me."

*Trust me...* the words echoed themselves in my mind as different memories started to flash in my head. *Trust me... Trust me, Eva... Just listen to me, you can trust me...* A man was saying it but it wasn't Jake or Luca. *Who was that man?* I wondered, as I let myself stand there zoning out, trying to concentrate on the memory.

"Who am I?" I asked, now letting my eyes blink out of their trance to look back into Luca's.

"Who... what?" He looked as confused by the question as I felt asking it. "It doesn't matter. Right now, you're Bria, my wife! You're pregnant with our child and you're going to do as I say and follow me. If you don't do it willingly, I will make you do it and punish you later for disobeying me."

I'm sure any confusion I was expressing at that moment quickly switched to frustration. I didn't know what he meant by it but now I was more concerned with why he would even say it, let alone mean it.

"Fine," I said, moving forward to finally follow him, "but if you touch me, you'll regret it." I didn't know how I would make good on my threat, or maybe if Jake would but I figured it wouldn't hurt to at least put it out there.

As we entered the building, we walked into a large open room that was decorated nicely and looked quite elaborate for the times. Chester motioned for Luca to follow him into what I assumed was his office. "Kyle will take her to your room for you, Luca," Chester said boisterously talking to Luca as he nodded to a man that I assumed was Kyle. The same man that walked up to us as we were talking and asked Luca who I was to him. "Room 122, Kyle, give them the Eleanor Suite for right now," he said, looking over his shoulder as he walked into his office, with Luca following closely behind him.

I looked over at what had to be Kyle, who appeared to be all business. "This way!" He said, reaching his arm out toward me, ready to herd me down the hall. His choice for a weapon must have been something he was concealing because he wasn't carrying anything in his hands and I couldn't detect anything on his body either.

"What's your name again?" He asked. Now that we weren't any

longer in earshot of Chester, he quickly changed his all-business demeanor to a more casual, friendly one.

"Bria Eva," I said, realizing it went against what Luca was telling them but I didn't care.

"Oh, really… I didn't know Eva was an Italian name," he said, sounding suspicious.

I instantly regretted not following along with Luca's lie and realized he really might have only meant the best saying it, even if he was being too forceful with me. "That's my middle name," I said, trying to cover for myself. Then realized I don't know Luca's last name so I couldn't continue with the lie even if I had wanted to. Now that Kyle had said that, I realized I didn't even know that Luca was Italian. The more I thought about it though, the more his looks and accent started to make sense.

"Oh, well, I never knew Luca all that well. The last time he was here the woman that he had with him wasn't nearly as pretty as you though, so…" he shrugged. I got the idea he knew the truth but it didn't really matter to him.

By his response, I figured they didn't really let women in on their business dealings so he probably didn't care if I was the same one Luca had before or not. "Are there other women here?" I asked now curious since I hadn't seen any among the dozen or so men that had been standing around.

"Yes, but not many. The grotto lands aren't really a good place for women. To be honest, not a ton of them made it out of the Sicari invasion." He stopped to pull out a key from his pocket, likely a master key, considering he already had it when Chester told him which room. "It's not common to have a wife these days. Luca is a lucky man. I can't say you're in danger here but you need to be careful, there are a lot of men that haven't been with a woman for a while," he said as he pushed the door in and held it open for me to enter.

"What do you mean?" I asked, now slightly frightened that this place wasn't as safe as Luca thought it was.

"Well… you're prettier than most. Luca should keep an eye out is all I'm saying. It's not always a good idea to flaunt your decadent steak dinner around a bunch of starving men," he said as he continued into the room behind me and let the door shut.

I was about to look around and examine where I was going to lie down and sleep, but the realization that he had entered the room with me, allowing the door to shut behind him, took me off guard. "I think I'm fine now. Luca will be here soon. Thank you, you may leave," I said, trying to encourage him to keep the friendly demeanor he'd had up to that point and not try to do anything stupid. I could tell the tension between us quickly changed, however, and leaving was not what he had in mind.

"How did Luca find you?" He asked, standing there looking at me as if I was the steak he'd referred to and he was a starving man.

"What do you mean?" I asked, full well knowing what he meant but trying to buy as much time as I could hoping Luca might come in and save me.

"You're not from the grotto lands, if you were you would have been assigned here to the inn, not to some cavern Chester assigned Luca to post guard at…" He paused as he slowly walked closer to me, cautiously eyeing me up and down. "The grotto lands aren't safe to wander around in, especially for women. So how did Luca find you?" Of the two beds in the room, he sat down on the edge of the one that was closest to the door, with his body facing mine.

"I don't remember," I said, thinking maybe if I was honest with him it might throw him off and decide to keep talking.

He squinted a little and brought his brows together, uncertain how what I was saying was realistic. Then he let his face relax, apparently having decided he didn't believe me and wanting to move on. "Look, I don't want to hurt you, that's not my nature… But you see it's been a really long time since I've had a woman under me, if you know what I mean." He stopped talking and just sat there, undressing me with his eyes, then moved his mouth in a way like he was trying to use his tongue to clean his teeth.

"I know what you want, but please… now isn't the time. Luca

could be here any minute. You don't want him to catch us. I don't know what he might do to you," I said, hoping it would either scare him, entice him to think I would allow it just at another time, or maybe both—though I never would. Either way, I wanted him to decide he didn't want to proceed with it, at least not right then.

"Luca doesn't have the key to get in… but it doesn't really matter, this isn't room 122," he said as he gave me a mischievous smile.

Instantly, I felt like my heart sunk to the bottom of my stomach. At the same time, I could feel a large lump develop in my throat. I didn't say anything else to him. I felt like I was about to pass out, throw up, or both.

"I meant it… I don't want to hurt you. That's no fun for me. I'm not a violent man, especially not like that. I don't enjoy forcing it. What if you allowed me to show you what you were missing, ya know… what Luca can't give you?" He said it calmly, showing no remorse or shame at the request.

I swallowed hard, hoping it would take the lump away with it. "Touch me and I'll kill you," I said finally, not thinking, just letting my mouth run away with what my mind was feeling.

His calmness escaped, going somewhere and leaving him with an irritated tension, forcing his face to glare at me. He stood up slowly and took a step toward me, making me take a step back. Not realizing how close I was to the second bed, I fell backward onto it. I started to scream, then stopped. Something in my mind switched. It felt like in a split second I went from flight to fight.

As he closed the short distance between us, I lifted my foot to kick him in the throat but I couldn't get it high enough fast enough before he just swatted it away like it was nothing. I quickly pivoted my weight and leaned forward to sit at the edge of the bed facing him. I took my right hand and made a fist, then punched him in the groin as hard as I could. He dropped to his knees in front of me, now with his head almost to the height of mine. Before I had a chance to think, my body jumped to its feet. My hands moved quickly, so quickly I had no time to analyze what they were doing. It looked like they moved up, then over; I wasn't sure. They grabbed a hold of his head and twisted hard, spinning his face around in a way I didn't know it could go. I felt more than heard the sickening crack in his neck as his body went limp.

"Holy shit!" I gasped as he dropped to the floor, realizing what I had just done. "Oh my gosh, did I just kill you?" I asked shakily, looking down at his limp body. I couldn't believe it. *How did I do that? Was that luck?* It didn't feel like luck. It felt like my body knew what the hell it was doing even if I didn't. Random thoughts instantly poured through my mind. *I just killed him. Oh my gosh, I just killed a man.* I started to internally freak out before something inside my head felt like a mental slap, telling me to snap out of it. "Who am I?" I whispered to myself, realizing I was capable of more than I previously thought.

I stood up and looked down at him for a moment, trying to rationalize what just happened and the idea that he deserved what he got. Then, after taking a moment to pull myself together, I leaned down and searched him for the key that he had used to get into the room. I took it from his pocket and walked out slowly, checking the hall to make sure no one saw me leaving, then let the door quietly shut and lock behind me.

I needed to find room 122. Surely Luca would be there waiting for me, maybe wondering where I was. I looked up to see the number of the room I was in—104. I turned around and headed down the hall, looking at all the numbers until there it was at the very end, 122. I put the key into the lock and let myself in. The room was larger than the other, likely a suite just as Chester had said it was. I looked around but didn't see anyone there.

I could feel the adrenaline in my system beginning to wane. I bolted the door and turned to lean my back against it. *Did that really just happen?* My knees felt weak. *What if the key I had now acquired had duplicates?* I didn't want other unwelcome visitors, so I turned with trembling fingers and engaged the second latch just to be sure. My legs felt like they couldn't hold me up much longer so I moved to the bed that was the furthest from the door and collapsed onto it. There were no sheets on either mattress but that one had a nice plush duvet. I pulled it up over my head and did my best to choke back the tears. If Luca returned, I couldn't be crying or he would know something had happened. He would find out what I had done. *I wish Jake were here. He wouldn't have left me with a strange man to fend for myself...* But I had. I had protected myself when no-one else did. Maybe I wasn't at helpless as they kept telling me. I lay there as the adrenaline dissipated while the low that followed pulled my brain in with it, forcing me to relax and fall asleep.

# 17
## WIVES PLURAL

I had barely dozed off before I heard a loud banging against the room door, followed by a low mumbling sound I couldn't comprehend.

"Go away!" I yelled to whoever was there. I was exhausted both mentally and emotionally. I wasn't in the mood to deal with any other men, whether it was Luca or someone else wanting to rape me. It didn't matter, I'd had enough.

"Bria!" The voice became clearer the louder it got. "Let me in, honey!"

"No, you can go away just like I said," I yelled again.

After a moment, I didn't hear anything anymore like he'd gone away as I said he should. *That was easy*, I thought to myself as I pulled the covers back over my head, trying to close my eyes again, hoping he would stay away and let me rest. About ten minutes later, I heard the doorknob jiggle like he'd found a key and was trying to use it to get in.

"Who is it?" I yelled, finally getting up from the bed to walk over to the door. I figured if I wasn't going to get any rest, then I might as well remove the second bolt so he could come in, since he had a way to get through the first lock.

"It's Luca, I need you to open the door. This key isn't working."

*Dammit*, I thought to myself; *I didn't have to get up after all*. I was already there though, so I figured I might as well let him in. "What's the password?" I asked loudly as I peeked through the peephole, making sure it really was him. I felt extra defiant and figured I would mess with him a little before actually releasing the bolt.

"What?… There isn't a password… Just let me in." He clearly wasn't in a playful mood, so I quit and just unlatched the door as he asked.

"Oh my gosh, Bria, why do you have to act like this?" He spoke quietly under his breath as he walked into the room. By his tone and the way his movements were short and swift, I quickly gathered he was irritable.

"Act like who… Bria? Or is it Eva? Who do you want me to be, Luca? Do you want me to be Bria? Apparently, I'm taking orders about who I am now. First it's Jake, then Kyle, now you… I would like if someone would just make up their damn mind and let me know because this shit is exhausting!" I didn't care how irritable he was. I doubt whatever happened to him was as bad as what just happened to me. He didn't get to be the one who was in the bad mood. I did. I turned to walk back to the bed so I could lie down again.

"What are you talking about? Where is Kyle? Chester was looking for him when I asked for the key to the room. Apparently, there's only one master key, and he has it." Luca asked as he took off his button-up shirt, revealing his bare arms and a small bit of chest peaking out from his undershirt.

"Are you serious? You're concerned about Kyle?" I looked at him, confused, not caring if my feelings of disdain for Kyle and his whereabouts were openly expressed on my face.

"Well, of course I'm concerned about Kyle. If the agents come for you, we're going to need all the manpower here we can get. Why are you so anxious? Is it because I'm calling you Bria?" He asked as he sat down on the bed beside me.

"How well do you even know these men? You just walked in and let one of them take me away. You didn't turn to approve, to check on me, you didn't—"

"Bria…" He said, interrupting me as he lifted his hand toward my mouth, "please, you need to calm down. You're getting all worked up, and it isn't good for—"

"Enough about the freakin' baby!" I cut him off. He was right. I was getting all worked up, but I didn't care. I was upset with him. "How well do you know Kyle, Luca? Answer the question, now!" I said it, letting myself get as worked up as I felt I needed.

The intense green of his eyes glimmered as he stared at me, perplexed by my behavior. I had to concentrate harder on being mad so his eyes didn't distract me. "I don't know him all that well. I'd met him before but that was years ago. I don't understand why you're asking me that." He said as he turned his body so it was easier for us to talk.

All I could think about was how mad I was at him. I was mad that he didn't protect me. I was mad that he was so naïve that he didn't even think of what Kyle was capable of before he let him take me away. I sat there and looked at him for a second, then without forethought of the consequences I said it… "You're a freakin' idiot," the words slipped out of my mouth in anger, even though I mostly meant them, I didn't really intend to say them. No sooner had they left my lips, his expression quickly went from blank to furious. He reached up and smacked me hard across my face. I instantly felt a searing sting in my cheek, accompanied by a ringing in the ear on that side.

I couldn't believe it. I brought my hand to my face to help try to massage the pain away as I sat there shocked, staring at him. I didn't say anything. I just turned and crawled to the top of the bed and pulled the duvet back over my head. My emotions were so mixed, I wanted to lie there and cry. I wanted Jake. I wanted to smack Luca back, or better yet break his neck like I did Kyle's.

"Shit… Bria… I'm sorry. I shouldn't have done that. Please… we can have a civilized conversation. Come back out from the covers… Bria," Luca said, hoping to try again, but I wasn't willing.

"That's not my name, asshole!" I knew I was antagonizing him further but I couldn't help it. I didn't know how to respond otherwise. "When Jake gets here, he won't be happy when I tell him you're treating me this way."

"Please, Bria… I said I was sorry. We need to talk… Jake isn't coming back." He knew the right thing to say to make me remove the duvet.

"Yes, he is…" I said, pulling my head back out, "You said he… was…" I stopped. I felt sick again. Maybe it was my naïveté, but I wanted to feel some stability and Jake was that. I needed him to come back and I didn't understand why Luca would say he wasn't.

"Please… just listen to me. Jake was lying to you. I couldn't tell you the truth until I made sure I got you here safely. Now, if you will let me, I will tell you who you really are, everything!" He said, leaning in across the bed toward me.

I was still upset and had half-a-mind to bring one of my feet out from under the duvet to kick him in the face but I didn't. "Fine, then tell me," I said as I sat up and leaned against the headboard, agreeing to listen but deep down I knew that wasn't me agreeing to believe him.

"Good," he said as he moved up toward the head of the bed to be next to me again. "Your name is Bria Luna Segreto. You *are* my wife, and that *is* my child you are carrying." He paused, staring at me with his magical green eyes, likely waiting for me to respond, but I didn't. I was frozen by the shock of his statement.

"We were both living in the cave together when about a month ago Jake came along. He was an agent with a gun… I didn't have any way to defend us against him. So I just did what I could, trying to appease him, hoping he would leave. But he wouldn't leave. He became infatuated with you; he wanted you to be his… He knew you would never leave me and go with him so when I wasn't watching, he gave you the serum he brought with him… that's what made you forget everything." He stopped again. His eyes were glossy like he was about to cry from having to bring up the distressing memories. "You're the love of my life, Bria. It killed me thinking another man was trying to steal you from me." His voice half cracked.

I started to feel bad. I still wasn't sure whether I could believe him but, again, he was making such a compelling argument. It was hard for me to judge it otherwise. I couldn't tell for sure but it didn't *feel* like he was lying. The way he was speaking was so genuine. The sincerity in his eyes made the love he appeared to have for me look so real. "Then what about everything Jake told me about who I was... Eva... his baby?" I asked, as I began to accept the lure of his eyes.

"He was lying to you! It was all a lie so you would go with him and let him have you. He was trying to take you from me. He knew you wouldn't go willingly, so he erased you," he said as he moved his hand up to my face where he hit me. "You have to believe me, sweetie... I'm sorry I smacked you. I've never done that before. I don't know what got into me. I'll never do it again, I swear. Will you forgive me?"

I was now completely lost in his eyes, his sincerity overwhelming my anger. "Yes... I'll forgive you," I said, trying to forget it and how much it hurt me emotionally to think he would do something like that.

He smiled, "Thank you, my Bella," he said as he leaned in to kiss me. I couldn't remember what his kiss felt like, but this one was smooth and strong, as if he was a passionate man. I figured I could get used to that.

"What does Bella mean?" I asked as we broke the kiss to look at each other.

"My beauty..." he said with a large smile, then leaned in to kiss me again. He brought his hand up, burying his fingers into my hair, then I felt him try to bring his other hand up to my chest.

"No..." I said, quickly pulling away from the kiss. I didn't know why I did it, though. It was like my body was acting on my behalf even when my brain wasn't telling it to.

He hesitated, then nodded, "I understand," he said with a weak smile, "this is a lot for you all in one day. I will give you some time. I'm sure you're pretty tired."

"I am," I said, looking away from his eyes so they wouldn't pull me back in. "Before I rest though, there's something that's bothering me now." I looked back up to him as I said it but hoped I would have the control to just talk to him and not let the lust for his eyes overtake me again.

"What is it?" He asked as he continued to gently caress my hair.

"Jake and I... you know... did things. Uh, we were together... intimately." I felt like I needed to tell him so I wasn't holding onto the guilt since we were married and I guess it was technically cheating even though I didn't know any better.

"Oh, my… Bria… Are you serious?" He froze, looking distraught.

I nodded, then looked away now feeling ashamed.

"It's okay…" he said lowering his hand from my hair to my chin to lift my face to look back at him, "Look at me, Bria… If you can forgive me for smacking you, I will forgive you for—" he paused and took a large breath like it was hard for him to say it, "for having relations with another man."

I smiled, glad to have that off my chest.

"You should lie down and rest now. Later, I agreed for us to sit down with Chester for dinner," he said as he leaned in to kiss the tip of my nose.

I agreed, then crawled back under the duvet. I closed my eyes to go to sleep but my mind had other plans. Thoughts began spinning through it; so many I couldn't keep up. *What if he's lying? Why should I believe him over Jake? What about Kyle saying I didn't look like Bria? But Kyle also wasn't sure where Luca would have gotten me if I wasn't Bria. If Kyle hadn't seen me in years, he could have been mistaken… Ugh, he was about to rape me, why would I listen to anything he said… What happened to Jake? Was he really upset with me for walking away from them? Was that why Jake didn't come to find me in the woods? Did he not want me anymore? Which of their stories made more sense—it feels like Luca's does.* I pushed the thoughts out as best as I could, hoping without them my mind would finally let my body fall asleep.

"Bria, honey, are you hungry?" Luca asked, waking me up rubbing my belly.

"If you're a doctor like you say you are, you should know that's not where my stomach is," I said, opening my eyes to look at him.

He smiled, then looked down at my stomach. "You're not quite showing yet but you will soon. In the next month or so, your chances of miscarriage decrease. I won't need to baby you so much then," he said it with an odd look on his face like it bothered him for some reason.

"I'm sure I'll be fine," I said, trying to make him feel better but not really knowing why he felt bad to begin with.

"Do you feel rested? If so, why don't you get yourself cleaned up? Chester was nice enough to have one of the girls bring you some fresh clothes. You've been in these filthy rags for ages. It's time you dress to your potential. I don't want my wife looking so disheveled." He reached over and held up a small, pale pink dress. My eyes lit up when I saw it, it was so pretty. Then I remembered what Kyle said about steak and starving men.

"Um, I'm not sure that's a good idea," I said, changing my expression from initial excitement to concern.

"Why?" He looked at me confused and disappointed like he had also been excited about the idea of seeing me in it.

"Well, Kyle said…" I paused to release a small sigh, "It might not be a good idea to make me a steak dinner when there are so many hungry men." I tried to recite it the way I thought I remembered Kyle saying it to me but it felt like I wasn't saying it quite right.

Luca started to laugh, then quickly quieted himself as he looked away from me. "That's probably true, sweetie," he said with an unpleasant look, casting his eyes to the floor, "but it won't really matter tonight. We can address that problem when it gets here." He handed the dress to me. "It's all right, go ahead and wear it. I'm afraid Chester insists."

I was confused by what he was saying and what he meant by it all but I chalked it up to having just woken up. My mind was never as sharp right after I woke up. I took the dress from him and put it on then went to look at it in the full-length mirror that was hanging on the back of the door. I didn't remember what I looked like. I moved closer to further examine myself.

Luca was right. I was quite disheveled looking. I took my fingers and gently combed them through a waterfall of chestnut tinged deep brown hair that fell well past my shoulders. Who knows the last time I'd had it cut. It wasn't straight, but it wasn't curly. It had a wave to it that created a nice amount of volume, almost too much if I hadn't combed it down. I turned to my side to analyze my baby bump, or in this case, lack thereof. The dress looked good on me and he was right. There wasn't really any bump there yet.

"You're as beautiful as the day I met you," Luca said with his thick accent. I looked up to see him in the mirror behind me, walking toward me. He wrapped his arms around my waist and rested his head on top of my shoulder, looking at me in the mirror now as well.

"How did we meet?" I asked.

His smile fell flat suddenly, like the memory was actually a painful one for him, then he blinked a couple of times and brought himself together, forcing the smile back on his face. "Before the war, our families actually brought us together. My parents were emphatic that I date another Italian girl." He stopped, seeing my face was now a bit baffled. "Are you confused because you don't look Italian?" He asked as he turned me around to look at him.

"Yes," I said, hoping he would clarify for me why that was.

"It's because you're only half," he said with a gentle smile. His eyes looked different this time as if he were recalling memories from a person he'd previously lost. Maybe that was how he felt when he thought Jake was going to take me from him.

"Your father was Italian and your mother was Scottish. That's where your fair skin comes from and the faint auburn highlights in your hair..." he said with another smile as his eyes trailed off for a moment, lost in a memory. "I love you, Bria."

That took me off guard. I didn't know how to respond to him. I felt compelled to say it back out of courtesy, but I didn't really feel that way for him, so I couldn't.

"Don't worry," he said, bringing his eyes back to mine when he sensed my hesitation. "You will learn to love me. I won't let anything happen to you this time." He shifted his eyes away again after he said it.

I tilted my head. *What did he mean by 'this time'?* I started to ask him when he quickly leaned down to kiss me, stopping my inquiry before it began.

"Let's go now," he said, releasing the kiss and leaning away finally. "Chester isn't a patient man so we shouldn't keep him waiting."

As we sat down to dinner, I looked around to assess who all was eating with us. There were seven men in total that were sitting and only two other women except myself. I was beginning to feel like Kyle was right. The ratio of men to women was way off and potentially problematic. I didn't know how many women there were total or how many men there were all together either, but all I could do was hope that Luca would be better at being vigilant about how other men were treating me. Up to that point, he'd done a piss-poor job, and I didn't like the idea of having to kill more of them but I would if I had to—if it wasn't just luck the first time.

"So, Bria... Luca tells me you are almost to your second trimester." Chester spoke first as we sat there and waited for our food to be served, by who, I wasn't sure.

"Um, yes," I said as I looked around at the other people sitting across the table, wondering why that was his selected topic of conversation. The two other women were older than me, or so I assumed, by the age lines that graced the sides of their faces. Both were smaller framed just as I was, but neither looked unhealthy nor underfed. One of them had thick, curly black hair and dark skin, while the other had lighter skin and dark blonde hair that was stick-straight and thin. They were both reasonably attractive for their age. The blonde one had a large overbite and if it hadn't been for that I thought she would have been very pretty.

"Oh forgive me, my dear, I haven't introduced you to my wives," Chester's booming voice spoke again straight to me, likely seeing that I was observing the appearance of them both.

"Wives?" I asked before I realized that I should have just kept my mouth shut. It probably wasn't the best to question him, since he appeared to be the one in full control of the place.

He laughed loudly at my response. I looked over at Luca, who wasn't as thrilled by my question. "Oh, yes, Bria, both of them are mine," Chester said, looking my way. I instantly felt uncomfortable with the way he let his eyes gaze at me.

"Oh, of course," I said with a smile like I was sure that was normal behavior.

"This is Ladona, and that is Morgan," he said as he pointed at them, each raising their hand a little with a polite smile as he spoke their name.

"Nice to meet you both," I said, smiling back pleasantly.

Before long, the food finally came. Two other women were serving it along with three other men. Chester began to talk to Luca and the other men sitting at the table with us about other subjects, leaving me to sit there and eat. I wasn't paying much attention to their conversation since I hadn't eaten all day and I was ravenous. While trying to put all my energy into eating, something Chester said still caught my ear, enticing it to perk up and listen.

"Luca, remember… this is a give and take community we have here. You have my protection but you will need to give back as well… as you've requested, you have a month. I'm sure the men will be happy when she's cleared to go. I know I will be."

I didn't look up. I sat there staring at my plate, trying to think about what he was saying and what exactly he meant by it. Surely he didn't mean what I thought he meant. That was absurd. Chester quickly moved on to other subjects and said no more about that one. I figured I would talk to Luca when we got back to our room to confirm my theory was wrong. *It better be wrong!*

# 18
## NOT JUST CHORES

"Bria, my dear, I have another question for you," Chester said, speaking to me again. I felt intimidated by how open and forward his demeanor was and didn't want to look directly at him, afraid of what he might say next. "Where's Kyle?" He asked, with his tone changing to be more stern and direct, as I'd feared.

I looked up at him finally to see if he was mad or just curious. "I don't know," I practically whispered, hoping being as vague as possible would help the lie progress without being caught.

"I was afraid you would say that," his demeanor changed, now no longer upset with me, just concerned more about where Kyle would be. "He's the only one with the master key. I gave him one job… carry the key. That's all he has to do. One damn job! The idiot, where did he run off to this time?" Now it was obvious he wasn't as concerned about Kyle's health as much as his incompetence.

"I'm sorry," I said without thinking. Apparently, my guilt over his death hadn't yet been released so my mind felt this was the proper timing.

"Please, Bria, there's no need to apologize," Luca corrected me. I thought it was odd, but I didn't reply. I lowered my face and nodded like he was right, agreeing I wouldn't say anymore.

Once the dinner was over, everybody quickly scattered off, leaving Luca and me to find our way back to our room. Each person must have had a key to their own room because they didn't seem to have any trouble even though the master key was still missing. The key Luca had been given didn't work in the lock for our room but Luca had thought ahead and left our door propped open so we could get back in. We hadn't been back long before he felt it was a good time to scold me for my dinner behavior. It would be an understatement to say I was surprised that he thought I behaved poorly.

"Why would you apologize about Kyle going missing?" He asked abruptly as he shut the door behind us and bolted it.

I hesitated to answer him. I was still a bit taken aback by the idea that he was mad at me when I felt like I was the one with questions he needed to answer, not the other way around. "Because I really was sorry," I said as I moved to open the curtains to the room so there would be a little moonlight for us to see each other better.

He let out a loud sigh, "Maybe it's because you're a woman and you don't understand how... ugh... the way it works here. If you're going to apologize for something, you better have been the one to cause it. If you didn't cause it, the last thing we need is Chester thinking you did!" He began to remove his shirt as he walked over to the bed.

*Because I'm a woman, huh?... Idiotic asshole...* I didn't know how to respond to him. I understood what he was saying, but that was the problem; I did cause it. *Crap*, I thought. *If they found out I killed him, what would they do to me?* "I'm sorry," I said defensively, not knowing what else to say.

The tension in his stance and expression relaxed a little with my apology as though he realized my perceived mis-step was unintentional and further scolding would be unproductive. "I understand you don't know a lot yet. You're just now learning who you are again. It's an easy mistake," he said as he sat down on the edge of the bed, still facing me.

"What did he mean when he said you had a month before I would be ready? Ready for what?" I asked, seeing he was calmer and maybe more willing to be honest with me. I walked over to the bathroom and picked up my old clothes, intending to take off the dress and re-wear them to go to sleep in.

"What are you doing?" He asked, watching me.

"I'm changing back into these," I said, noticing that he hadn't answered my question yet, and I wasn't about to let him forget it.

"No, you're not. Those things need burned. You can come to bed with just your panties if you don't want to be naked with me yet. I would understand that, but I'd prefer you not put those back on —ever."

I couldn't help but sigh, seeing I wasn't being left with any options that I felt comfortable with. "Please?" I asked, hoping he would allow it just for another night or two.

"Bria, you don't need to be ashamed of your body. Believe it or not, I've seen you naked before!" His tone was kind and endearing, with a bit of his Italian accent thrown in. He made it hard to disagree with him.

"Fine," I said, realizing it was dark anyway and he wouldn't likely get that good of a look at me. I dropped the clothes and pulled the dress straps off my shoulders then let it fall to the floor before I picked it back up to fold it and place it on the second bed. "Will you answer my question now?" I asked again as I walked past him and around to the far side of the bed, avoiding getting within arm's reach of him so as not to temp him to touch me.

"I'm sorry, you've distracted me and I've forgotten what it was you asked about. Your skin has the prettiest soft white glow when the moonlight hits it," he said, as he stood up to remove his pants.

"What did Chester mean when he told you I would need to be ready in a month? What was he talking about?" I asked now pulling the duvet up over me, hoping to hide any skin that might entice Luca further.

He hesitated and didn't respond right away while he stood there like he was debating if he wanted to remove everything or keep his underwear on. "Chores..." He said finally, "just chores... you will have some, and I will have some." He decided and left his underwear on as he climbed into the bed and pulled the duvet up over him. "It's not as late as it looks outside, did you know that?" He asked as if either to change the subject or allude to another one that I wasn't ready to tackle yet.

"What kind of chores?" I asked, feeling a bit more anxious by his lack of description.

"We will see how you're feeling in a month and then we can talk about it," he said, deflecting from the subject again.

I realized it was probably easy for my mind to take what happened with Kyle and twist it to think all the other men had the same motives, and I was likely coming up with the wrong idea of what Chester meant. "Why a month?" I asked, hoping for more validation that my initial idea was completely skewed.

"Well, that's the longest I was able to get from him. He wanted you... to start doing chores right away, but I didn't feel like you would be ready yet so we agreed until you were far enough along that it wouldn't hurt you," he said as he rolled onto his side to face me.

I didn't understand how normal house chores would be dangerous for me and the baby but I didn't want to argue with him since I liked that I had another month before I would need to do anything. "All right," I said softly, finally giving up on the subject.

"Bria..." he took his hand and placed it at my waist then pulled me over to be closer to him. "What do you remember about us when we were at the cave?" He pulled his elbow up to his pillow and let his head rest in his hand to look down at me.

"Us? Nothing... I mean the last day before we left, Jake said that you'd kissed me once and that he wouldn't let you do it again. He said he'd kill you if you tried," I grinned, but only because it sounded funny coming out of my mouth, not because it was actually funny.

Luca slightly chuckled to himself. "Yes, he was quite protective of you. He made it hard for me for sure. I could barely find time to get you alone when he wasn't hovering over you like a vulture."

"He said the only reason he hadn't already killed you yet was because I would need a doctor in six months," I wanted to see what

Luca said when I told him, maybe it would clear up more of my confusion surrounding my identity.

He didn't say anything for a moment, he just lifted his hand to my face and began to stroke my cheek with the back of his fingers. "I knew it was dangerous for me to try to kiss you while he thought you were his… but I did it, anyway. I wanted you so badly… Do you know how long I've been waiting to finally have you in my bed with me?"

Before I could reply, he leaned down and kissed me again. Despite all of my timorous behavior since we re-entered the room, he was still interested and didn't act like he would take no for an answer. He slowly moved his hand from my cheek down to my side then down to my thigh. It must have been a long time since we'd last been intimate, because his hands felt like they were exploring me for the first time.

His kiss quickly went from soft to firm as his mouth communicated his increasing level of arousal. Obviously, I couldn't remember what it was like being with him but he came across as more assertive than I would have expected. His hand didn't linger at my outer thigh long until it quickly moved farther down.

"Luca, wait…" I said, moving my head to free my lips from his. "I'm not ready."

He didn't say anything, he just moved his hand back up to my chest, then leaned back in to continue kissing me again.

"Luca!" I said it again, but firmer.

He stopped kissing me and pulled his face back to look at mine then sighed. "If you really mean it, I will stop… but I don't think you mean it, Bria. You know you want it as much as I do. That bastard kept us apart for months…" he said, letting the intensity of his eyes try to mesmerize me.

"Uh… okay…" no sooner had I spoken the words than his mouth was back, kissing mine.

He moved slower this time. His hand stayed on my chest, caressing it longer before he let it slowly drift its way down to my inner thighs again. He continued to kiss me, letting his lips softly pepper down my neck. Until he stopped suddenly, lifting his head again to say something. "Bria, you're stiff as a board, sweetheart. Am I not turning you on?"

I gently shook my head without saying the word no. I didn't want to upset him any more than my body's response likely already had.

"Is it Miles? It is, isn't it… You're attracted to him more than you are to me!" He said, his voice coarse with rejection. It was clear he could easily snap like he had before and I needed to proceed with caution.

"No, baby," I said quickly, trying to make him feel better. I was lying, though. I didn't even realize it until he accused me, but he was right. There was something about Jake that I longed for and Luca didn't have it, but I wasn't sure what 'it' was. "You're enough… I'm sorry I'm so tense. Maybe it's the pregnancy… maybe my hormones?" I asked, hoping to give him an alternate solution to help relieve his anxiety.

Before he could answer, there was a knock at the door. His body stiffened then relaxed again as he let out a long sigh. "Stay here," he said as he quickly got up and put his pants back on. He went and opened it, leaning out to briefly talk to someone before he shut it again then returned to stand at the foot of the bed.

"Who was it?" I asked, hoping everything was all right, and they weren't still trying to inquire about Kyle.

"Ryan, he was the big bearded guy that sat across from me tonight at dinner," Luca said as he picked up his shirts and started to put them both back on.

"Where are you going?" I asked, seeing he was getting dressed again.

"Chester is asking all the men that aren't on guard duty to help him find Kyle so he has the master key again. A few of the men can't find their individual room key so they can't get in to sleep," he said, hurrying to get going.

"What if you can't find him? Is the key all they really need?" I asked, looking at him, not wanting to divulge what I knew, but realizing I could get myself in more trouble the longer I kept the secret to myself.

"Bria, do you know something you aren't telling me?" He asked, now with tension in his voice and posture as though waiting for news he hoped wouldn't come.

"I don't want to be in trouble," I said, pulling the duvet up over me until it reached my neck.

"You're going to be in trouble if you keep secrets from me. Tell me now! What do you know?" He didn't sound happy that I hadn't already told him.

I wasn't sure what exactly I wanted to disclose, some of it, all of it, or none of it. "I have the key," I said finally, after thinking about it for a moment.

"You what?" He asked, glaring at me.

"Kyle gave it to me..." I said, trying to lie, then realizing it might have not been the best route to take.

He walked over to my side of the bed and looked down at me. I couldn't see his face very well, but what I could see didn't look happy whatsoever. "Tell me everything right now, Bria. If you lie to me you're going to regret it."

That scared me. I didn't know if he was exaggerating but it felt like he meant every word. "He took me to room 104, not room 122. He was going to rape me. He said that the men were hungry, like sexually, and there aren't enough women for them all to get one..." I couldn't help it, I started to cry, thinking about what happened and how difficult it was trying to bring it back up. "I didn't mean to... I killed him, but I didn't mean to. I don't even know how I did it. He just fell to the floor, dead!" I relaxed as soon as it all finished pouring out of me. It felt good to have it out, but I was still scared how Luca would take it and if he would be mad enough that he still wanted to hit me again.

"I can't believe you," he said, clearly disappointed with me. "Give me the key. I'm going to have to go clean up this mess and try to keep anyone from finding out."

"I'm sorry!" I said, hoping he wouldn't still be angry. "It wasn't my fault." I got up and walked over to the end table between the beds where I had hidden the key.

"You killed him! How is that not your fault? Do you even realize the jeopardy this puts us in? We have to stay here, we have nowhere else to go, Bria!" He began to yell, then quieted himself likely realizing the walls weren't very thick and he didn't want anyone else to hear. "I don't have any other way to keep Miles from coming and trying to take you away again!" He seethed, then snatched the key out of my hand and turned to leave.

When I heard the door shut behind him, I crawled back into bed and closed my eyes. I felt awful but I couldn't determine exactly why. I didn't like getting yelled at but I couldn't argue with him. He was right; I did put us in jeopardy. But he was wrong, too. It *was* an accident. I felt so torn. Part of me wanted to lie there and stew, feeling guilty for my actions. Then part of me wanted to stand up for myself and tell him he could go to hell because I didn't do anything wrong. Kyle was the one who did something wrong. Kyle got exactly what Kyle deserved.

I didn't like that Luca would talk to me like that. *Would Jake have talked to me like that?* I wondered. He said the only reason we were here was so Jake wouldn't come back to get me… *Did that mean Jake was coming back?*

My thoughts were endless, feeding me one after another. Once I consumed them, my brain had more ready to take their place. I tried to clear my mind as best I could, then go to sleep. I figured I would deal with Luca when he came back.

L uca must have slipped in while I slept. When I woke up the next morning, he was laying in the bed next to me. I didn't want to wake him up; I was afraid he would still be upset with me, or maybe more so, depending on how much work it took him to cover up what I had done. I got up and put the little pink dress back on. I would have put my other clothes on, but I knew it would've just upset him more. The dress was pretty, but not all that comfortable, and way more revealing than I liked.

I stood there staring at myself in the mirror again, trying to do something with my hair when I heard a soft knock at the door. I initially felt trapped between the idea of waking Luca up to answer it, since I wasn't comfortable with the men around there, and keeping Luca asleep since I didn't want him to yell at me again. I figured before I decided which route I was going to take, I would look through the peephole and see how scary the man that was knocking really was first. If he looked less scary than Luca, I considered just going ahead and answering it myself.

Initially, I didn't see anyone when I looked through the hole, then I saw a stripe of what looked like long blonde hair. It wasn't a man; it was a woman. A woman was definitely less scary than Luca was right now. Upon that conclusion, I opened the door. I was shocked when I first saw her. She had the richest blue eyes, like deep-set sapphires; I couldn't help but stare. She wasn't one of Chester's wives or one of the girls who served us at dinner. She looked younger like me. I was pleased to see I wasn't the only woman there that was my age.

"Hey… uh, it's Bria, right?" She said quietly, like she was shy.

"Yes," I said, smiling at her initially, wondering what she needed with either Luca or myself.

"I was just coming to tell you that Chester would like to see you both at breakfast. It will be served in the next hour or so…" she hesitated, like that wasn't all the news she intended to deliver.

"Okay… is that it?" I asked curious to see what she might have been holding back.

She smiled really big as she looked down at her hands. "I'm just happy that you're here," she said. "Oh, my name is Amy, by the way."

I initially thought the same. It would be neat to have a friend. I couldn't remember if I ever had a friend that was a female after the war. I smiled back at her. "Do you not have any other female friends, either?" I asked, assuming that was what she meant by her comment.

"Uh no, not really, there are only six of us women… Well, you make six," she said lowering her smile a touch, "I'm just happy that you're going to be helping me keep up with all the men."

"Like with chores, right?" I asked in agreement, knowing she must have felt some relief, thinking she wouldn't have as many chores to do now that there would be another woman around to help.

She looked at me blankly for a moment as she blinked a few times, trying to figure out what I was saying. Then she half-smiled with a small chuckle, "Well, sure if that's what you want to call it, I guess."

"Wh-what do you call it?" I furrowed my brow, now curious about her comment.

She looked at me innocently. "Um… sleeping with the men, making love, f—"

"Woo, woo, woo… What?" I couldn't help but say it loud and obnoxious. "Is that what you think I am going to help you with?" I seethed.

She immediately acted shy again like she thought I was verbally attacking her. "Well, that is what Luca agreed to. Chester has to keep the men happy so they will stay and protect everyone and in return, well… we don't have to worry about food or agents attacking us again. You only have to be with a few a day, and most of them are gentle…"

My eyes felt like they were about to bulge out of my head. I didn't even know what to say to her. "We might or might not make it to breakfast," finally it came out of my mouth as I thought about whether Luca could still eat after I was done with him.

"Um… okay, I… I can tell Chester, I guess." She stammered a little, acting a bit skittish.

"You do that… You tell Chester he can go f—" I felt the air quickly escape me as a hand covered my mouth as well as another strongly wrapped around my waist, pulling me backward.

"Tell Chester we will be there for breakfast! Thank you," Luca quickly spoke from behind me.

# 19

## MAN IN BLACK

"You son of a bitch!" I spun around and screamed at him. I'm sure he regretted removing his hand from my mouth so soon after the door shut. He froze, uncertain how to respond. "You even think about hitting me again and it'll be the last time," I said, warning him not to even try raising his hand to me.

"Bria, calm down!" He said low and slow, clearly scared of my reaction, but whether it was fear of me or someone hearing me, I didn't know or care.

"No! I'm not calming down! I'm not going to let you turn me into a whore! Chores? Really? Did you not expect me to find out what I was really signed up for? You lied to me, you freakin' bastard! I should break your neck right here just like I did Kyle's!" I took a threatening step toward him, forcing him to slowly back away from me and into the main part of the room. I must have been scaring him. His whole body was tense like he was prepared to run from me if he needed to.

"You're right! Okay, now calm down… please, so I can explain myself," he said, raising both his hands to guard himself in case I tried to attack him.

"You think I am going to listen to you after you lied to me? You think I'm going to believe anything you tell me ever again?" I stepped closer to him, enjoying that he was frightened by me for once.

"I wasn't going to allow it! I don't want you to have to do it as much as you don't want to do it. Do you think I want to share my wife with twenty other men?" He paused, seeing he had my attention now with what he was saying. "That's why I asked for a month. You're farther along than that, you're probably already in your second trimester. I just needed for us to stay here long enough to make sure any agents following us lost our trail."

"What if they try to attack me again before we leave, like Kyle did? You didn't stop him; you weren't even there! He could have done whatever he wanted to me and you… you piece of—"

"Bria, calling me names won't make you feel better. Don't say things that you can't take back. I'm sorry I wasn't there to protect you from Kyle. I didn't realize you needed protecting. I wasn't all that wrong was I? Look what you did to him. You didn't need me to stop him; you took care of yourself just fine." He started to lower his arms, apparently no longer concerned I was about to strike him.

"It doesn't matter that I took care of myself. I needed you and you weren't there. I shouldn't *have* to protect myself! That's what a husband is supposed to do; stop other men from attacking me!" I didn't lower my voice. I kept it the same volume as before, making him lift his arms again in a defensive position.

"Are you angry about Kyle or what you thought I agreed for you to do in a month?" He asked, though I wasn't sure how it was going to help him for me to clarify everything I was mad at him for.

"Both!" I yelled it again, refusing to dampen my temper. "I wake up with no memory. One man says I'm his, and it's his baby… Cool, fine, weird as shit, but fine. I can handle it, I guess. Next thing I know, you take me away, I'm not his, I'm yours… it's your baby… Then Kyle tries to rape me… I kill him… I freakin' killed a man… Next, you want to have sex with me, when I'm not ready, then smack me, then yell at me for killing Kyle and hiding the key… Not all in that order but it doesn't freaking matter. Now I find out you lied and really did agree for me to turn into everyone's pleasure puppet…" I paused to take a long breath, "It's f'd up, Luca… Do you even get what all of this is doing to me?" I started to feel completely overwhelmed, I walked over and sat on the second bed and pulled my legs up to rest my head on my knees.

"Bria… I'm sorry you feel that way, but—"

"You're seriously going to say *but*… 'you're sorry, but'? You're sorry I feel this way? Are you freakin' serious right now? How about being sorry for the shit you did, not just about how it made me feel. Take responsibility for your own actions for once! Get the hell away from me! You can go eat breakfast with your head up Chester's ass and leave me here." I quieted my voice but only because my throat was starting to hurt from all the yelling I had been doing.

"Will that help you calm down so when I get back we can talk without you screaming at me?" He asked calmly as he bent forward a little, ready to console me.

"I don't want you to come back, get out, and leave me alone." I dropped my legs so I could say it as I put my face closer to his, trying to intimidate him.

He stood up and took a step back. "Will you be here when I return?" He asked like I had an option not to be.

"Do I have a choice?" I asked, thinking if his answer was yes then my response would probably be no, I wouldn't still be here.

"No," he said as he straightened up his shirt a little and began to tuck it into his pants the way he usually wore it.

I didn't say anything else to him; I wasn't going to give him the satisfaction of thinking I would listen to any demands he wanted to make on me. Even though every fiber of my being wanted to leave, I knew I couldn't. I didn't know where I would go, if I was even able to get past all the guards, and that was without them trying to attack me again on top of it.

"I know you don't think so but we are only here because I'm trying to protect you. You don't know what Miles was going to do to you. If he caught you again… ugh… Bria, I love you… I won't let him take you from me," he said it then turned to walk toward the door. "I'll tell Chester you couldn't come because you weren't feeling well. When I come back, I'll bring you some food." He finished, then opened the door and shut it quietly behind him.

I sat there and stared off into space, trying to think of what options I had and which of those I wanted to take. I hated to think that Luca was right about Jake but so many of the things he told me made more sense than the things Jake told me. I secretly wished deep down that Jake was the one that was right and Luca was the one that was lying but even with all my logical thinking I couldn't make it make sense.

I tried to remember what things Jake told me before we left the cave so I could compare them with the things Luca was telling me now. Maybe I could catch a hole in one of their stories. I was looking for any kind of inconsistency to help guide me to believe one over the other. The harder I thought the less productive it seemed to be for my mind or my current level of anxiety. Then a new thought popped into my head. *Why do I need to stay with Luca?*

Luca hadn't really told me what Jake intended to do with me. *What about him did Luca think was so bad?* I didn't think just him wanting to steal me away from Luca was all that bad. My thought process quickly diverted paths without my knowledge, leading me to suddenly feel the opposite.

If Luca was right and Jake was willing to steal me away from my husband, it didn't matter if he was acting all loving during the two weeks we were together. *What kind of man would do that?* If he was willing to do that to me, maybe he did have other bad intentions. I didn't know if he was a good guy, a bad guy or if he was just hiding who he really was until I was trapped with him, with no way out.

I began to develop a headache the longer I sat there. I knew it was likely from my over-analytical processing but I suspected it had something to do with being hungry and thirsty as well. I broke my long gaze at the floor and looked up at the curtains that were covering one of the windows. Maybe I would feel better if I let in more sunlight.

I got up and opened them, anticipating only seeing the tall grass and weeds of the front lawn, maybe with a few men scattered around it. I saw more men than that though, way more. Chester must have been heeding Luca's warnings about there being more agents in the area. It looked like the guard count was probably close to double what I had been used to seeing out my window. *Great, more men mean even more pressure on the women to keep them satisfied.* Then, from the corner of my eye, I caught movement… something that I didn't think looked like it belonged.

I turned my head to look. There was a dark shadowy figure standing in between the trees on the other side of the parking lot. I stood there, then leaned in closer to the glass, trying to make my eyes focus so I could see it better.

It was a man, a man dressed in all black, hiding himself half behind a large tree and half in the denseness of the wood's foliage. *How had I even seen him?* The next question I asked myself was if that was Jake or another agent? *Is he here to get me? Do I want him to get me? Does he see me looking at him? How can he get past all these guards?*

I don't know how long I stood there wondering, wading through all the questions, but suddenly I realized I couldn't see him anymore. He had disappeared. He must have slipped back behind the tree and left.

T he next few weeks went by quickly. I went over to the window daily to gaze through it, hoping for another glimpse of the man in black, but I didn't tell Luca about him, or what I thought I saw in the woods. I didn't want him to freak out about it and sign me up for any other stupid chores, thinking it would help give us more protection. I saw nothing out of my window except all the '*starving*' men posted out front to keep me safe, more like keep me a prisoner. I wasn't sure which. I still wasn't sure where Luca planned on taking us when the month's deadline was up and it weighed heavily on my mind. It didn't matter how many times I asked him about it, every time he said it wasn't something I needed to worry about and he would handle it.

His demeanor since our fight had been less abrasive and more caring. I suspected it was only so I would forget about it all and finally let him touch me again, but it wasn't working. I didn't plan on letting him do anything with me until I saw how he planned on getting me away from there before the end of the month was up. I knew it frustrated him. Every night, he seemed more and more agitated that I continued to refuse him, but I didn't care. He'd be allowed to touch me again when I knew he was willing to stop other men from having me. If not, I'd decided he'd only get what he forced me to give just the same as all the others.

He didn't appear to still be upset about the Kyle incident and having to clean up the mess. I asked him what happened and how he was able to cover it up. He said he gave the key to Chester and told him he found it outside room 104 when he was looking for Kyle. Apparently, they weren't happy when they went in and found Kyle lying there dead but with no obvious evidence of a struggle, Luca said he was able to convince them it was likely a heart attack. After that, any other time we spoke about the incident, he had been very kind to me. I think he finally saw how traumatic it was and he didn't want to make it worse by accusing me of any more wrong-doing.

"We only have a week left," I tried to talk to Luca quietly as we walked through the halls to return to our room. He had been kind enough to take me for a walk outside so I could get some fresh air.

"This is the third time you've brought it up today. Are you anxious about it?" He asked in his doctor's voice like I was his patient.

"Oh no, not at all... I'm *so* sure you've got it handled." I said sarcastically.

"Don't talk to me like that, Bria." He quickly corrected me. I don't think he was used to anyone speaking down to him, especially a woman. I figured it was probably from all his doctor training. He was used to being the one in control, with everyone listening to his every command without questioning him.

"What is your plan, then? Where are we going to go?" I asked, ignoring his correction and continuing with my attitude. I was irritated that not only had he not answered me yet but also that I'd had to keep bringing it up before he finally would.

He put the key into the lock to unlock the door, then held it open for me with one hand. "Get inside, now!" He said now sounding irritated that I hadn't stopped with my behavior as he had asked.

"You don't have a plan, do you? You lied again… You're just going to let them have me." I said it hoping I was wrong, hoping he would be so upset with my false perception of his character that he would defend himself by going ahead and telling me what his plan was.

"I told you not to talk to me like that… You're going to start listening to me, Bria," he said as he shut the door behind him and locked both the knob and the bolt. "You were never this rebellious before. What has gotten into you?" He turned to look at me, with his eyes showing a mixture of frustration and intense desire.

"Don't touch me," I said immediately, knowing what that look meant.

"Which way?" He asked, taking a step closer toward me, making me take a step back.

"Either way!" I snapped, taking another step back, increasing the space between us even further.

"I've been nothing but kind to you, and you still won't let me have you… Why?" He asked, looking frustrated but still letting his face relax a little.

"If you don't tell me how you're getting us out of here within the next week, I'm leaving you. I'll run into the woods and you will never see me again." I said, deflecting his question and answering it all at the same time.

"You wouldn't last two minutes out there alone…" he huffed, then stopped to look at me as if wondering if I really meant it or if I was just trying to threaten him. Then he started to walk toward me again, slowly. "Let me make love to you, then I will tell you everything you want to know. Everything I have planned for us."

I stood there, staring at him, furrowing my brow in disgust, making it obvious I wasn't thrilled with his offer. He didn't say anything else, he just looked at me, waiting for my response. I couldn't help it. I began to laugh. *He's insane if he thinks it's just that easy*, I thought to myself.

"How about this? I'll do it with you once you prove to me you aren't going to let Chester turn me into the inn's new whore." I said it, but didn't mean it. Then I sat down on the nightstand that was between the beds. Just in case he decided to force me to do anything it wouldn't be as easy for him to make me lie down.

"I should have let Miles have you… You are a whore remember, you already gave yourself to him," he said flatly, with disdain on his face like he meant every word.

I immediately looked away from him and crawled into the bed and pulled the duvet over my head. I didn't respond with words; I had none. I couldn't believe he would say something like that to me.

"Bria, dammit, I'm sorry, baby. I shouldn't have said that. I didn't mean it. I swear I didn't mean it." He continued to apologize, but I stopped listening. My mind caught one of the words he said and immediately took me into a trance of memories, as it did the first day we arrived at the inn.

'*Baby*' he called me baby. I began to have flashes, memories funneling their way into my mind. I saw Jake in some memories, then I saw another man in others. *Who were all these men, and why couldn't I remember more?* I was frustrated with my lack of recognition for each of them. The flashes with Jake weren't in the cave, though. They were somewhere else, a house or cabin, I couldn't tell. I lay there trying to think harder about them when I felt Luca pulling on the cover, trying to get me to release it.

"Bria, I said I was sorry. Please, just come back out here and talk to me. We don't need to fight like this. I love you. I want you to learn to love me again."

"Again?" I threw the duvet off and sat up to glare at him, "You stupid lying piece of shit! I never loved you and I never will. You—" Before I could finish, he reached up and smacked me again across my face like he had the first time, but harder. It stung. I tasted the metallic tang of the blood in my mouth and felt a throbbing pain begin to radiate across my cheek. What hurt more than that though, was the insult to both my pride and my dignity.

I didn't think before I reacted; I reached up to grab him,

somewhere, anywhere. I wanted to hurt him back, but I wasn't fast enough. He grabbed both of my arms and pushed them down against the bed, pinning me under his weight. I couldn't move and knew it wouldn't do any good to yell for anyone.

"Bria, stop this, please... I don't want to hurt the baby," he grumbled, trying to keep himself on top of me, despite how hard I was fighting against him.

"Get off me, now!" I tried yelling back but was quickly running out of extra breath.

"Please..." he said, sounding like it was distressing him having to hold me down.

"Or what? You'll hit me again? Hit me!" I said intentionally not relaxing but realized I was beginning to without trying. I didn't have enough stamina to keep fighting.

He didn't say anything else, he just lay there holding me for a few more seconds, then slowly relaxed and let go of my wrists before pushing himself up off of me. "It wasn't supposed to go like this." His shoulders slumped as he ran his hand through his hair. With pain in his voice he continued, "I love you... I don't want to hurt you... I don't want other men to have you, either. That wasn't ever the plan. I didn't know that's what would happen if I brought you here. I don't have another plan, all right? Is that what you wanted to hear?" He turned and sat down beside the bed on the floor, bringing his knees up to rest his forearms on. "I don't know what else to do. If I take you away from here, then Miles will find us. If I keep you here... Chester wouldn't accept anything else. I thought if I had a month that would give me enough time to think about what else to do... I just need more time. I don't want to lose you..."

I didn't respond to him. I knew my silence would be more painful for him than if I tried to come back with anything verbally. I didn't care what he said; I was still angry with him and I didn't believe him anymore. Maybe some of the things he was saying were true but with the flashbacks I had of Jake, I didn't know if Luca really was telling me the truth about who I was or if he made it all up so he could have me to himself.

"Are you not going to say anything?" He asked feeling the pain of the silence as I intended he would.

"Why should I? Anytime I say anything you don't like, you hit me." I said finally, after a few more moments of silence.

"I don't like when you disobey me. I'm sorry. I promise I won't ever do it again." He mumbled as if he regretted it.

"You said that last time," I retorted.

"You're right, there's never a good reason to hit a woman and I feel utterly ashamed of myself, all right? It hurts me to think that I could do something like that to you, to the baby…" He moaned a little as he sat forward on his knees and turned around to face me, kneeling beside the bed. "I am not perfect. When we met, I told you I had demons. I meant it… I have a past that I am not proud of. But despite how it looks, the things I've done to you, or the times I've lied… you must believe me when I say I love you."

I didn't know how to respond, whether I liked it or not—I did believe him on that account. I didn't know if that changed anything about how I felt about him and what he was willing to do to me, but I could see he was being genuine.

"I'm hungry… Will you go get me something to eat?" I asked, hoping it would defuse the tension between us without relenting to him and accepting his apology. I didn't want to accept it yet. I still wasn't sure if he deserved it.

His face relaxed, looking relieved. "Uh, yes, of course!" He said it quickly like he too wanted to be released from the painful tension that had now settled between us. He probably also thought that I might be more forgiving if he were kind again and did me a favor. He got up, stood there for a moment, straightening his now rumpled shirt, and walked out, slowly shutting the door behind him.

I sat there trying to think about what just happened, how I felt about it, and what I intended to do from there. I looked out the window for a minute. Seeing it was now later in the day, I didn't have much time before it would be dark. *What if I had wanted to leave, to run away? If so, where would I go and how many guards would I have to escape past?*

I got up out of the bed and walked over to the window to get a better look at the area around the inn. The longer I stood there though, the more my eyes began to play tricks on me. I thought I saw the man in black again, or maybe two. I couldn't tell. There was a dense fog that was beginning to set in around the trees so everything looked like shadows at first. But the more I stared, the more I could see I was right. It wasn't just shadows that were out in the woods; it was more than that… Everything in me wanted it to be more than that… I wanted it to be Jake.

# 20

## BLOODY DUVET

"Jake?" I whispered to the glass, trying to lean in as far as I could. The distance was too far to really see if it was him, but I wanted it to be. I hoped it would be so bad that a part of me was concerned that I was delusional. Maybe there wasn't anything there at all. I wondered if I was seeing things. Maybe it wasn't a man in black. Maybe it was just a tall, muscular tree stump. Delusion or not, he stood there like he was trying to stare back at me, seeing if it was really me. I expected him to disappear again as he did three weeks before when I first saw him, but he didn't. He didn't move.

"Jake…" I said again softly, more certain that it wasn't just a manly-looking tree. I wanted to go to him, I wanted him to come to me. I wanted to leave and be free again. I didn't want to do the things Luca signed me up to do. I didn't want to be with Luca. I didn't love Luca. I didn't know if he was lying but I didn't care anymore. I would take my chances with Jake. Any plans he had for me surely were better than what Luca's plans for my future were.

I turned around to assess the room, looking to see what I needed to grab before I left. Nothing… I didn't have anything that was mine. That was easy, I thought. I stood there for a moment, trying to think about the best way to escape. Thoughts about Luca kept coming into my mind the more I tried to think about Jake and wanting to be with him. *What if Luca really was my husband? Would it kill him if I left? Should I say goodbye?* I knew there was no time. If I didn't get out at that moment, then when would I be able to? I caught myself pacing, going one way toward the door as I thought about Jake then going the other way back toward the bed as I thought about Luca.

I sat down on the bed, forcing myself to stop and really think about what I was about to do and make sure I wasn't being impulsive. I thought about the memory flashes that I'd had and the different men I saw that weren't Luca. I thought about the way I felt about Jake versus Luca, and which one felt more genuine. The deeper I dug, the more I felt a connection with Jake, one that I didn't understand but knew to be there when it wasn't with Luca. That had to mean something. That had to be an indicator of which man I really belonged to. Finally, I knew what I wanted to do. I had decided.

I stood up and walked over to the door, took a deep breath, and opened it. I stepped out of the room, first looking to my left at an empty hall then to my right at the emergency exit door. I had never been out that door before but I figured I might as well try it first. Maybe it would open and wasn't locked. I walked up to it hesitantly, realizing once I walked out I might not be able to come back. I knew it was my last chance to change my mind, but I didn't. I knew what I wanted to do now, and I was going to do it. I started to push the large lever to release it when I heard someone behind me.

"Bria, no!"

The door opened. I took a step out, then turned back to see Luca, having just entered the long corridor, holding a plate in one hand and a cup in the other. For a moment he stood there, his expression distraught and broken, then suddenly he dropped everything and began to run toward me.

"Stop! Bria, don't!"

I turned back and pushed the door open fully to leave. I pivoted to my right to run in the direction I thought Jake was in. I heard the door shut behind me as I passed the side of the building and started out into the grass then paused to look at the tree-line on the other side of the parking lot where I hoped to see Jake. I wanted to see him again. I wanted to run to him.

Before I saw or heard anything else, though, everything changed. A violent blow forced me to stagger backward, sucking every ounce of air from my chest as I landed in a crumpled heap of excruciating pain, shock, and confusion. My stomach felt like it had imploded as I frantically gasped for breath.

Moaning, I tried to turn to focus on the grass that was scratching the side of my face, anything to ground my thoughts. My mind was swirling, trying to fill in the blanks with what it thought had just happened. Something strong had hit me in the stomach. I wanted to look around to see what it was, but I couldn't. The pain kept me grounded and held my focus. The intensity completely overtook me. Before I could see anything clearly, I heard voices—Luca's voice. I tried not to close my eyes, but my eyelids were going to do what they wanted.

"What the hell? Why did you do that?" Luca screamed at someone.

"I didn't recognize her... I'm sorry," the gruff voice came from another man.

My stomach was throbbing. The pain kept me folded into a fetal position lying on the ground. Before long, I felt my mind begin to slip. It wanted to retreat. My consciousness did as well.

"She should be fine. It's just a bat. At least I aimed low... I could have hit her in the head. That'd have been way worse... right?"

"She's pregnant, you stupid idiot!"

"Bria, honey... Bria, look at me..."

I felt him pick me up. I wanted to be gone. I wanted to have passed out, but I hadn't yet. Why hadn't I yet? The pain was so intense, I'd never felt anything like it before. It was a fierce throbbing deep inside me, almost within my groin.

"Open the door dammit, I need to get her inside."

I felt a warm liquid trickle out of me like I was peeing but I couldn't stop it. The pain was so unbearable, I couldn't stop the groaning sounds my body was releasing deep within my chest, either. I wanted to black it out, but I couldn't. My mind wouldn't cooperate and just let me go. It kept me there, so I could feel every ounce of agony my body was wrenching from.

"Bria, honey… you're going to be fine, just lay still. Don't move." I felt him lay me down. The duvet was soft against the skin of my face. I tried to embrace any comfort I could from it, hoping it would distract my mind from the severity of the pain I was in.

"Go get me some water, now!" Luca snapped. His demands of someone were filled with urgency and his own form of pain.

"Bria, can you open your eyes for me? Look at me, sweetie, I need you to look at me." I felt him slide his hand in under my head and gently lift it. "Bria?"

I opened my eyes as he'd asked, but my body wasn't cooperating and insisted I look up instead of at him.

"Bria, you're bleeding everywhere." His voice was pitchy with concern.

I blinked a couple of times, hoping my eyes would roll back down to look at him. Then I felt them begin to water. My mind knew what it was doing, apparently. It wasn't just in physical pain but now I realized my torment was a deep emotional one as well. I blinked again and finally was able to look at him. He was staring at me, but the greenness of his eyes were clouded by their own watery glaze.

"I'm… sorry…" I whispered through the pain with what strength I had left. I wanted to say more, but I couldn't. I knew what I had done. I knew it was my fault.

"Bria…"

"Here! I got the water. Man, I'm so sorry. I swear I didn't know it was her. She just came out of nowhere. I thought she was an agent…"

My mind felt dejected, fragmented like it was breaking away from itself. I felt it slip slowly out of consciousness, then back again. I heard Luca speaking to me, then the man speaking to him. Then I was caught by a third voice that I had never heard before. It sounded like someone else had come into the room.

*"What have you done? This is your fault! The life that was in you is now gone, and it's your fault! How selfish can you be? It should have been you... It still can be. Just let go. You know you want to."*

I tried to open my eyes to see who was speaking, but I didn't have the energy. It had all been drained out of me. I felt myself drifting off again; I thought about what the voice said and considered it. Maybe it was right. The light slowly funneled away from my eyes and I let myself go with it—somewhere it wouldn't be as painful, I'd hoped.

"Bria," I woke up. The pain was now less intense and my eyes opened just as they should have. Luca was sitting next to me, holding what looked like bloody rags in one hand. His expression was dull and bleak, offering no smile as he moved his other hand up to wipe something away from his eye.

"Is this what you wanted?" He asked solemnly. I knew what he meant, but couldn't answer him. "Were you trying to punish me for slapping you again? Is that why you ran?"

I didn't respond. I looked down at my stomach. All I could see was blood all over the cream duvet. It looked like a murder scene.

"Well... you got your way. You ruined everything. I'm certain you've lost the baby," he said, angry with me. I felt the anger deeper than he probably intended for me to, though. It felt like shame. A deep seed, a silent curse... guilt weighing so heavy I could barely breath—I was ashamed. I didn't disagree with him. I knew he was right. I was on his side this time. I blamed myself as well. I relaxed my head back against the pillow and looked up at the ceiling. I couldn't look into his eyes. I was ashamed of myself and what I'd done.

He got up and walked over to the end of the bed. "Go back to sleep. I'm going to leave for a little bit. I can't stand to look at you right now. I'm too upset. You're a mess... I'll deal with you when I get back. Try not to do anything else that's stupid while I'm gone, will you?" His voice cracked on the last few words, clearly in pain himself. I knew he didn't mean everything he was saying. He was just hurt. I'd hurt him by leaving.

I nodded, feeling a tear begin to roll down my cheek. I brought my hand up to wipe it away when I noticed it seemed like I was adding more moisture to my face than I was removing. I pulled my hand away to see it was bloody as well. I slowly lowered it and did as he said. I let my eyes close again, hoping I could relax. Maybe that would ease the lingering pain.

I don't know how long I was asleep when suddenly I heard the door being flung open and multiple men's voices speaking like they were all coming in.

"She's in here," one said.

"You're not gonna like what you see, Boss…" another spoke with a long pause.

"Find. Him. Now!" I opened my eyes when I thought I heard Jake's voice. I was right, it was him. He walked in and stood at the end of the bed. His eyes slowly moved from my head to my feet. He didn't say anything else, he just stared at me like he couldn't believe what he was seeing.

"Jake?" I said faintly. I was so happy to see him, I tried to smile as best as I could.

"FIND! HIM! NOW!" He turned to yell again at one of the other men. Then he slowly walked around the bed to stand close beside me as he looked down at my stomach, then at the duvet. He looked distraught as he let his eyes trail from the duvet to mine, back to my legs then back up. "Oh, baby… what has he done to you?" His whisper was ragged, almost under his breath.

His face grew flush as he quickly looked away while he brought his hand up to press his palm against his forehead. Then he let out a guttural groan as he moved his hand away and brought his eyes back to mine. "Baby…" he groaned again, holding back intense emotions.

Then my eye caught the movement of his hand as he began to raise it again. I couldn't help but flinch as he brought it toward my face. He stopped and quickly lowered it, creating a fist as he turned around. "Andry, when they find him, bring him straight to me. Do you hear me? Go tell Carver he can kill the others now. I don't give a shit anymore, just not the women."

"Boss, this wasn't supposed to be that kind of mission… You know Carver only suggested it because he's a cutthroat. You sure you want to give those orders?" the man said. He was also dressed in black, standing behind Jake where I couldn't see him fully. He was larger than Jake though, a lot larger. I could see the top of his head and the outsides of both of his arms, like he was a giant and Jake, merely his shadow.

Jake hesitated to answer him, probably rethinking what his anger was asking of his men. "Fine, just bring me Luca. But you can kill anyone who tries to stop you or gets in the way."

"Are you good here, alone?" The man asked before he walked out.

Jake gave a curt nod. "Shut the door when you leave, when you get back knock with your name in Morse and I'll know it's you."

The man eyed the room before nodding to agree to Jake's orders, then walked out. Jake turned back around again to look at me. His face was full of quiet devastation, like he had waited for the other men to leave before he was willing to show his true feelings. He slowly leaned against the bed, then lowered himself to his knees beside it so his head would be level with mine. He didn't say anything at first, he just fixed his tormented eyes on mine.

"I'm sorry I didn't find you before he did…" He said softly, finally releasing it, like it had been killing him to hold it in.

I didn't know what to tell him. I didn't know if it really was his baby that I'd lost or if it was Luca's. A part of me was still scared that Luca was right and Jake wasn't really who I was with in the beginning, and now he was about to drag Luca back in here and kill him just as he promised me he would do if Luca ever touched me again.

"Are you going to hurt me?" I asked without thinking.

He furrowed his brow, then closed his eyes tightly, bringing his hand up to cover them like he was even more distraught that I would think to ask him that. He swallowed hard and slowly slid his hands down his face as he looked away, trying to restrain his emotions again, then looked back at me. "Baby, I would die a thousand times trying to save you before I would even think to lay a hand on you in anger."

I began to cry. I wanted it to be him, the one who I was with, not Luca. I hoped Luca had been lying. I didn't want to be married to him. "But I killed the baby…" I said as I lay there sobbing like I was asking for it, feeling like I needed to be punished.

He slowly brought his hand up to my forehead to sweep the hair back out of my face. His lower lip started to quiver, but he pulled his jaws tight together, clenching his teeth to stop it. "You didn't do anything! Do you hear me?" He paused as anger momentarily displaced his other emotions. He gently pulled his hand back from my face, then turned and hit the wall, hard, releasing the overflow of anger that had become too much for him to keep bottled. Then he sat there and stared at the floor for a second as he breathed deeply a couple of times. When he looked back up at me, it was sorrow I now saw in his eyes. "I saw it. I saw the whole thing. You were just trying to get to me… I'm sorry we didn't move in sooner. I was coming for you, baby… Ehh… I'm going to kill that bastard!" He quickly switched from being sorrowful to angry again the more he thought about Luca.

"You can't…" I said, feeling scared of him again even though I knew he wasn't angry with me. "He was just mad that I lost his baby, he didn't—"

"It was my baby!" He said sternly, stopping me. "What else has he lied to you about?"

"Please don't kill him," I begged, seeing his anger continue to escalate past where I thought it topped out.

"What else has he told you, baby?" He said suddenly as calmly as a psycho would before they committed mass murder.

"He told me my name is Bria and I'm his wife and it was his baby. You came to the cave and wanted me for yourself so you erased my memory so you could take me away from him. He brought me here to try to protect me from you." I said everything I could remember like it was a big secret and I wanted to spill my guts, hoping for relief.

He stayed calm while I continued. He didn't say anything, he just nodded, letting me know he was listening. Then he stroked my forehead with his thumb before he pushed the rest of his hand back into my hair.

"He loves me… you can't kill him. I don't know who's telling the truth!" My voice broke as tears welled in my eyes again. "Please…" I begged, hoping he would have mercy on Luca, even if he was the one that was lying.

He nodded again with a short up and down movement, agreeing to a truce to not kill him. "Okay…" He said finally like it was difficult for him. "Has he…" He started to ask another question before he closed his eyes and looked away then took another deep breath, "Has he…" he stopped again, unable to say it.

*Touched me… forced me?* "No… well… he, uh…" I tried to answer what I thought he was asking but didn't know exactly what to say when I heard a knock at the door that sounded unusual.

Jake looked at me and nodded again as he gently cradled the side of my head with his hand then stood up to go to the door. I didn't hear anything for a moment, then I heard the door open and the voices of a couple of men talking quietly.

"Miles… please…" Luca pleaded after the man holding him uncovered his mouth as they all came further into the room, letting the door quietly shut behind them.

"Luca…" Jake said calmly. I tried to sit up a little to see them and what he was about to do to him. There were four other agents now surrounding both men. One of them was holding Luca's arms behind his back. "What did I tell you would happen if you touched her again?" Jake asked him.

"Please don't kill me. I'm sorry!" Luca said as he began to shrink away.

"Let his arms go, Turner," Jake ordered of the man who was holding Luca.

"Luca… hit me like you hit her," Jake said as he moved over directly in front of him.

"I didn't hi—"

"Hit me like you hit her, now!" Jake growled, cutting him off. I saw one of the other men turn and peek out the peephole as Jake got louder.

Luca stood there, looking pathetic like he was willing to take a beating to avoid the embarrassment he was now receiving. Then he leaned in and smacked Jake across the face just as he had done to me.

Jake reached up and rubbed his face a little as he stood there staring at Luca. The room was silent. Then without warning he took a small step back with his left leg and brought his left arm back as far as it looked like he could, then with one explosive movement, quickly swung it, hitting Luca square in the face with as much force as he probably had in him. Luca immediately brought his hands up to hold back the blood as he stumbled backward before falling against the wall, then to the ground. Jake stood there for a moment, staring down at him before speaking again.

"Stand up, you piece of shit," he said, shaking off his fist.

Luca slowly brought himself back to a standing position, which didn't look easy for him. Then he looked over at me, letting his eyes connect with mine almost like a plea for help.

"Don't look at her!" Jake growled again, bringing Luca's eyes back to his immediately.

"You stealing her is one thing, but the other shit you've done to her while she was in your care…" I could see Jake ball his fist again as he continued, "I would kill you right here, right now if she hadn't asked me not to! You don't even get it… you don't deserve her. Everything you've done to her and she still—" he stopped. I could see him relax his fist then reshape it repeatedly like he was getting angrier but trying to stop himself. "Tell her the truth…" he said through gritted teeth, obviously fighting to bring his emotions back level.

Luca nodded in fear then looked over at me, about to speak but hesitated.

"This is the last time you're going to speak to her so I suggest you make it count," Jake said, urging him to begin. "Tell her the truth. She was never yours… Tell her now!"

"I'm sorry…" Luca said looking at me, finally letting himself speak, "I do love you. That wasn't a lie. But you can't be with him. He hadn't told you who you really are. You're a Si—"

Before he was able to finish, Jake leaned in and quickly punched him again in the gut as hard as he could to stop him from saying any more. Luca's body went limp and dropped to the floor. He lay there writhing in the pain from the sudden blow.

Jake stepped up closer to him and with his boot turned Luca's face up to look at his. "You'll wish she let me kill you by the time I'm done with you."

# 21
## MARCHING ORDERS

Luca didn't say anything, he just spit blood out of his mouth onto the floor, probably hoping to hit Jake's boots, with no luck.

The man closest to the door leaned over to look out the peephole again, then motioned to the man next to him as he brought his hand to the handle to open the door. Jake looked up, taking his attention from Luca for a second to address them. "Go! Do what you need to do. I'll be done with him soon." Jake said as he motioned for them to leave. They both pulled out large knives, one from the small of his back and one from his side, then turned the handle and walked out as they quietly shut the door behind them. The larger man that was originally behind Jake while he was next to me at the bed moved over and took the spot next to the door, ready to keep watch through the peephole.

Jake looked back down at Luca who was now just laying there, gripping his stomach. Jake stared at him for a second, probably trying to decide what to do with him. Then he squatted down next to him, letting one knee rest against the floor, as he leaned in to whisper something to him. Then Jake leaned back to stand back up and wait for Luca's response.

Luca began to laugh, then cough as he spit up more blood. He pulled himself up a little so he could look up at Jake to answer. "Threaten me all you want. I don't care what she told you, she lied. You don't think I had her?... Look at me, you want the truth?" He asked loudly, then chuckled again to himself as he looked at me then back to Jake. "Yeah, I did! She begged me to because she wasn't satisfi—"

Jake kicked him again in the gut as soon as he realized what Luca was saying, stopping him from being able to continue. Luca didn't stop, though. He kept talking, trying to taunt Jake more when he got his breath back.

Luca finally pushed him too far. Jake couldn't keep himself restrained any longer. He dropped to one knee on Luca's chest and began to pummel him with punches to the head. I wanted to scream at him but didn't when I saw one of the other agents that were left in the room step in and stop Jake before he had the chance to finish Luca off.

"Miles…" the man said gently as he tried to restrain Jake's arms and pull him off Luca. He began to say something else to help Jake calm down but Jake stopped and pulled himself away from the man's grip before any more words were needed. He rounded his shoulders with a shrug like he was readjusting their tension then paced slowly back over to Luca, peering down at him again.

"Lane…" He said, speaking to the man that had just pulled him off of Luca, "Check on Kaleah, see what she needs before we can go." Then he turned to the man standing at the door and motioned something, referencing Luca and what they were going to do with him.

"Are you cool now, then?" Lane asked Jake, making sure he wasn't just ordering him away so he could kill Luca without restraint.

"Yes, now do what I asked," Jake said firmly, pointing toward me.

Lane nodded, then turned quickly and walked over to me. He didn't say anything at first, he just slowed himself as he got closer, letting his eyes quietly assess the mess I was laying in. His face wasn't as stoic as Jake's had been when he first saw me. He stood there, unsure what to do with me, then finally he spoke with a gentle demeanor. "Do you have any more clothes?"

I looked over to the other bed where I had last laid my folded clothes that I had been wearing before I put on the dress; but they weren't there anymore. I looked down beside me at the bloody rags Luca left, realizing what they were and where he'd got them. I looked back at Lane, feeling apologetic not knowing any way to give him what he was asking of me. "No," I said softly, trying to reserve as much energy as I felt I had left. "I'm sorry."

He furrowed his brow, confused at why I was apologizing, then continued, "That's fine. You're fine..." he said, trying to be quick with the exchange as he began to look around. "Where are your shoes?"

"I don't know," I said as I tried to sit up a little to look at the floor, thinking they surely were around there somewhere.

"No... stop!" He put his hand against my shoulder and gently pushed me back against the bed. "I'll find them, just lay there." He said softly, looking at me. His eyes glistened with an open sincerity that I hadn't seen in any other man's eyes before.

I rested back against the pillow, then I heard a knock at the door like before, one with an unusual pattern to it. I looked over to see another man now entering, carrying a thin blue fleece blanket. Jake held the door for him and two other men. I counted six agents now in the room.

Jake took the blanket from the man and started to walk over to me as he continued to give orders to them all. "Andry, pick up that piece of shit and carry him out. If he gets too heavy, feel free to drag his ass. I don't care."

Another man chuckled, "Nothing's too heavy for Andry."

I looked over at Luca, who was now laying there lifeless. His face was a bloody mess, but it looked like he was still breathing so I hoped Jake had kept his word and hadn't actually killed him, even though he wanted to.

Jake walked over beside my bed and looked down at me, then as Lane bent to retrieve something from the floor Jack asked him, "Lane, what's she need?"

"I got 'em," Lane said as he stood up, now holding both of my shoes. One still looked relatively clean, while the other had a good bit of blood splatter on it.

Jake nodded, looking at the shoes, then looked back at me. "Kaleah, baby…" he paused. I could see that he was trying to maintain some semblance of self-control but as he looked at me on the bloody duvet, his already strained composure was visibly shaken. "I'm gonna wrap you up in this and carry you out, okay? Moving you might be painful. I'm sorry… I'll be as gentle as I can be." He let out a deep breath. "All right?"

I nodded in agreement. He handed the blanket to Lane, then gently gathered me in his arms and lifted me off the bed. Lane draped the blanket over me and tucked it in around my body as well as he could until Jake nodded that it was enough and began moving toward the door.

Jake began barking orders to the men who quickly assumed their positions. He walked up behind the man in the middle who was following the tall man that was now carrying Luca thrown over his shoulder. "Carver, take point. Andry, Lawson, you back up Carver at 10 and 2. I'll take center with Lane behind me. Turner, you cover our six."

"Kaleah, baby, close your eyes and rest against me now. I don't know what you might see out here, but none of it's gonna be good for you." Jake said, looking down at me.

I looked back at him, thinking about what he asked of me, then relaxed and closed my eyes, pressing my face against his chest. He pulled me in tighter, trying not to reposition his arms too much so he wouldn't cause me any unnecessary pain.

"Carver, go now!" Jake's voice reverberated through his chest. It was deep and strong. Then I felt him begin to walk.

I tried everything I could to follow his orders even though I wanted to open my eyes and look around so badly. I wanted to see what the men had done, who they had killed, all just to retrieve me. But I didn't open them. I kept them shut just as he'd asked. I didn't want to disobey him. I realized the last time I disobeyed; I got myself in more trouble than if I would have just listened, so I decided I would try to start listening more.

I didn't hear much, if anything, at first since all the men were so quiet. Then I heard the lever of the emergency door exit—the same one I took when I tried to leave. After a moment, I heard some talking before whoever it was got louder and began to shout. I couldn't understand what the voice was saying, but as soon as I heard it, I felt Jake's walk turn into a trot.

I heard a gunshot, then another. I dug my face further into his chest, hoping for solace. After a minute of what felt like him running, he stopped quickly with a sharp turn. I tried not to groan from the shooting pain that began to increase deep within me when I felt my weight shift. I opened my eyes to look, seeing if he was intending to put me down. I would have understood if he needed to put me down.

"No, baby, relax. I got you." He whispered softly down to me, seeing I'd opened my eyes. "Lawson… fall back with Turner, secure the rear," he ordered the men. His words were calm and low, but still firm and direct all at the same time.

"Let me go, I'll cover you." The voice that spoke sounded like Lane's.

"No!" I felt Jake tense up. "You stay with us; Carver can go if they need another man."

He must have nodded in agreement because I didn't hear anything else from him. Jake started walking again but his movement felt different like he was trying to be stealthy.

After a few minutes, I heard more voices returning like the men that he had ordered to fall back were now catching up to us.

"We're all clear," one said with a slight husk in his voice.

"Good. Is anyone hurt?" Jake asked.

"I'm good, Miles." The voice sounded like Lanes.

"I'm great!" said a new voice, one I hadn't heard speak yet. "It's been years since I've gotten to kill that many Gypsyin bastards."

Jake tensed up again and stopped walking after the man said it.

"Uh… Carver?" Lane's voice spoke again.

"Oh, Miles… shit. I'm sorry… Really, man, I'm sorry I said that. I didn't mean anything by it, you know, nothing against her and all. I just… I just need to watch my mouth. I—"

"Enough…" Jake said, stopping the man from rambling before he began to walk again.

I didn't know where we were going or how long he would have to carry me but I was beginning to feel more tired than I had, likely from the adrenaline of Jake's return wearing off, or maybe from blood loss, I wasn't sure. I kept my eyes closed and tried to block all the voices out so I could fall asleep.

I woke up with a sudden movement change; it felt like I was falling. I jerked, trying to cling onto something, trying to stop myself from hitting the ground.

"Kaleah! I've got you, you're fine…. Shh, you're fine, baby." I opened my eyes to see Jake, now sitting, holding me in his lap, close to a campfire. I looked around for a minute, seeing the other men now sitting around it as well, then I turned back to look up at Jake as he continued to gently stroke my hair away from my face. "You're fine now, angel. I've got you. Shh, baby, just go back to sleep. I won't let anything happen to you."

I relaxed and closed my eyes again. My stomach had begun to throb. I didn't know how to help it feel better, so I figured it would be best to listen and let myself fall back to sleep if I could.

"Miles… the blood might draw predat… uh…" The man stopped to clear his throat, "I just didn't know if you thought of it, or if you already had a plan."

"You're fine, Andry. I know, I already thought of it… The cars are too far to try to make it there tonight. I need to get her cleaned up but I'm concerned the water from the last creek we passed would be too cold on her right now. I don't want to give her a chill on top of what she's already dealing with."

"Miles, if I had something to bring it back in, I could get some and heat it up over the fire for her, if you think it would help."

"No, Lane, thank you though. I don't want anyone out in the woods alone now that it's gotten dark. I'm just glad we were all able to make it out without anyone getting hurt. All that would be for nothing if you went and got yourself eaten at the watering hole."

"Ugh, I forgot… the foxes…"

"It's not the foxes I'm concerned about, Lane, it's the wolves and whatever else might be out there."

"Is she…"

"It's okay, don't worry. I think she went back to sleep. We can talk. She won't hear us now."

"Miles, what do you plan on doing with him? He's quite bloody himself. I doubt you care about that, but—"

"You're right, I don't! If the wolves don't get him tonight, I'm going to send him with you four back to Nashville. He's a Gypsyin, so Nashville is perfect for him. They won't let them be taken in as bondservants like they will in New York. My guess is he'll have a nice brain wiping session before they toss his ass back out in the woods to wander around. Let the woods take his newfound innocence from him like he did to her… freakin' bastard!"

"So you and Lane are going to take her back to New York?"

"Yeah, I'm going to take her to my parents' place. New York is out of Miller's jurisdiction so he won't try to look for her there. Andry, you still good with our plan?"

"Yeah, Boss, me and Turner will dig around at Miller's place and find whatever we can and get back to you within the month. Do you think the girl is real?"

"I don't know… It was just a picture. It could be anything. He's lied to me before and I wouldn't put it past him to do it again. He wants something from Kaleah that she doesn't have. I'm afraid he'd kill her trying to get it out of her if he ever got a hold of her again."

"Miles, what about me and Lawson? We want in on this too. You know we got your back. I'm sorry about what I said earlier. I didn't mean to offend you; I forgot she's a Gypsyin."

"Carver, I appreciate it, man, but I feel like I've asked too much of you both already."

"I'm not loyal to Miller. Is that what you're worried about, Miles? Doing the right thing means more than rank. Everyone knows he's a dirtbag."

"That's not it, Lawson, I trust you both. If not, I wouldn't have asked you to come back here with me to get Kaleah. It's Miller that I don't trust. He's a vindictive son of a bitch."

"What can we do? Carver's right, I wanna help too. You've not asked too much of us, man. We owe you our lives. None of us would be here if you weren't our lead when we fought the Sicari at Knoxville."

"All right… If you want to help, when you go back to Nashville keep an eye on Cortez, I gotta feeling he's the one who's been pulling strings for Miller… We all know Miller's an asshole. I don't know how he's kept his rank with all the shit he's done so my guess is someone's covering for him."

"You're right, I never liked him. Miller's the worst commanding officer I ever served under for sure… We'll do that for you, Miles, and let you know if we see anything… If you don't mind me asking, man, how did you get reassigned to New York?"

"Truth is, I didn't… Miller put in the system that I went rogue. It doesn't matter anywhere except for Miller's jurisdiction, though. Not many know but the two cities don't share the same agency boards in the central system. When I go back to New York, I'll still have my rank as a Track and Capture agent like I did under Miller."

"What were you doing with her out here in the grotto lands, then? Why didn't you take her to New York before?"

"Turner, I wish I could answer you, man, but it's complicated."

"It's 'cause she's a Gypsyin… He loves her… You know what his folks would do if they found out he loved a Gypsyin?"

"Lane… that's enough…"

"Sorry, Miles, I just… they don't know you like I do, man. I just thought it would help."

"It's fine… You're driving tomorrow, so I suggest you lie down and get some sleep."

"Yeah, sure thing, bro!"

.  .  .

I woke up shivering. It was still dark, but it looked like it wouldn't be long before the sun was up. "Jake?" I said as I tried to sit up, looking for him. It was the first time I had awakened without someone laying next to me and, for whatever reason, that made me feel insecure and scared. *What if he left me here?* "Jake?" I tried again not sure what I was seeing around me. It just looked like shadows, not men. Where were the men that were with Jake? Where was Jake? I started to feel like I was close to becoming frantic. "Luca?" I screamed out again, wanting someone, anyone.

**"You're alone. No one wants you. They left you here for the wolves."**

Who said that? Who was talking to me? I tried looking around again, panic beginning to set in. I still couldn't see anyone.

"Jake!" I screamed. "Jake…" *No… no… he's here. He didn't leave me.* I tried to calm myself.

"Jake!" I screamed again, as loud as I could.

"Kaleah!" I opened my eyes, this time for real—I hoped. The sun *was* up. Lane was kneeling next to me. "Kaleah… you all right? You were yelling in your sleep."

I looked up at him. "Where's Jake?" I asked still frantic. I needed him. I didn't want him to leave me.

"You're shivering… Here, hang on…" He stood up and took his jacket off then laid it across me. "Miles just went to check the water temperature in the creek. He'll be right back, promise."

"Don't make promises you can't keep." It came out of my mouth without forethought. He squinted his eyes slightly, trying to figure me out.

"Okay… okay, yeah… you're right, sorry," he said as he rested against his heels, "Are you hungry?"

"Where's Luca?" I asked as I slowly sat up. A strong aching feeling overwhelmed my senses as I began to look around. "I wanna see him."

"Uh… he's uh… yeeeah," he hesitated as he looked at me, clearly confused by my request. "Um, he's not supposed to talk to you… see you… touch you… you know—nothing *you* again. But he's not dead, so there's that. Feel better?"

Leaving my face intentionally blank, I stared at him, not saying anything, just staring.

"Uh, are you in pain? Is that why you want to see him? Do you need a doctor? I mean I still can't… oh boy… Miles would kill me if I—"

"Lane!" I said his name. He acted surprised by my assertive tone.

"Okay… well, he *is* tied up. I don't guess he could hurt you again being tied up and all."

"Thank you, Lane," I said, seeing he was going to give in and let me have what I wanted.

"Can you get up on your own or uh?" He asked as he stood up and looked down at me, probably unsure if he was allowed to touch me.

"I'm fine," I said as I began to push myself up off the ground. I lied though, I wasn't fine. My stomach was already throbbing again with the same intense pain as it had the night before, but I wanted to see Luca, so I didn't let the pain stop me. I knew I probably wouldn't ever get to talk to him again. I needed to say goodbye, even if it didn't make any sense to anyone else.

I stood up as quickly as I could, trying to prove to Lane I was fine. I clutched the thin blue blanket around me. I still had on the pink dress from the night before but it was so blood-stained I didn't want anyone to see me in it. I looked around. The other men were all sitting a ways away, next to a second fire. The longer I stood there staring at them the more they began to turn like they weren't level with the ground any longer, or like my head felt heavy to one side. I tilted it, trying to adjust before I began to walk but it all happened too quick. Lane gasped as I felt myself falling into him before my eyes forced themselves shut, no longer feeling or hearing anything else.

. . .

"Bria? Can you hear me? Wake up…"

"Lane, if Miles comes back and sees you untied him… Dude, you're gonna be in so much shit. I'm not taking the fall for this one."

"Shut up, Lawson, what else was I supposed to do. She passed out. He's a doctor!"

"Guys… She's lost a lot of blood."

"See, I told you, he's a doctor… he knows shit."

"Whatever, Lane, when heads roll, it's yours."

"It's fine, we just gotta make sure he doesn't touch her… or ugh, shit!"

# 22

# A BROKEN GOODBYE

"Luca?" I opened my eyes, thinking I heard his voice.

"You passed out. Just lay still. You don't need to move. You've lost a lot of blood but you'll be fine. You need to drink so you can replenish it. Do you understand me?" He said hastily, as if he knew this encounter was brief and he wouldn't get to say much more.

"Uh, dude, that's enough, she's awake now so I need to take you back." Lane spoke up, speaking to Luca.

"Wait! I won't touch her, just give me a minute, please!" Luca said not looking away, keeping his eyes connected to mine but talking to Lane.

"Ugh… man, this wasn't a good idea." It sounded like Lane was now talking to himself, but he wasn't reaching down dragging Luca away so he must have been willing to give Luca the time he requested.

"Bria… I'm sorry. I never meant to hurt you. I wish I could take it all back and do everything differently," he said still looking at me then lifted his head to look around to make sure Jake wasn't about to come up to strangle him from behind.

"I forgive you. Will you forgive me?" I asked. I didn't know how long we would have to speak before one of the men decided it was enough.

Luca looked at me confused, "What fo—"

Before he could finish, the largest of the men, I believed to be Andry, had now walked over and decided to intervene on Lane's behalf. "Enough!" He said with a voice deep down in his chest, as he pulled Luca to his feet then restrained his hands again behind him. "I can't sit there and watch you allow this, Lane," Andry huffed.

"Luca, forgive me... please!" I said again, trying to get the response out of him before they took him away. Just in case I was wrong, and it *was* his baby that I lost, I wanted to feel free from the shame of my decisions.

"Kaleah, you didn't do anything." Lane spoke to me again, not understanding the reason for my request.

I ignored him to ask again, now attempting to sit up as I did. "Luca... please?" I tried to look at him, but the large man walked him away before he could turn to say anything else to me.

"You're freakin' lucky Andry stepped in, Lane..." I looked back to where Lane was standing above me. Now one of the other men was standing next to him, speaking.

"Whatever, man. I did what I thought she needed." Lane said flatly, addressing his concern then looked back down at me. "What do you need? Water, right? He said water would fix you?"

I nodded as I finished sitting up the rest of the way, then reached over to where the blanket had fallen when I had passed out and used it to cover myself since my dress was now revealing more than I had wanted it to. I sat there and looked around at all the men. The tall one had taken Luca far enough away that I couldn't see him anymore. I had heard Jake say all their names at one point or another but I didn't know which one was which, except for Lane, and I thought I remembered the giant being Andry.

Lane was now rummaging through a bag over at the second fire where the other three men sat. Andry hadn't returned from retying Luca yet. They all looked so different from each other. The one that was standing scolding Lane about letting Luca speak to me was sitting in the middle. He was of average height but had long blonde hair tied up in a little topknot at the back of his head. Something made me think he was the one Jake called Lawson, but I wasn't sure.

The other two men were almost the opposites of each other. One was tall and stocky, with dark mahogany skin. His hair was short and thick with small, tight, dense curls. The other was of average height, pale skin and lean—not lean like Luca, though. He was lean like he didn't eat a lot, for whatever reason. I knew one was named Carver and one was I thought Taylor or maybe it was Turner; I couldn't remember. The taller one looked like he was more ornery. From what I remember Andry saying about Carver, I would assume that was him and the pale, lean man was Turner.

I looked back over to watch Lane, now pouring something into a container, probably about to bring it to me. I didn't know who he was to Jake, but they looked similar. Related or not, there was something about him that was familiar, something I must have seen in Jake before. He was smaller than Jake in stature, but just about as muscular. By appearance, they looked the same age but by their mannerisms he seemed younger than Jake. I didn't figure his demeanor was a good way to calculate his age, though.

"Hey, baby, did I hear you yelling?" I jumped not realizing someone was behind me, then quickly calmed when I recognized it as Jake's voice. I turned to see him walking up with a couple of large containers, filled with water I would assume. "I'm sorry. I didn't mean to scare you. Where's Lane?" He asked as he looked away from me to see where he went. "Never mind, I see him. What's he doing?… Ugh… he wasn't supposed to leave your side," he said it more to himself than to me.

"I asked him to speak to Luca; don't yell at him. It wasn't his fault," I said, watching Jake as he sat the water down next to me. I was trying to be as transparent as I could, hoping it would be better for everyone if I was as honest as possible going forward.

"What?" He frowned, looking confused, apparently not taking what I said very well, which was the opposite of what I had intended. "What wasn't his fault?" He scowled.

"Miles, I'm glad you're back," Lane spoke loudly, now walking back over to us.

"Lane!" Jake said, about to scold him for something he didn't even know about.

Lane's smile quickly diminished, and he looked over at me as if I'd tattled and tried to get him in trouble.

"Jake, stop! I said that so you wouldn't be upset with Lane. If you're just going to yell at him anyway, why would I try to be honest with you again in the future?" I said, looking back at him. His face relaxed like he couldn't argue with my logic. We both looked at Lane as he stopped in front of me and reached down to hand me a canteen.

"Thank you," I said, taking it from him. His face relaxed as well, looking relieved and happy that I stopped Jake from scolding him.

"Tell me what happened, Lane," Jake said calmly, just wanting the truth.

"Okay, well, it all started when she woke up… she was cold, so I gave her my jacket, then—"

"Quick version, Lane, we don't have all day," Jake said, rushing him as if he was known for drawing out stories.

Lane sat down in front of us like he wasn't listening and was getting comfortable enough to go on with a lengthy tale. "She asked to see the doctor, I said no at first but… well, you know, she doesn't seem like the type that was going to take no for an answer," he said then looked from me to Jake with a little smile like Jake would know what he was talking about.

"Are you serious? What, were you afraid she was going to hurt you?" Jake interrupted, sounding irritated.

Lane dropped the smile with a shrug and continued, "Okay, well, after that she stood up too fast and passed out… but don't worry, I caught her, so she didn't hit her head or anything." He stopped and smiled again, pleased with his role thus far in the story.

"Go on…" Jake said still urging him to get to the point, the part he knew he wasn't likely to be happy about.

Lane cleared his throat a little then went on, "Well she wasn't waking up so I thought about it and I thought, you'd be way more pissed with me if you came back to her not breathing than if you came back and the doctor was trying to fix her."

Jake took a deep breath in, trying to decide how to address it now that Lane finished telling him. "Okay... so you just went and asked him what he thought you should do?"

Lane's face froze as his eyes started to wander off, stumped by why he hadn't thought of that. "Um... well..."

"Hey, uh Miles?" The tall man I mentally labeled as Carver had now walked up behind Lane. Lane's face looked like it was instantly relieved and he hoped he wouldn't have to finish the conversation.

Jake stood up and walked around Lane to address Carver, as they touched shoulders like they were going to tell secrets.

"Drink, Kaleah," Lane looked over at me now to talk in Jake's absence.

"Okay." I brought the canteen to my mouth to take a few sips. "I didn't mean to get you in trouble, I'm sorry," I said finally after I brought it back down to my lap.

"It's no big deal. It wouldn't be the first time Miles has been upset with me," he said with a chuckle as he readjusted his position.

"Who is Jake to you?" I asked now trying to observe his mannerisms closer than I had previously. I couldn't get over what about him was so oddly familiar.

He smiled, happy to tell, "He's my cousin. Our moms are sisters... We were raised more like brothers, though, so you're gonna be seeing a lot of me. I hope you don't mind."

I didn't respond. I just slowly nodded, acknowledging what he said as I kept staring at him. It made so much sense after he said it. Their build looked the same, their hair was the same sandy brown color, they even pronounced their words the same way.

"He's told me all about you," he said with another smile, one that I realized was also just like Jake's except Lane had small dimples on both sides.

I half-heartedly smiled back, "You probably know more about me than I do about myself then, I suppose." I said it, then looked down. I had begun to feel cold again. The blanket wasn't all that insulating, and it reminded me that I was still a bloody mess underneath it.

"He loves you. If you don't know much else, you should at least know that," he said, drawing my eyes back up to him. "I've never seen him like this… in love that is. Not like he is with you, anyway. I mean he's had other girlfriends and stuff, but… he talks about you differently… especially with the bab… oh, uh…"

I looked down at my stomach, then back up at him, hesitating for a moment, "It's okay, I know what you meant."

"I'm sorry… It would have been his first… he's always wanted kids, but with the agency and him always working so much… you know, he just never…" he slowly trailed off from what he was saying, realizing he wasn't making me feel better like he probably had intended to do with that comment.

"What does he plan on doing with me?" I asked, diverting the subject.

"Uh, what do you mean?" He asked, furrowing his brow in confusion, probably from the way I asked the question.

"I just… uh," I didn't know how to say it. I didn't know if he would still want me if I wasn't carrying his baby. "Never mind," I sighed, hoping he would just forget it.

"Kaleah…" Jake said now coming back. "The men agreed to wait here while I take you to the creek to help you get cleaned up. The closer it gets to mid-day the more the water should have heated up. Are you feeling better now? You think you can handle it if I take you down there?" He walked around and sat down next to me again, then looked down at the canteen.

"The doctor said she just needed to drink more. If she did, then she'd make more blood to replenish what she lost," Lane said, looking at Jake, trying to be helpful.

"Yeah," he nodded thoughtfully, "she's going to need to eat some red meat, too. I'm sure her iron is low now as well." He said, lifting his hand to gently rub my back.

"I think I'll be fine for you to take me there," I looked back at him. I missed him. I missed the connection that we'd had the couple of weeks that we were in the cave before Luca took me. I wanted to be cleaned up, but I was also nervous to speak to him again on my own without anyone around. I was afraid to talk about what had happened. I didn't know if he thought that I intentionally left him the day Luca took me or if he knew it was an accident and I just got lost. I knew I needed to talk to him about the baby as well but I was afraid to. I was afraid to see the disappointment on his face.

"Good," he said with a warm smile, looking at my eyes, then brought his other hand up to sweep the hair from my face and tuck behind my ear.

"Lane, I brought extra clothes for her. They're in a gunny sack in my small bag. Would you mind getting them? I'm going to carry her down there. Will you go with us and stay at the top of the hill to keep watch for predators or anything that might smell the blood in the water?"

"Sure, man!" Lane quickly got up and turned to go get what Jake asked for.

# 23

## FEELINGS YOU CAN'T FORGET

Jake went straight to a large rock that was positioned perfectly in the sun and set me down on it like he'd already scouted out the best place for me to sit when he'd been to the creek earlier that morning.

"Is this all right, baby? Are you comfortable enough?" He asked as he began to unwrap the blanket from around me.

"Uh… yeah," I said quietly, feeling a bit anxious and tense.

He stopped what he was doing and sat down on the rock in front of me. "Kaleah…" he said, looking straight into my eyes.

"What?" I mumbled, trying not to let him see my timidity.

"What's wrong, baby?" He asked, sensing I wasn't acting like myself, whoever that was.

"I feel like I'm a burden to you," I said the first thing that came to my mind when I thought about his question.

"Oh, baby! You're not! That's not true… You've never been a burden to me," he said as he leaned in to wrap his arms around me and let me rest my head on his shoulder. "Why would you think that?"

"I just see what all you had to do to get me back… the men you got to come with you… Then, everyone who died just so you could get me out. It's all too much; I'm not worth it." I was trying to be honest with him about how I felt. It was hard to explain myself with all the thoughts that were forcing their way into my mind.

"Oh my gosh, Kaleah… no!" He pulled back away from me to look at me again. "I'm going to tell you something and I need you to listen, okay? Are you listening? You need to hear me!"

I nodded, looking at him, trying to show him he had all my attention and I was going to listen as best I could.

"Good! The things that have happened to you the last three weeks are not your fault! Do you hear me? Luca saw your vulnerability and used you. He found you before I could and took you from me! There was nothing you could have done… it's not your fault!" He moved his head down to keep eye contact, seeing I had started to let my eyes drop away from his. "Look at me, baby, this is important." He said, gently placing a finger under my chin to tilt my head back up.

I brought my eyes back up to his and nodded.

"Luca abused you! That's never your fault. I don't care what he said to make you think you deserved it. You're innocent! Hear me? I don't know what all he did to you but I never want you to think it was your fault."

"What about the baby?" I asked, trying everything I could to stop myself from breaking in half and melting into a puddle of tears and pain.

"I love *you*! The baby was just going to be a bonus, a happy little unplanned bonus. If we never have kids, I don't care, you're enough. You're always going to be enough!"

"I know," I said, interrupting him, "but it feels like it's my fault, like I'm the reason we lost it."

He looked down briefly to think about how to respond before looking back up at me. "Did you want the baby?" He asked as he swiped away a tear under my eye with his thumb.

I furrowed my brow a little confused why he would ask me that.

"Did you…?" He asked again.

"Yes, when I thought it was yours I did…" I answered, wondering where he was going to take it.

"If you wanted the baby, and you were only hit in the stomach trying to escape, then it can't be your fault. If anything, it's Luca's for making you want to escape! Don't put something like that on yourself, baby. It's too heavy and you shouldn't have to carry it!"

I nodded like I was willing to take what he was saying and try to internalize it.

He smiled, then reached over for a rag that he had brought and dipped it in the water. "It's warmer now. Let me clean you up."

"Okay…" I said, looking down at my dress. I reached up to slide each of the straps off of my shoulders one at a time, then slid it down to rest at my waist.

"If you're concerned about being topless in front of Lane, I can put my jacket—"

"I'm not…" I stopped him. "I trust Lane. He feels safe."

Jake smiled, "Good, he is… I don't trust anyone—except you of course—more than him. He's my cousin, but really he's more like my brother. We're even the same age, almost… Our moms were both pregnant at the same time." He began to take the rag and wipe the blood off of me with it as he kept talking. "I know there were a lot of things I still hadn't gotten a chance to tell you about your past after you lost your memory. I've decided I'm going to tell you everything, though. We're going to go to New York… My parents live there. They've agreed to take us in for the time being. It's a long drive from here to there, so I figured it would be the best time to give you all your secrets back." He smiled brightly as if he hoped that would cheer me up.

"But I'm a Gypsyin… your parents won't like me."

He stopped suddenly, looking at me with his mouth agape. "Who told you that?" His face hardened.

"I don't know… I just thought of it… no one, I guess." I said, being honest.

He squinted his eyes, trying to figure something out, then he brought his hand up to scratch his chin. "It's true. They have their own prejudices, but it's more my mom than my dad. It doesn't matter though, they don't have to ever find out what you really are." He turned and dipped the rag back into the water then looked down at my legs, where the majority of the mess remained.

"I don't have a tag. How am I supposed to hide that?" I asked as I finished pulling my dress off so it would be easier for him to clean my legs.

"It doesn't have to be hard. In the summer, when it's hot, you can just wear loose clothing and keep your arms covered. Besides, if they're not expecting anything, then they won't be suspicious."

"What about everything else, where we'll live... Will you keep working for the agency? Will you keep going out on missions? If not, how could we possibly afford to stay there?" I had so many questions but had a hard time without the memory of my past, knowing which ones were relevant and which weren't.

He started to chuckle a little as he dipped the rag again, then brought it back up to my thighs. "No, I won't keep working missions. You don't need to be concerned about that. My commanding officer doesn't have jurisdiction in New York, so it wouldn't do me any good to report for duty there. It doesn't matter, I never needed to work to start with. I just did it because I wanted something to do."

"What do you mean?"

"You wouldn't remember it, but when we were first together, I told you I worked for my dad's company... Well, I could again if I needed, or not, it doesn't matter..." he said acting a bit flustered. "The point I'm trying to make is we don't need to worry about money, or where we'll stay or anything else."

"Why... is your family rich?" I said joking. I didn't know if that was what he was trying or rather not trying to say but that was the idea that had come across, nonetheless.

He worked his way from my upper thigh down lower, gently making small strokes with the rag before re-dipping it in the water. "No... well, I mean I wouldn't call it that..." he hesitated. "Ok, well, I don't like to call it that. The word rich is subjective... Affluent sounds better... We have enough money for whatever we need and that with my agency rank helps give me influence. So take that however you want, I guess."

"I don't know if my lack of memory has any effect or not but it sounds like you're rich." I said, letting myself smile at him.

He stopped and looked up at me, trying not to smile but giving in. "I just never wanted anyone to look at me like I got where I was because of the family I was born into. You know?" He asked, looking back down to continue what he was doing.

"So you could have anyone…" I mumbled, looking away.

"What do you mean, instead of you?" He asked softly like he knew what I meant.

"Yes… Why me? I'm just a Gypsyin."

He lifted his head to look at me again briefly, "You're not… You're so much more than that! You're beautiful, intelligent, feisty, witty… sweet, caring… You're mine, that's really all that matters… and whether you know it or not, you're a hell of a fighter."

"I am?" I wasn't sure if he meant in life in general or physically.

"Mm-hmm," he mumbled as he worked the rag now down to my lower legs.

"Well, I did kill a guy that tried to rape me when I first got to the inn," I said it matter-of-factly trying to validate what he'd just told me, not realizing what I was actually telling him and how he would take it.

"What?" He lifted his head and stopped working on my leg. His eyes widened as he gasped, shocked and likely upset by what I said. "Where the hell was Luca?" He scowled.

"Well, he… uh…" I didn't want to say anything that would entice him to go back to the camp with a new grudge to finally finish Luca off. "He wasn't paying attention, that's all."

"That's ridiculous, I can't believe him!" He turned to dip the rag again, then paused and looked back at me, "Wait… you said you killed the man?"

"Yeah, it was like a freak thing… luck I think… I don't know how I did it. My hands just moved without me thinking about how to move them, and I twisted his neck and he fell over, dead."

He didn't say anything at first, just looked at me, thinking about what that meant. Like it meant something, but he didn't respond to help clue me in on what that something was. Then he turned away again to re-dip the rag. "You're amazing," he said as he turned back toward me. "Too bad you didn't kill Luca yourself."

I could tell he meant it. "Jake…" I said softly, wanting him to listen this time. "He lied… when he said… He didn't, we didn't…" I didn't know how to say it nicely. I just didn't want Jake to believe Luca and feel like he took that from me, too.

"I know, baby, you don't need to say it. Whatever you did do together… you don't have to tell me if you don't want to. He manipulated you. Anything you did was a result of him lying to you, so it's not your fault. You don't need to be ashamed, all right?" He said, softening his expression.

"We didn't do anything," I said it finally, letting out a silent sigh of relief. I wanted him to really know. "He tried, but something in me knew he wasn't the one, even though he lied. He stopped when he knew I wasn't getting turned on. I think it bothered him. He knew I didn't want him."

Jake smiled, but it looked different from his usual smile, like he was using it to try to hold back other emotions, probably ones that would cause him to tear up. "Thank you for telling me that. I know it probably wasn't easy for you," he said then swallowed hard. "You might not understand it since you're not a man, but just knowing that helps." He smiled again, then quickly turned back to the water probably trying to keep from showing me more emotions.

He turned back around with more fresh water in the rag, but stopped as he looked down to where he'd taken it last. "I think I got it all," he said as he set it down and reached for the gunny sack. "After New York, when Lane and I stopped in Nashville to get the rest of the men, I wasn't sure at first what condition you would be in when we got back to get you. I never thought it would be as bad as it was." He pulled the clothes out of the bag and leaned in to help put them on me. "I'm sorry I didn't find you before he did and I'm sorry you had to go through all this pain. I hate seeing you in pain."

"Jake…" I said as he finished helping me pull the shirt on over my head, "I love you. I know I don't remember anything from more than a month ago, but apparently, that doesn't matter. I don't guess I have to have the memories to keep the feelings… I just wanted you to know."

He smiled really big, then leaned in to kiss me. "I don't think those three words have ever meant more to me than they do right now… I love you too, baby." He said as he pulled back to look at me deep in the eyes almost as if he was trying to see my soul. "I love you too!"

**Jake and Kaleah's love story continues with book three of the ERASEHER series - Hearing Hidden Voices. CLICK HERE to download now.**

# About the Author

SARA NICHOL QUINCY is a website designer and novelist born and raised in Indiana. She's a mother, wife, and entrepreneur. The ERASEHER Series reflects her passion for writing romances that are sexy, twisty and edgy. Add in a little dystopian suspense and a touch of crazy and you have yourself an epic love story that only she can tell.

To read more of her personal story and see what other books are in the works, you can visit her website at:

**SaraNicholQuincy.com**

There you can subscribe to get new release updates and exclusive offers!

*Plus... only subscribers get:*
*- Launch date perks (1st week sales get 20% off!)*
*- Cover reveals before launch date!*
*- Exclusive Bonus Chapters that aren't available*
*  anywhere else!*
*- FREE books! (When available)*

*- ARC Reader offers for new book series and much more…*

Got a question or comment about her work? She'd love to hear from you. Reach her anytime at **Sara@SaraNicholQuincy.Com**

**Thank you again for taking your time to read Finding Fallen Angels. Please consider leaving an honest review. It would help immensely!**

facebook.com/saranicholquincy
twitter.com/SaraNQuincy
tiktok.com/@saranicholquincy
instagram.com/saranicholquincy